Dangerous

Creatures

Patricia Fisher Mystery
Adventures

Book 11

Steve Higgs

Dedication

To a lady called Sharon Kay Webb.

I asked for plot ideas and hers was a corker.

Table of Contents

Stretch

'It's George. He's gone missing!' Lady Mary's words reverberated in my head as Barbie and I ran up the steps to my house. Just minutes ago, enjoying a relaxing lunch in West Malling, the panicked call from my friend arrived and scuppered whatever plans I might have had for the rest of the day.

Bursting through the front door, we found my boyfriend, Alistair, and two of our friends from the cruise ship, Lieutenants Pippin and Schneider, in the entrance lobby. Pippin and Schneider were just about to leave. Their time away from the ship was over and they were heading back.

The other lieutenants, Deepa and Martin, whose wedding we all attended just two days ago, were now on their honeymoon in Sri Lanka where they were staying in an elephant sanctuary. It sounded heavenly. They would return to the ship when they were done.

Barbie blurted, 'Lady Mary's husband's been kidnapped.'

'We don't know that,' I corrected her, 'Lady Mary said he has gone missing.' However, the seed was sown, and the three men were staring at me with wide eyes.

'Should we stay?' Lieutenant Schneider asked me, cutting his eyes at Alistair, his captain, for his opinion as well.

'No, chaps,' I shook my head. 'This will be a simple thing.'

Barbie was on her way to pack a bag but paused halfway up the stairs to question my advice.

'Really, Patty?' she cocked an eyebrow at me. 'You don't think maybe we should keep the two trained security guys around until we know what is going on?'

I frowned at her. 'It's Lady Mary. Her husband is a writer, and she is sozzled on gin most of the day, every day. There will be a simple answer for George's absence. Pippin and Schneider will be bored if they come with us. They should get back to the ship.'

Barbie snorted with derision. 'Patty, since when are any of your investigations ever boring or simple? I bet you twenty bucks we get shot at before the end of the day.'

'Maybe we ought to stay, Mrs Fisher,' suggested Lieutenant Pippin.

Schneider added his thoughts, 'Yeah, Barbie kind of has a point.'

Now I was getting defensive. 'Nothing terrible will happen, thank you very much.' I cut my eyes at Barbie, still hanging over the banister. 'I'll take that bet. You'll see. This will all be resolved without a fuss.'

Barbie shrugged and started to run up the stairs again. 'Okay, Patty. Just make sure you have some cash in your purse.'

Schneider and Pippin were yet to move.

'It's all right, gentlemen. You can go,' I assured them.

They shifted their gaze to check with Alistair. A smile creased his face.

'If Mrs Fisher believes you are surplus to requirement, I guess there is no reason to delay your return to the ship.'

Both men snapped out smart salutes. 'Very good, sir.'

I waited for them to pick up their bags, gave them each a quick hug and promised to see them in a few days. They were to meet the ship in Naples tomorrow. We were set to fly out in three days to meet it before it left Rome. I had mixed feelings about going back and all the changes to my life that were coming with it, but this was not the time to discuss that.

2

It was time to ask Alistair if he too believed Barbie had a point. When Pippin and Schneider left the house, I speared him with my eyes.

The smile didn't leave his face and he raised his hands in mock surrender. 'Darling, you do have a certain ... magnetism when it comes to bullets. They never hit you, but I cannot for the life of me work out how.' Like a coward, he then clapped his hands and ran off to pack a bag of his own, leaving me to scowl at his back.

Less than thirty minutes later we were driving south down the M2 Motorway in my Range Rover. Jermaine was at the wheel with Barbie sitting next to him. Alistair and I were in the back, my two dachshunds snuggled in next to me.

My assistant, Sam Chalk, a man in his early thirties with Downs Syndrome, was to join us later. When I called him, he was out with his parents attending a show in London. They would arrive home later and drop him to Lady Mary's house. I knew he would want to be part of the investigation and ... well, what's the good of hiring an assistant if I don't then let him assist?

'You say Lady Mary lives in the zoo?' questioned Alistair. I suspected he already knew the answer and was just making conversation to take my mind off the very real possibility that something might have happened to my socialite friend's husband.

'Her house is within the grounds,' I explained. I hadn't been to Lady Mary's house. We met on the ship a few months ago and hit it off immediately. Given how close we live to one another, it seemed odd now that I hadn't found the time to visit her.

I knew the house though if that makes any kind of sense. As a child, my parents had taken me to the zoo. It was just a zoo to me, though wildlife park might be a more accurate term. They had acres of ground and large

3

paddocks for all their creatures. The collection, started several generations before Lady Mary came to inherit it, contained tigers, elephants, hippos, crocodiles … you name it, they probably had one. Or a herd.

Doing some rough arithmetic in my head, I calculated that it was more than three decades since I last walked through the visitors' gate with my soon-to-be ex-husband, Charlie. We were newly married or still dating, I could not now recall which it was, but that was the last time I saw her house and the grounds of the zoo.

'Should I take this turning, madam?' asked Jermaine from the driver's seat.

I leaned forward to peer through the gap between the front seats and shook my head.

'No, we want an unmarked turning,' I replied, remembering Lady Mary's instructions. Naturally, the way to her house wasn't through the visitors' entrance and carpark. Squinting into the distance, I pointed at a gap in the tall hedgerow. 'It might be that one.'

I was guessing a little; Lady Mary had done her best to describe how to find her house, but she had been fraught with worry and had the police knocking on her door because she'd called them before she called me.

Jermaine flicked the indicator stalk and slowed the Range Rover to take the turning, gliding across the road and up a narrow strip of tarmac that led between trees.

No one spoke as we all searched the dark foliage for a sign that we were on the right path. The road wound slightly left and as the trees parted, Lady Mary's grand residence filled the windscreen.

4

Barbie said, 'Wow. This place is even bigger than yours, Patty.'

She wasn't wrong.

If you feel like I have jumped forward and you are not too sure what is going on, then I should tell you my name is Patricia Fisher. There is kind of a long story about how I came to be riding to the rescue of an aristocrat who I get to call a friend. To catch you up really quickly I will tell you that I caught my husband cheating, ran away to sea, had some adventures, met a Maharaja who has rather a lot of money, and I somehow came to be known as a quasi-famous sleuth. I have a large house courtesy of the same Maharaja, a butler who I adore, my boyfriend is the captain of the cruise ship on which most of my adventures took place, and I feel utterly blessed.

Parked in front of the house were two police cars. One was the traditional white squad car with all the markings and light bar on top. The other was a silver Ford Mondeo. To many, it might have looked like just another car, but the addition of an extra antenna was a sure-fire giveaway. The unmarked car would have arrived with at least one detective in it.

No officers were visible; I guessed they were inside talking to Lady Mary already, or perhaps inspecting the grounds for evidence that George had been snatched.

I didn't get a lot of detail from Lady Mary, just that George was gone, and she was desperate for help.

Jermaine cruised to a gentle stop next to the police cars, the lot of us bailing out before he could kill the engine.

Anna and Georgie, my two Dachshunds, bounced from the car, keen to stretch their legs. They were happy to travel, snoozing contentedly on the

5

backseat, both with their heads on my left thigh, but travelling was all about arriving and now they wanted to explore.

We were standing on a wide expanse of gravel with managed gardens all around us. I could see pleached trees, trimmed Buxus bushes, and freshly mowed lawns. Thinking the girls might want to 'do their business', I let them scamper off. They could come to no harm here and we would be in the house soon where opportunities for a dog to relieve herself would be non-existent.

Jermaine and Barbie walked directly to the large front door. It was double width and double height, set centrally in the front façade between six pillars that rose twenty feet into the air. There were six steps to get up to it, the ground floor of the house set several feet above ground level.

This was an old house, built when England's great houses were filled with servants who lived on the bottom floor set partially below ground. A row of windows poking up seemingly out of the earth were spread equidistant on either side. In my head, the parties Lady Mary's grandparents and great-grandparents must have thrown would be exactly like those seen on *Downton Abbey*. I had no other frame of reference with which to imagine them.

Alistair was waiting for me, partway between the car and the house as I watched for the dogs. I was about to call them, so we could get on and get inside, when I heard them both yelping in fright.

I started forward; a startled reaction born of fear that my tiny fur babies might be in peril. They exploded out from under a bush before I could take another step, running for all they were worth and as if the devil himself were trying to catch their tails.

I saw why a heartbeat later when a large peacock burst through the same bush. It had manic eyes and was squawking its displeasure at the two retreating forms. It was fast too and coming my way because the girls were running to me for safety.

My feet reversed direction, propelling me backward and toward the house where I planned to shut the door in Devil Bird's face.

I wasn't going to get there though.

The peacock darted its head forward, nipping Anna's tail and drawing a squeal of pain and horror from the little dog.

'Alistair!' I shouted, caught between wanting to scoop my dogs and the feeling that doing so would result in terrible peacock-related injuries to my face and arms.

The dogs whipped between and around my legs. Not stopping to use me as cover, they sprinted onwards for the house. I turned to follow and squealed in fright as I came face to face with an ugly grimace.

'Go on! Gertcha!' growled a large man in a zookeeper's outfit. He was dressed for the outdoors and evidently spent a lot of time there if his ruddy complexion was anything to go by.

He flapped a meaty arm at the peacock who immediately gave up the chase. It didn't run away though. Instead, it eyed the man as if respectfully choosing to back down on this occasion while simultaneously plotting his demise.

'Gertcha!' the man repeated, flapping his arm at the bird again.

A large, brushed-steel watch clattered on the man's wrist. I'd seen men wear their timepieces like this before – as a statement. Brash younger men with more money than manners would wear them loose so they could show off the Rolex or Patek Philippe that cost the same as a car. I guess it was intended to impress.

That's not what this man was doing. At least, not overtly, but perhaps that had been the original intention and he had never grown out of wearing it that way.

The peacock turned and walked away. Its pace was unhurried; complying but making sure to show it didn't think the man was scary.

Breathing a sigh of relief, I put my hand to my chest and turned to face my saviour.

'Thank you.'

'Who are you?' the man asked impertinently. 'Have you business here?'

My eyebrows reached for the sky.

I was about to retort in kind when Alistair arrived at my side. He stretched out his right arm to shake the man's hand.

'Alistair Huntley. Good of you to step in like that.'

'William Gill,' the man took Alistair's hand, but let it go after nothing more than a quick grip. 'I'm the head keeper. If you've no business here, I'll have to ask you to leave. There's trouble at the house and they'll not need any additional interruptions.'

My eyes were narrowed down to two small slits as I glared up at him.

'I am a friend of Lady Mary's and here to give her my support.' I could have told him I was here to investigate, but I prefer to keep my identity and purpose secret if I can.

There was something behind his eyes, something he wasn't saying. Alistair stirred; he didn't like the way the man was looking at me. Mr Gill had wary judgement on his face. Before any one of us could speak again, the front door clanged open.

'Is everyone all right?' asked Lady Mary, crossing the gravel a second later.

I turned away from the zoo's head keeper to greet her. She had Barbie and Jermaine in tow; they were carrying a dachshund each and hobbling behind them was a man in butler's tails who had to be in his eighties. 'Jeeves let me know you had arrived. I should have warned you about Stretch.'

'Stretch?' I repeated, unsure what she meant.

'The peacock. Come along, let's get inside. I'll have the maid bring us some tea.' She talked as we walked. 'We have two dozen peacocks here; they roam freely around the grounds, but only Stretch is ever aggressive. I might have to let someone shoot him. Or feed him to the tigers; they might like a feathery snack.'

Barbie pulled a face at me – she didn't like to think about the peacock getting eaten even if he was a little headstrong.

I glanced back to see what Mr Gill might be doing, only to discover he was nowhere in sight.

Inside the house, Lady Mary continued to chat. 'I'll take you through to George's study. The police are in there now looking at his things. I rather think you might need to have a word with them Patricia, they are not taking me seriously at all.'

We turned a corner, and the faint murmur of voices we had been able to hear coalesced into speech. Through an open door to our front, I could see several uniformed officers.

One looked up as he caught sight of us approaching. There was a moment when our eyes met and when recognition occurred a half heartbeat later, we both had very different reactions.

I smiled, relishing what was to come.

In contrast, he bowed his head, leaned on the desk, and looked as if he had just been handed the worst news imaginable.

Approaching the study, we all heard him sigh and say, 'Lord save me from amateur sleuths.'

My smile broadened. 'Hello, Chief Inspector Quinn.'

I didn't stop at the door to the study, I swept right through it, my entourage following close behind. All the officers inside stopped what they were doing to see who the new people were. Their expressions revealed they all knew my face.

Chief Inspector Quinn lifted his chin, regaining his composure as he folded his arms and narrowed his eyes at me.

'Were you invited here, Mrs Fisher?' he enquired, somewhat impolitely.

'Indeed, she was,' snapped Lady Mary, answering for me.

'Lady Mary and I are friends.' I couldn't stop the grin spreading across my face at his discomfort.

He sighed and I got to see his shoulders slump in defeat. 'Of course you are. I suppose you are here to solve Lady Mary's mystery?'

Lady Mary jumped in before I could reply again. 'Yes. And I dare say she will do a better job too.' The lady of the house swung her attention from the senior police officer to me. 'They have been complaining that there is nothing to investigate,' she accused them directly.

Chief Inspector Quinn harrumphed, 'That's because there isn't, Lady Mary. You advised the dispatch officer that your husband had been kidnapped.'

'That's because he has, man!'

'Then where is the ransom note? Why is there no sign of a struggle?' I kept quiet, letting Quinn tell me the things I did not yet know. 'At this

11

time, we have a man who has chosen to be elsewhere. He could have gone to the supermarket, or the local public house.'

'His car is in the garage,' Lady Mary shot him down.

'Which proves nothing,' Quinn argued. 'There is no evidence of foul play and no sign that he was taken. You said he went to check the tigers?'

'Tiger,' Lady Mary corrected him. 'We lost the male last year. A new one has been purchased from a zoo in Greece and will arrive in a few weeks. They have a successful breeding programme. Look, nevermind all that,' Lady Mary realised she was off topic, 'George left the house to visit the tiger because she is pregnant and due to deliver any day.'

Quinn frowned. 'I thought you said the male died.'

Lady Mary pursed her lips in annoyance. 'Yes, well that is another matter that requires some investigation.'

Quinn hitched an eyebrow. 'You're suggesting tiger immaculate conception?' A smile teased the corners of his mouth.

My socialite friend scowled; she was not used to being spoken to in a derogatory way by public servants.

'I shall be having lunch with the chief constable of Kent's wife next week, Chief Inspector. Would you like to be a highlight of our conversation?'

Quinn hadn't expected her reply and was about to say something that wouldn't be an apology – Chief Inspector Quinn didn't do that – but would be a retraction of some form. He didn't get the chance.

'I feel, Chief Inspector,' said Lady Mary haughtily, 'that I can manage from here without your assistance.'

'This is a matter for the police,' he argued, sparing a quick glance in my direction.

Lady Mary scoffed at him. 'You just claimed there was nothing to investigate, man. Which is it?'

Momentarily dumbfounded – he probably believed George's absence was nothing more than a husband wanting a few hours peace from his henpecking wife, but also didn't want to turn a possible crime over to me – he missed his chance to recover his position.

Lady Mary is no slouch and she dropped him neatly into a verbal meatgrinder.

'I see your wit matches your face, Chief Inspector – dull and a little pointless.'

One of his sergeants couldn't help but snigger. It probably didn't help that Barbie guffawed. Had she been taking a sip of a drink at the time she would have choked and have it dripping from her nose as Lady Mary continued to fire.

'Since you are too dim-witted to find the evidence that will lead you to find my husband, I shall bid you good day and hand this investigation over to someone with skill as a detective.'

The chief inspector had just been invited to leave but was gawping uncertainly at his host.

'Good day, Chief Inspector,' she stated firmly. He got a two count before she said it again with some force behind the words. 'Good day, Chief Inspector.'

The two detectives in their suits started toward the door. The sergeant in uniform went with them which left just Chief Inspector Quinn in the study.

'Must I invite you to leave once more?' enquired Lady Mary cruelly.

It had taken him a good thirty seconds to recover his composure, but finally, the version of the chief inspector I was more used to made a comeback.

He forced a smile onto his face, nodding politely in my direction as he said, 'Good luck, Mrs Fisher. If in the unlikely event that you do receive a demand for a ransom, I expect to be the first to hear about it. Otherwise, I hope you do not have too much of your time wasted before Lady Mary's husband returns of his own accord.'

It was a senseless parting comment that got treated with the disdain it deserved. Not one of those of us remaining in the study bothered to respond, choosing instead to move farther into the room now that there was more space.

Jeeves the butler led the police officers to the door as I turned to Lady Mary and got down to business. We had been moving since we arrived, either physically or verbally and this was the first lull. I got to take a proper look at my friend, meeting her eyes and seeing the worry behind them for the first time.

I closed the distance between us and pulled her into a hug. 'Oh, Mary, this is so terrible.' I held her like that, certain she was far too British to shed a tear but giving her a shoulder to cry on just in case.

I held the embrace for just long enough, then let her go and backed away a pace.

Alistair begged, 'Tell us what happened, Lady Mary.'

It was just as she opened her mouth to start speaking that Barbie squealed in fright and the dachshunds started barking again.

The dogs took off as if shot from a catapult, zipping across the carpet and out of the door. Had they been moving any faster, they would have created a vacuum in the air behind them.

Barbie was laughing now, leaning against Jermaine for support as she clutched her chest.

'Ooh, wow. That's not something you see every day,' she gasped.

'What?' I frowned at her, wondering what on earth I might have failed to notice. Her eyes and Jermaine's were trained outside of the study to somewhere deeper in the house. They were still near to the door and thus had a view out into the hallway.

Lady Mary tutted loudly. 'That will be Octavia. I should have warned you. My mind is really not with it today.'

Assuming Octavia was a housemaid or cleaner or something, I stalked into the hallway outside the study to call the dogs back. Imagine my surprise when the dogs, still barking, chased a fully grown ostrich along the hallway in front of me.

'Arrrrgh!' I screamed in both shocked surprise and absolute terror as the giant bird – easily six inches taller than me – began pounding in my direction. Its beady bird eyes were filled with avian insanity. 'Arrrrgh!' I repeated just in case no one heard me the first time.

Jermaine was rushing to my rescue, but Alistair was closer. He didn't attempt to stop the bird; he just did what anyone with a brain would have done: he shifted me out of its path.

I hadn't been able to get my brain to function lucidly enough to think to do that for myself. Yanked to safety by the sleeve of my coat, I spun

16

into Alistair's arms as Jermaine whipped out behind the ostrich as it passed.

My efficient ninja butler/bodyguard scooped both of my dogs as they attempted to evade his hands. They wanted to chase the giant chicken thing and were most put out to have been thwarted. I found it ironic that they ran terrified from the peacock but were content to chase something fifty times the size.

I guess the difference is that the ostrich ran away and in so doing gave them something to chase.

The bird vanished through a door and from sight as my pulse continued to race.

'Mary,' I gasped. 'Mary, why on earth is there an ostrich in the house?'

'There's always an ostrich in the house, Patricia,' she replied as if that was any kind of an explanation. 'While we are on the subject, I should also warn you about Freddie.'

'What's Freddie?' asked Barbie suspiciously.

Lady Mary crossed her husband's study to a bookshelf whereupon she opened what I took to be a row of books. It wasn't, it was a cocktail cabinet complete with freezer compartment for the ice.

'Freddie is the house octopus,' she told us as she pulled out a glass.

Barbie made a choking noise of surprise.

'Something the matter, dear?' asked Lady Mary as she put the glass back in the cupboard.

Barbie chuckled at herself. 'No, sorry. For a moment there I thought you were making a gin and tonic.'

'Goodness, no.' Lady Mary looked surprised by the suggestion. 'It's far too early for gin.' She selected a different glass. 'I was going to make a mimosa. Anyone else?' she asked, holding up a bottle of champagne and a pair of glasses.

I bit my lip but decided a clear head would be better for me. 'No, thank you. Any other creatures we should know about?'

There was, it turned out, quite a menagerie with which Lady Mary shared her house. The list included a large boa constrictor, the ostrich and octopus, two chameleons which she said she wanted to relocate to the reptile house but could never find. I couldn't tell if that was a joke or not but chose to keep my eye out for them just in case. Topping off the list was a zebra called Dotty. According to our host, the stripey horse let itself in and out as it pleased and could sometimes be found watching television.

'Don't they make a mess?' Barbie wanted to know, her face screwed up a little as she imagined piles of poop in the halls.

Lady Mary was surprised by the question. 'Goodness, no.' She downed her first cocktail and began refilling her glass as she added, 'They are all house trained.'

'How does one house train a zebra?' Alistair enquired, like me questioning if our host might be pulling our leg.

'Oh, it's surprisingly easy,' she replied, eyeballing the champagne level in her glass and adding some for good measure.

Before we could head off on that tangent, I wrangled her back to the purpose of our presence.

'George,' I reminded her. 'Tell us what happened. What are you even doing here? Aren't you supposed to be out of the country with him on a book promotion tour?'

Lady Mary flopped into the soft office chair behind George's desk.

'He broke his big toe,' she revealed. 'It was the darndest thing. He opened the overhead locker as we landed in Denver and a bag of duty-free spirits dropped right out and onto his feet. Well, he always takes his shoes off to fly; he says his feet swell otherwise. The bottles landed right on the knuckle of his big toe and that was that. We had to call the whole thing off.'

I wondered if anyone else thought the duty-free spirits most likely belonged to Lady Mary. No one thought it necessary to comment.

'Tell us when you last saw George, what was happening at the time, where you were, and don't leave out any detail.'

Lady Mary levered herself back out of the office chair.

'I think we ought to retire to one of the drawing rooms. I'll have Jeeves drum up some tea.'

Tea

Over a pot of tea and some petit fours, we listened to Lady Mary talking about returning home this morning. Their flight got into Heathrow just after breakfast and her privately owned helicopter collected them shortly thereafter.

They arrived ravenous because even the food in first class isn't all that, according to Lady Mary. Once home, she began to prepare a small brunch, 'It wasn't worth bothering to call Cook,' she confided, sounding proud that she'd fended for herself. 'While I did that, George went to check on Esme. That's our pregnant Caspian tiger,' she expanded to clarify. 'One of the only ones left in the world. They were hunted to extinction – for game, of course,' she added sadly. 'My great-grandfather was wise enough to bring several here. Breeding programmes have not been effective though and by the time artificial insemination technology advanced, there were too few left for the species to be saved.'

I chose to interrupt her, not wanting to let her get too far ahead of my understanding.

'Yes, did I misunderstand the part about her getting pregnant? You have a pregnant lady tiger, but no man tiger. Is that right?'

Barbie skewed her lips to one side. 'Yeah, how does that work?'

Lady Mary took a sip of her tea. It had been served to a low table as we reclined on her chintz sofa set. We were in a room overlooking her garden, which is to say overlooking the zoo. A rhinoceros walked between two trees in the middle distance.

'If memory serves,' she said between sips, 'it doesn't work like that at all. It's something of a mystery. We had the head vet, Ashley Montague, examine her when she first started to display odd behaviour. I assumed it

20

was a phantom pregnancy, but apparently there are several cubs in her belly.'

'Ooh,' squeaked Barbie. 'That's exciting. How many do you think there might be?'

'Typically, tigers have two or three cubs at a time. But the question remains as to how she came to get pregnant in the first place. Old Tony the tiger has been dead for nearly eighteen months, bless his soul.'

I felt a little itch at the back of my head – the mysteriously pregnant tiger meant something. Pressing on, I asked her what happened next.

Lady Mary finished her tea and set the cup aside. 'Well, nothing, truth be told. George went to check on Esme and never came back. I served our brunches – a venison loin and fennel salad – and waited for him to come back. When he didn't appear, I called his phone.'

'Ah,' Barbie's eyes lit up. 'We might be able to use that to locate him.'

Lady Mary swung her attention to my young Californian friend. 'I doubt that very much. It's in the kitchen, sweetie.'

Barbie pulled a disappointed face.

'So that's it?' I pulled Lady Mary's attention back to me. 'George went to see the tiger and vanished?'

Our host looked rather glum when she nodded her head. 'That's about it, yes. George never goes anywhere, that's how I know he has been taken by someone. It would never cross his mind to go to the pub like that idiot Quinn suggested. George lives in this strange little make-believe world where all his characters exist. He only comes out of it to talk to me and eat food.'

I didn't want to challenge my friend's conviction – she was certain her husband was in trouble at the hands of person or persons unknown, yet I needed to eliminate some other possibilities.

'Is it possible he could have chanced upon an idea for a new book and been so caught up in it he is tucked away somewhere scribbling notes and plotting merry mayhem?'

Lady Mary sucked some air between her teeth and was good enough to consider my question.

'I suppose it is not beyond the scope of possibility, but I already searched the house and the route to the tiger enclosure. There was no sign of him, and he would have come to his senses by now and remembered to let me know what he was doing. And he would have got hungry. That man cannot abide being hungry.'

'Could he have fallen or become incapacitated?' Alistair suggested carefully. 'I've no wish to alarm you, Lady Mary, but is it possible that he suffered a dizzy spell, or strayed from the path? Are there sinkholes on the property?'

I think Alistair was actually asking if the poor man might have suffered a stroke or heart attack and be lying dead or in a desperate state somewhere. That he skirted around the subject was probably for the best - Lady Mary looked a little delicate today.

'Sinkholes are not something I have ever heard of occurring here. I did have a look around the ground, as did the police when they first arrived. The chief inspector sent the two detectives with my head keeper, Mr Gill - that's that chap you were talking to outside. They returned without finding anything though. They reported no sign of a struggle and I have to say I agree with them. That doesn't mean he wasn't taken at gunpoint though.'

22

'And his health?' I prompted her to answer the other part of Alistair's question.

'I cannot rule it out, but I am doubtful George would wander deeper into the park grounds if he felt less than chipper. He would have returned to the house, not found a remote spot to crawl into and die.'

We were about done with the question-and-answer element. I needed to get out and see what there was to see. George's study would need to be examined with a fine-toothed comb, and there were house staff, ground staff, and the zookeepers, vets, and goodness knows who else to interview. If something had happened to George – I was quite prepared to take Lady Mary's word for it, then someone had to know something or must have seen something. They might not know what they saw was a clue, but we were less than an hour into this case and I was keen to get something onto the blank page of notes I currently possessed.

'One last question, Mary,' I promised. 'Is there anything else you feel might be pertinent to our investigation? However obscure, it might be the one clue that ties everything together.'

Lady Mary frowned slightly, giving my question some thought before deciding there was nothing she could think of.

The tea was finished, and the petit fours had been devoured, not that Barbie succumbed to eating any of the delightful treats. She would probably perform fifty crunches later just for looking at them. It was time to divide our team and get to work.

Barbie and Jermaine took George's study. It was as good a place as any to mine for clues. Alistair and I were heading to the tiger enclosure.

Just as we all got to our feet, the doorbell rang.

Chasing Someone Already?

Naturally, we expected Jeeves the butler to answer the door. Lady Mary was leading us in that direction and questioning where he could be when she heard the doorbell ring again.

Given his age and the size of the house, I didn't find it surprising that it might sometimes take him a while to get to the door. Jermaine always moved with a dignified unhurried cadence when he was in my house and in the role of my butler. I knew he thought it unseemly to rush.

The doorbell rang yet again.

'Perhaps one of us should answer it?' I suggested.

Lady Mary's expression could only be described as aghast.

'Answer one's own door? Have you gone quite mad, Patricia? It could be anyone outside.' She turned away from me and raised her voice. 'Jeeves? Jeeves?'

His reply echoed back from somewhere. 'Coming, M'Lady.'

Another ten seconds ticked by before he shuffled into sight.

'My apologies, M'Lady. I felt it prudent to check on the wine cellar situation since you have guests.'

'Yes, very good, Jeeves.' I got the impression Lady Mary was used to hiding her impatience. I also felt sure I knew who was outside, but we waited patiently in the lobby while Jeeves made his way to the door at a pace only slightly faster than glacial.

'Has he been the butler here for long?' I asked our host, my voice quiet so the geriatric butler wouldn't hear me.

'It was my grandfather who hired him. Jeeves was third footman when he first came to the house. That was in nineteen twenty-seven.'

I blinked. Then I did some mental arithmetic. 'Nineteen twenty-seven. How old is he?'

My socialite friend sniggered. 'I'm kidding, Patricia. Jeeves has been here since before I was born, and I honestly couldn't tell you when he started or how many years he has been in service. I couldn't possibly get rid of him though. It would kill him.'

Watching him amble slowly to the door, his butler's livery hanging from his near-skeletal frame, I wondered if he might expire before we could confirm the identity of the person pressing the buzzer.

The doorbell rang again, and this time a voice came with it.

'Come on!' a lady shouted, spoiling my guess because I expected the person outside to be my assistant, Sam. 'I needs to pee,' the lady shouted through the door. I checked to see if there was a letter box, half expecting a finger to poke through so the person outside could see in.

The door was not fitted with one, mail presumably coming to the tradesman's entrance to the side of the house.

However, Jeeves was finally at the door, and it swung open to reveal a lady of approximately eighty years of age. I didn't know her, and neither did Lady Mary if I was reading her facial expression correctly.

The door continued to swing though, and as the view to outside widened, I saw Sam. He was standing next to the old lady, a small suitcase in his hand and a big beaming smile on his face. Spotting me, he gave an enthusiastic wave.

26

Sam Chalk is the best assistant I could have asked for. He's a little scruffy, but he sees things I never would and asks questions I could never perceive. He is perpetually happy and generally just fun to be around. When we leave for the ship, he is coming too.

'Hello, Sam,' I greeted him as he stepped across the threshold and Jeeves swung the large door shut behind him. I offered the lady at his side my hand. 'Hello, I'm Patricia Fisher.'

'Gloria Chalk,' the lady replied, taking my hand with a bone-crushing grip. 'I'm Sam's granny.'

I had already made the connection from her name. Gloria stood about five feet and two inches tall. She had wellington boots on her feet beneath a hopsack calf-length skirt. Covering her top half was a Paddington Bear blue duffle coat complete with chunky toggles. Her glasses were thick round things that as kids we used to refer to as the bottom of milk bottles and her hair was a jungle of white curls. 'Nice to meet you,' I replied as I rescued my hand and began to massage some life back into it.

'Gran's coming to the ship to look after me,' boasted Sam excitedly.

This was news to me. The subject of how Sam would manage living by himself had been discussed but not settled. I was returning to the Aurelia to take up a paid position and Sam was coming along as my assistant. It was a PR thing for Purple Star Cruise Lines – they were equal opportunity employers and keen to prove it.

My opinion might be unfair or harsh, I didn't know that was why they employed him, but it really made no difference because he and I both got what we wanted.

'That's so exciting,' gushed Barbie, who was always great with Sam. 'Patty, you never told me Sam's grandmother was going to be joining us.'

'That's because I didn't know,' I admitted, pursing my lips, and turning an accusatory eye to the one man who must have known.

Alistair didn't bother to protest his innocence.

'Can a man not be trusted to have a few secrets?' he asked.

Barbie, Lady Mary, and I all folded our arms and gave him a hard stare.

'Generally, no,' said Lady Mary.

Barbie agreed wholeheartedly. 'Men and secrets do not good bedfellows make.'

Alistair chuckled at us. 'I think you may be talking about a different kind of secret. Whatever the case, Mrs Chalk will be joining us. I have been discussing the matter with Sam's parents for some time.'

I felt both relieved and a little undermined. However, this was not the time to dwell on trivial things.

'We were just splitting up to begin our investigation,' I let Sam know. 'Do you want to explore the grounds with me and Alistair to see if we can find a clue to what might have happened, or head to the study with Barbie and Jermaine to look for clues there?'

I expected him to fall over himself to get outside into the zoo's grounds, but he pulled his trusty magnifying glass from his jacket pocket and picked the study instead. I guess the lure of bits of paper to magnify was just too great.

'What shall I do?' asked Gloria.

Lady Mary checked her watch. 'I dare say it's not too early for a cocktail if one is inclined,' she teased the concept tantalisingly under Gloria's nose.

It was way past time in Lady Mary's books, of course, as she often started her days with a breakfast cocktail of some form and had already downed three mimosas that I had seen.

Gloria clapped her hands and rubbed them together.

'I can see you and I are going to get on famously,' she cackled. 'Lead the way.'

A few minutes later, I had the collar of my winter coat turned up to protect my neck from the cool air outside and a mental note to unpack a scarf later. It was cold out, but not so cold that I felt a need to scurry back to the house. My hand was looped through Alistair's elbow, and it was almost like we were taking a stroll through the countryside as we set out on the path from Lady Mary's house.

The dachshunds were leading, their noses in the air as they strained against my arm to get to wherever we were going.

We had directions from the house to the tiger enclosure. George vanished on his way there. Or perhaps it was on his way back. We wouldn't know until we found him.

'Do you have any initial thoughts?' Alistair asked as we wandered.

I suspected he was making conversation rather than leading me to form a conclusion.

'Not yet,' I replied, 'Other than to say I believe her. If Mary says George has been taken, then I think we have to assume we are dealing with a kidnapping.'

'Why?' Alistair asked the obvious question. 'I could understand someone taking him if they demanded money, but with no ransom note and no contact from anyone, that seems less likely.'

'Unless they want to make Lady Mary desperate before they call. They might make her stew for a day first,' I suggested.

He dipped his head to acknowledge my point. He opened his mouth to say something, but I cut him off.

'Shhhh!' I hissed as quietly and urgently as I could. I didn't need to make the sound twice or explain why because he heard it too – two people arguing ahead of us.

We ducked into the foliage at the side of the path so we would be less visible and strained our ears to hear.

It was two men, but I couldn't make out what I was hearing. Whatever they were saying, their discussion was heated.

'We need to get closer,' I whispered.

Alistair nodded and knew better than to try to leave me behind to go forward chivalrously by himself.

I scooped the dogs. One bark from them and any chance to overhear the argument raging around the corner would be lost. I passed Georgie to Alistair and crept around the side of a tree.

I couldn't see our targets, but with each yard their voices became clearer. However, just when I thought I was starting to make out words, there was a loud exclamation and the sound of air leaving someone's lungs at speed.

One of the men had just hit the other!

A cry of pain rang out and that caused Anna to bark.

I hadn't yet had time to react but now we needed to move fast because we could hear retreating footsteps. The men heard Anna, realised they were being spied on, and chose to run away.

Darting forward, I swore at my choice of footwear, but plopped Anna on the ground and started running. I wasn't wearing a tall heel, but any heel is a poor choice for running on damp grass.

Faster on his feet, Alistair zipped around me, tiny Georgie pulling him along as she raced to see what the noise ahead might be.

I rounded the corner to see a man vanish into the trees to our right.

Alistair, already five yards ahead of me was in pursuit, but the other man, the one I expected to be holding his gut and recovering, was nowhere in sight.

'He went that way!' yelled my boyfriend, twisting at the waist to shoot an arm at the trees of the opposite side of the path to the one he was heading for.

A glance showed me the branches of two pine trees settling back into position where the passage of something large had disturbed them. I ran at them.

Alistair and I were separating. It didn't feel safe; I knew Jermaine would not approve, but there was no time for discussion.

I pushed through the trees, Anna yanking the lead as she tried to get me to go faster. Branches whipped at my face as I pushed through the undergrowth. Anna just ran beneath it all, oblivious to the fight I had to endure.

The foliage was so thick I could barely see what was ahead, other than more trees. I found myself cursing the coniferous plants, wishing they could be deciduous instead. At this time of year there would be no foliage, just leaves on the ground for my shoes to trample.

Abruptly, I burst through the last of it, spinning into free space as the pressure against me fell away. On the other side of the trees was free space and a gentle downward slope.

There was also wet grass again and I hadn't been prepared for it. If the sudden lack of trees to batter through hadn't been enough, my lead foot slipping was.

I tumbled, releasing the dog lead for Anna's safety, but also so I wouldn't strangle myself with it. I didn't fall far, the slope wasn't steep enough to keep me tumbling once I started, but I came to rest on my bottom with my feet facing down the slope and the damp from the grass soaking through to my knickers.

My trousers were dirty, loose bits of my hair were stuck to my face, and when I tried to get up, I discovered one of my heels had snapped off. I muttered some choice expressions under my breath, looked around for the missing heel, and gave up when it didn't immediately present itself.

It was a perfect start to my investigation.

Anna, her tongue lolling to one side as she panted, gave me a curious look.

Getting back to my feet, and hobbling in my unbalanced shoes, I scanned for any sign of the man I had chased.

From my elevated position, I could see various parts of the zoo: buildings, enclosures, and habitats housing all manner of dangerous

32

creatures. However, as I scanned around for the man I was trying to follow, it was obvious I had lost him.

Gritting my teeth to keep me from verbalising my frustration, I was about to head back through the trees when I spotted the footprints. The grass was just a couple of inches high; the perfect length for holding moisture to make sure any accident-prone, middle-aged women who happened along and fell over were going to get soaked. But also, the perfect height to show which direction my quarry went.

I set off again, hurrying as best I could and running on my toes to minimise the problem of the missing heel. The ground levelled out, the grass giving way to tarmac as it met a road broad enough for vehicle traffic. I was looking at the back end of the zoo, the parts people would not see so the fences to my right were the far reaches of the enclosures when viewed by the guests visiting for the day.

The footsteps ended at the road, but I followed in the direction they were heading, hoping to pick them up again. I scanned the dirt at the side of the tarmac for a fresh shoeprint and sure enough, there was one.

It was my first proper look at the print of the person I was following. It looked like a generic boot print from a rugged outdoor shoe – the sort of thing a zookeeper might wear.

The man I did see, the one Alistair chased, had been wearing zookeeper uniform: fawn trousers, the kind with lots of pockets, rugged brown boots with ankle support, a dark green gilet with the word 'Zookeeper' embroidered between the shoulder blades and a light brown shirt almost the same shade as the trousers.

That I was also chasing a zookeeper seemed probable because there had to be a limited number of people who had access to the zoo's back areas. I wouldn't know unless I found him though, so I pressed on, my

33

pace hurried but not running as I skirted the fence and followed the boot prints.

Peering through the fence, I spotted a herd of wildebeest and then both giraffes and zebras, all three mixed in together. Something that looked like an antelope bounced and pranced in the distance.

I was a little out of breath, the sudden burst of energy had caught me by surprise, and I was beginning to wonder if there had been any point to it, because the man was surely long gone by now. Undeterred by the pessimistic voice in my head, I kept going for there were buildings ahead and the boot prints, getting fainter, were leading to them.

I rounded a corner of the fence a few yards farther along and found the entrance to one of the buildings right in front of me. The boot prints met the tarmac once more and vanished. Since they were pointing toward the door, and I had no other lead to follow, I kept on going.

The building was three stories high, a big steel-framed industrial unit built for purpose not aesthetics. I looked for a name on the outside to show me what that purpose might be, but the only marking was a number: fourteen.

It could mean anything, but as I pulled the door open and stepped inside, I discovered it was a food storage warehouse. A yellow forklift with a rotating orange light on top went by twenty yards ahead of me with a giant bale of hay on the front.

I picked Anna up and held her to my chest, cradling her for safety.

There were pallets stacked up to the ceiling in places and sacks, boxes, and cartons on steel shelves reaching twenty feet in the air. Apart from the bales of hay, I had no idea what any of it was or what creature it might be for. Acting as if I possessed every right to be where I was, I marched into the warehouse and stopped in the open, spinning slowly on the spot as I tried to find someone who looked shady.

They would be out of breath, have mud on their shoes if my own ruined heels were anything to go by, and might even be holding their gut if the outrush of air I heard was indeed a punch to the stomach.

'Hey!'

The shout was not entirely unexpected. I was a woman in everyday clothes in a behind-the-scenes area. Anyone seeing me would assume I was a lost visitor.

I turned in the direction of the voice to find a man in his fifties heading my way. He was short and a little doughy around his middle. He had a ring of brown hair sitting above his ears, but none on the top of his head, and a pair of black plastic spectacles above an angry expression.

'Before you tell me I shouldn't be here,' I cut him off before he had a chance to say anything. 'I am here at the request of Lady Mary and a guest in her house. My name is Patricia Fisher ...'

The man took in my appearance and his angry expression dropped away, replaced by one of fearful concern.

'Oh, my goodness!' he gasped, his eyes widening.

'It's okay,' I attempted to calm him down, but the man wasn't listening.

'Help!' he shouted. 'Help! This woman needs help!'

Surely, I didn't look that bad? The sound of people running came from all around me and the forklift truck ground to a halt.

'No, I'm fine,' I insisted. 'I just need to ask you some questions.'

'She's in shock,' the man shouted to his colleagues as they began to arrive. His focus shifted to me. 'It will be all right. You're safe here. Can you tell us what happened?' His words came fast like a torrent, and he grabbed for my arm. I think he meant to guide me to an office somewhere so I could sit down.

He looked startled when I ripped it from his grip. Anna was getting riled, her top lip peeled back to reveal her teeth in a threat display. She might be small, but that just means her teeth are like needles.

'Now don't panic, love,' said a woman in her forties. 'We're here to help.'

'What happened to her?' asked a teenage woman, arriving with a first aid kit tucked under her right arm.

'Take the dog, someone,' instructed a man's voice. I didn't see who said it, but the doughy bald man with the black glasses reached for Anna and she snapped at him, biting his index finger.

'Yowww!' He jumped back, holding his wounded digit, and staring at me as if it were I who had bitten him.

It gave me a moment of stunned silence and that was all I needed.

'Thank you all for your concern,' I forced myself to remain polite even though I was speaking through gritted teeth. 'I am not, however, in any distress. I fell over while pursuing a man who I need to speak with. My name is Patricia Fisher.'

'Patricia Fisher?' more than one person questioned.

'You don't look like Patricia Fisher,' the woman in her forties scoffed.

The doughy, bald man agreed. 'No, you most certainly do not. Patricia Fisher is elegant and refined. I have seen her pictures.'

The teenage woman sniggered. 'Yeah, you look like a ….'

I cut her off before she could complete whatever she was going to say. 'Have you seen the one of me when I fell off the stage at the Maharaja's coronation?'

It was true that my pictures had been in the papers. Mostly they were head shots and reflected me in a good light because the papers were running positive articles on my exploits. The reports would have stuck in the minds of the people around me because they were recent, and because I am sure they knew of my association with their boss, Lady Mary.

However, the picture of my bum sticking up to the sky and the poor choice of knickers I'd gone with that day remained a scar on my ego and it was out there forever on the internet. It worked though - reminding the press of people around me that I was not always the elegant image they had in their heads did the trick.

A second of silence ended when a young man burst out laughing. He'd found the picture on his phone and was showing it to everyone. My cheeks coloured as more and more people saw the shot. Some of them remembered it, but none had connected the dots.

'I can't tell if that's you or not,' cackled the young man. 'All I can see is your gusset!'

'Thank you.' I growled. 'Now then. I chased a man in here and it is imperative I find out who it was.'

If I expected them to now cooperate, I was sorely mistaken.

'That's as may be,' the doughy, bald man snapped rudely, not even slightly put off by my statement. 'Health and safety dictates that you cannot be in this area. The operations here are continuous and you are not wearing the correct personal protective equipment, nor have you been given the mandatory safety brief.'

'Stop all operations,' I insisted. Whether it was the force in my voice or that my demand had never occurred to him I did not know. He stopped talking though and that was good enough for me. 'Someone ran in here and I want to know who it was. Lady Mary's husband went missing a few hours ago and I am here to find out what happened to him.'

The man blinked a couple of times. 'George is missing? George Brown?'

'George is missing?' echoed at least three other people in the small crowd surrounding me.

'Yes,' I replied simply. 'He vanished on his way to the tiger house just a few hours ago. Now please do as I ask.'

Doughy, bald man gave a small shake of his head. 'I'll have to check with the head keeper.'

'William Gill?' I supplied the name to show how much I already knew. Again, it caught the small man off guard.

'Yes. Oh, here he is now,' the man lifted his arm and waved to someone behind me.

I turned to see the head keeper coming my way. He had a determined gait to his stride and to my surprise, Alistair was right by his side. The two were arguing about something.

I was relieved to see Georgie, my other dachshund, wriggling in Alistair's arms. She'd spotted me and Anna and wanted to get to us. Alistair was forced to adjust his grip to prevent her from getting free. A few strokes and whispered words calmed her, but in so doing, William Gill strode ahead of him and got to me first.

The short man concerned about health and safety started talking the moment the head keeper was in range. I planned that he would – I wanted to hear what he might say.

'This lady says George has gone missing, Will. Is that right?'

'Aye,' replied William Gill, the zoo's head keeper. 'That's no excuse for being back here though, Mrs Fisher. These areas are out of bounds to all except zoo staff.'

'Then you can consider me zoo staff,' I snapped in reply. I wasn't going to be argued with. 'If the police came, you would have no option but to comply. You can consider me the same.'

'But you are not the same,' he argued.

Before I could retort, Alistair said something that surprised me.

'Mr Gill here is the man I chased through the woods.'

'Aye,' the head keeper agreed. 'Breaking a dozen safety protocols in so doing. You had no right to interfere.'

'Who were you arguing with?' I demanded to know.

He kept his lips pressed tightly together and shook his head. 'That's not any of your business and nothing to do with what might or might not have happened to Lady Mary's husband.'

39

'I'll be the judge of that, thank you. Now, who were you arguing with and what was it about?' I was being more forceful than usual. My confidence as an investigator had grown over the months and, if I am being honest, having Alistair standing just a few feet away made me feel braver than I otherwise might.

I expected an answer. What I got instead was a chuckle. 'You've no sway over me, missy. This place cannot operate without me, and I'll manage it in the way I see fit. That means no one gets to poke their nose into my business. Understand?'

'Mind your manners, sir,' warned Alistair.

William Gill was taller and broader than Alistair and not only looked stronger but had the look of a man who was doing hard manual work every day. Such things made a person tough but if he thought he could intimidate Captain Huntley when he turned to glower down at him, he was sadly mistaken.

The two men faced off against each other, neither saying anything and neither blinking as the tension ratcheted upward.

I didn't want to see how that would play out, so I stepped in to stop things before a fist fight started.

Wedging myself in the middle, I pushed Alistair backward and broke the spell. It was clear we were going to get nothing from Mr Gill without Lady Mary getting involved, but I had one last go at finding out what we had walked into earlier.

'I chased a man in here,' I stated loudly so that everyone in sight would hear me. Most of the background noise had died away since everyone had stopped to watch the *almost* fight. 'He would be out of breath and have wet trousers and muddy shoes from running cross-country. Someone saw him come inside.'

Mr Gill raised a meaty arm to wave to someone while saying, 'That's enough now. It's time I returned you to the house. If you wish to stray from the house again, I will be happy to assign an escort to keep you safe, Mrs Fisher. Given the state of you already,' he took in my dishevelled appearance, twig-filled hair, and broken shoe, 'I don't see how you could possibly argue.' He caught the attention of the person he wanted, a young man in his early twenties. Shouting to him, he said, 'Hewitt, get a Rover and take Lady Bostihill-Swank's guests back to the house.'

I narrowed my eyes at his face. 'What do you imagine Lady Mary is going to say when she hears you deliberately impeded my investigation? Her husband is missing.'

'I have impeded nothing,' he replied, his tone amused. 'I am keeping you safe, Mrs Fisher. There is heavy machinery here and people driving vehicles. Occasionally an animal gets out of its enclosure. For your own safety, you will need an escort when you want to go anywhere. You will find me quite cooperative; we all like George very much.'

'Yet you are not cooperating,' I pointed out. 'I want to know who you were arguing with and why. I want to know why the other man ran away, and,' I placed my hands on my hips and glared up at his smug face, 'I especially want to know why you are keeping it a secret from me.'

His amused expression didn't twitch.

'It's none of your business, missy,' he dismissed me, yet again, using a derogatory term. It was like being spoken to by an adult when I was a child. 'And it's nothing to do with whatever might have happened to George. If it were … well, it would still be none of your business.'

41

A huff of angry breath left me as I continued to stare at his frustrating face. A Land Rover painted with black and white zebra stripes drove in through the large roller door at the front of the warehouse, Hewitt at the wheel.

Defeated, for now, but certain we were not done, I climbed into the car with Alistair beside me and the dogs on our laps, and let the young man drive us back to Lady Mary's house.

At least, that's what I had planned. As usual with my plans, that's not what happened.

I called Barbie from the back seat of the zebra Land Rover.

'Patty!' she blurted my name. 'Are you on your way back to the house?' Her tone made it clear she had something to show me.

'Yes. We didn't make it to the tiger house though. I'll need to pop out again.'

'I can take you to the tiger house,' volunteered Hewitt from the driver's seat.

I almost questioned if that would get him into trouble with Mr Gill, but stopped myself when I realised I didn't need to care.

'That would be super,' Alistair replied for both of us.

Barbie's voice cut over his, 'You are not going to believe some of the notes we've found,' she declared breathlessly. 'I don't know what he was caught up in, but this is big, Patty. Big and dangerous.'

Flicking my eyes to the driver, it was no surprise when I caught him doing his best to listen in.

I stopped her from saying anything further. 'Tell me about it when we get back. We will be there shortly.'

I got an, 'Okay, Patty,' before the line disconnected, and I brought my attention back to where we were going.

We were still in the rear area of the zoo, tucked out of sight of the visitors behind the paddocks and enclosures. The road wound around, following the fence line before it reached an open area.

'The tigers are just across here,' Hewitt pointed through the window. 'Tiger, I should say. The keepers are getting very excited about the prospect of getting another one. No one likes to see any of the creatures kept in solitary unless that is their natural state.'

Since Hewitt was being talkative, I tried to wheedle some information from him.

'Who was Mr Gill fighting with earlier?'

Hewitt chuckled. 'That could have been anyone. He's not very good with people.'

'Really?' Alistair voiced my question. 'How did he get to be head keeper? Surely, all the other keepers are in his charge.'

Hewitt gave a half shrug as the Land Rover bounced over a pothole. We were nearing the tiger enclosure and he was beginning to brake.

'I've not worked here long. Just a few months. I heard he used to be much nicer, but his wife died last year, and he's not been the same since.' He checked the rear-view mirror, meeting my eyes to see how I reacted to his news. 'That's what I heard, anyway,' he repeated.

I could think of nothing to say, and he was pulling to a stop at the tiger enclosure, so it was time to do what we left the house for in the first place.

Standing on the tarmac at the rear of the zebra-striped car, I looked back up the hill toward the house. George set out this morning to check on Esme the tiger.

'Is there a log or some such that people mark when they go into the buildings?' I asked, my eyes still on the route down through the grass and trees.

44

Hewitt's voice came from behind me. 'No, nothing like that.'

Turning to face him, I asked, 'Did you see George Brown, Lady Mary's husband, around the zoo very often?'

'Occasionally, yes. When he was here, I guess.'

'Can we see the tiger?'

Hewitt hadn't thought about getting us into the enclosure, the slightly panicked look on his face showed me he now needed to find someone else. He reached for his radio.

Alistair touched Hewitt's arm as he raised it.

'Best not use that, eh? Mr Gill probably wouldn't approve of you helping us. Perhaps you can see if there is a keeper around who can let us in.'

'Um, yeah, okay,' the young man mumbled, twisting around to see if he could spot someone. There was no one in sight. 'Um, I'll just have a scout around.'

As he jogged away, Alistair said, 'That was your plan, yes? To get rid of him so you can poke around?'

I nodded, pleased that he knew me well enough to read my intentions.

'He'll be back in a few minutes, and I want to talk to the keepers responsible for this area anyway. For now, though, we get to have a nose around unguarded.'

Making best use of our time, Alistair and I started to snoop. The dachshunds happily sniffed – they weren't much good as tracker dogs. I couldn't give them George's sock from yesterday and hope they would find him. Any clues we found in this area would be down to sharp eyeballs.

It was a long shot at best since we didn't know if George had even made it this far. However, this is my version of investigating - I poke my nose in and hope for the best. Somehow, it always seems to work out. I just need to expose my brain to enough of the mystery. If I do that, sooner or later, I work it out.

Anna and Georgie were doing their best to get to the tiger cage. It caused me to frown because I felt a large predator would be the last thing they would want to get close to. Surely, they could smell what it was?

'Come along, girls,' I insisted, tugging their leads hard enough to make them go the way I wanted. It was then that I spotted something in the weeds and stinging nettles growing at the base of the steel bars.

The tiger cage didn't have an outer protective barrier on this side the same way it did in the visitor area. It meant I could walk right up to it.

The girls, now that I was going the direction they wanted, pulled hard to get there, digging in with their little paws to scramble across the ground when we left the tarmac.

What I had seen, turned out to be a piece of paper. It was caught in the nettles, held in place by damp as well as entanglement.

Coming closer, I spotted what was getting my dogs so excited; just through the bars was a large piece of meat. What looked like a hip bone, complete with upper leg, was on the grass just inside the bars. There were teeth marks in the bone where the tiger had been rasping at it to get the last of the meat off.

Small pieces of red flesh still clung here and there. A horrible thought hit me like an electric shock, but I calmed again, stilling my pulse and leaning against the cage for support as I assured myself the hip bone I was looking at was far too large to be from a human.

In the last months I had seen death in many forms; eaten by a tiger would be a new one. Dismissing the notion that George was missing because he'd become a snack for a large predator, I focussed again on the piece of paper.

It was probably nothing, I accepted, peering at it but unable to determine what it was. I would need to fish it out of the nettles if I wanted to examine it more closely. It looked like a receipt, but not one from a shop. Rather, my brain wanted to believe it was an invoice from a wholesaler.

There was only one way to find out.

Huffing a breath and wishing I had someone else to do it for me, I pulled my coat sleeve down to hide as much of my hand as possible, then shoved it into the mess of stinging weeds and suffered the consequences.

I winced and swore at the beastly stings but gripped the piece of paper between two fingers. With a yank, it popped free.

Nasty lumps were already beginning to rise on my hand where the stings touched my skin. I did my best to ignore them and looked instead at my prize.

It was a soggy piece of paper.

In truth, I was right about it being an invoice from a wholesalers. The logo at the top listed the firm as Brenchley Premier Goods. I let my eyes flick down the list of items purchased and found myself starting to frown.

Expecting to see animal feed and all manner of products related to feeding the exotic wildlife, it struck me as odd to see twelve cases of champagne, other alcohol, and mixers. Together with some snacks, I had what looked like the ingredients for a grand party.

The lead for the dogs twitched in my hand, going taut as they moved away from me. I gave it a little tug as I continued to stare at the list of foods.

When Anna let out an excited yip, I decided I'd been holding a crouch for quite long enough and got back to my feet to see what she was getting all excited about.

Expecting to see that it was Alistair coming my way, or perhaps Hewitt returning with a keeper to let us in to see the tiger, I hadn't anticipated that the girls would be staring into the cage.

I turned my head, my eyes widening as I sensed the presence of something large in my shadow.

The tiger's face was inches from mine!

A colourful word slipped from my mouth as I danced back a yard. The girls didn't follow. They were wagging their tails like mad and hopping onto their back feet to get a better look. Had it not been for the barrier of stinging nettles, I think they might have tried to squeeze through the bars.

'Nice, kitty,' I cooed in a terrified manner as I reeled the dogs in.

I like tigers; they are so beautiful, but I like them on my television; I do not want to pet one and give it a hug.

'Find anything?' asked Alistair from right behind my head.

'Arrrgh!' I squealed, jerking away from the sudden and unexpected danger to my rear. It was times like these that I felt lucky to have not had children and thus potentially suffer the weak bladder problems so many ladies endure. Had that been the case for me, I would now be embarrassingly damp.

Alistair was chuckling at my expense – the horrible git had snuck up behind me on purpose.

I swiped at his arm, holding up the damp invoice with my other hand.

'Just an old invoice that blew in on the breeze. It's mostly alcohol so it's probably Mary's weekly supply.' I was being flippant, of course.

Alistair took it, muttering that he found nothing, but pointed out something I hadn't spotted.

'This isn't old. The date is two days ago.'

I leaned over his arm to see.

Alistair handed it back to me, muttering, 'It must have blown in on the breeze from somewhere. People are so careless.'

He wasn't wrong.

The sound of voices approaching turned into Hewitt and a plump woman in her forties sporting green and blue hair pulled into bunches. They came into sight at the far end of the tiger enclosure just as I was tucking the soggy invoice into my bag. It was just a lost piece of paper; I didn't for one moment believe it held any significance and would have thrown it away had there been a bin nearby.

The lady approaching had a bunch of keys in her hands and was sifting through them as she came closer.

'Hewitt here says you are guests of Lady Mary,' she stated as she approached, her focus still on the keys. When she found the one she wanted, she looked up and I got to see her expression change from confused, to quizzical and into recognition. 'Oh. You're that lady on the cruise ship.'

Hewitt frowned. 'What lady?'

I put my hand out. 'Patricia Fisher. This is Alistair Huntley,' I introduced the handsome man standing next to me. 'He's the captain of the cruise ship.'

The lady flicked her eyes across to Alistair as she let my hand go and flared them as a gesture of appreciation – he really is a fine-looking man. It was a bit like getting a round of applause for being able to attract him.

The lady introduced herself as Madison. She was devoid of makeup, her job not requiring it. Nor haircare it seemed, as her colourful locks were yanked into submission and subdued there with two elastic bands.

'You want to see the tiger?' she asked, no doubt assuming we were there because we were accorded special privileges as guests of the zoo's owner.

Esme was still staring at us through the bars, but magnificent though she was, I couldn't imagine she was involved in George's disappearance. I wanted to see the tiger enclosure and the area around it more than I wanted to see the animal. George was coming here when he left the house this morning, but I was forming the opinion that he hadn't made it this far.

The tiger cage was big when compared to my mental image of zoo enclosures. Measuring at least fifty yards in each direction, it was landscaped too with a water feature Esme could swim in on a hot day, and high rocks she might wish to laze on to get a view over the surrounding land. No doubt visitors would line the bars on the other side, excited to see her take a dip or climb up high.

Next to us, the habitat became a building. It would contain Esme's sleeping area and a place where she could be trapped for the vet to examine her. I had never been in the rear area of a tiger house so was making assumptions from shows on TV.

'Are you aware that George vanished this morning?' I asked Madison.

She made a suitably worried face. 'Yes, but only because Hewitt just told me. He said George was visiting Esme.'

I nodded but didn't verbally confirm or deny what she said. 'You are one of the tiger keepers?'

It was her turn to nod. She looked nervous, like someone at a job interview who knows they are on the back foot.

'I am a big cat specialist. I've worked here with the cats for twenty-three years.'

I dipped my head to acknowledge how proud she sounded of her dedication and pushed on with the purpose for my visit.

'Did you see George Brown today?'

'No,' she replied without hesitating.

'Did he often visit the tiger?'

'Oh, yes. He was fond of them. They knew him very well and would let him pet them. He was quite teary when we lost Tony last year. Not that it was a shock. He'd lived well past the normal lifespan for a tiger.'

51

'Can you offer any insight into how Esme comes to be pregnant?' The lead in my hand tugged again. I hadn't been paying attention and the dachshunds were back at the edge of the cage, almost nose to nose with the giant stripey cat.

I frowned and tugged them back again, missing whatever expression crossed Madison's face. It was a shame because when she spoke, I didn't think she was telling me the truth.

'No. Goodness, it's a total mystery to all of us. Heaven knows how it could have happened. I mean, the vets are all scratching their heads and talking to specialists from around the world to see if there are any other examples of delayed insemination like this one.'

Most of her answers had been close to monosyllabic, and now she was rambling, trying to fill the air with words.

I quizzed her a little more, unable to decide if she was hiding something or not and whether that something might be pertinent. I was on the cusp of challenging her, but held back, wanting to observe for a while longer before I started firing off accusations.

Instead, I thanked her for making time to answer my questions and shook her hand again. If she was up to something, she would now be at ease, telling herself I didn't suspect. That, in turn, would make her more likely to do something else.

Something that would get her, and whoever else was involved, caught.

For now, I wanted to see what Barbie had unearthed.

Who is George Brown?

Hewitt dropped us at the house, wheeling the zebra car around in front of the palatial façade.

'Thank you, Hewitt,' I gave him a pat on the shoulder as I swung my legs around to get out.

I got a nod of acknowledgement from the young man. He had been pleasant and helpful, which stood him apart from most of the zookeepers I'd met so far. I doubted I would see him again, but sliding from the car, I paused when I saw a question in his eyes.

A tilt of my head in question was all it took to prompt him to speak.

'Is there something going on here, Mrs Fisher? Should I be worried about my job?'

Interest piqued, I slid back into the car.

'What makes you ask that?' I wanted him to tell me more.

He wriggled his lips to one side and then the other, trying to organise his thoughts. In the end, he shrugged.

'I dunno. People behave oddly sometimes. They stop talking when I come into the room, or they send me away. Like I said earlier, I haven't been here all that long. At first, I thought it was just a new guy thing, but now ... well, you said Lady Mary's husband vanished inside the zoo today. That's just one more weird thing. Like with the tiger.'

'Is there someone you suspect?' I enquired, hoping he would supply a name.

'Suspect?' he repeated my word but in a tone that made it sound like a rude term to employ. 'I don't know what I should suspect them of, Mrs

Fisher. I don't think any of my colleagues have kidnapped Lady Mary's husband if that is what you are asking. If I did, I would already have spoken to the police.'

I nodded my understanding.

'Can I give you my phone number, Hewitt?' I took a business card from my purse. I had folded the company – I was leaving to take up a new job elsewhere – but the cards had my number on them. 'If you think of anything or you see something you believe to be suspicious behaviour, please call me. Night or day.'

Hewitt took the card, reading it and silently mouthing the words it displayed before tucking it into a breast pocket.

Sliding my legs around to get out again, I had a parting comment.

'To answer your first question, yes, I think there is something going on here. I must admit that I do not know what it is yet.' There was nothing left to say, and Alistair was waiting for me.

The sun was beginning to set, my thoughts turning to food as my belly chimed its emptiness with a loud grumble. An evening meal would be necessary, but my greater concern as we jogged up the steps and into the house, was for George.

Whatever had happened to him was still happening. Unless he was dead, someone had him and the longer he was in their possession, the more likely it was that they would feel a need to dispose of him. However, there was still no ransom note or call from the kidnappers that I knew of.

'What did you make of that Gill chap?' asked Alistair as I paused in the lobby to remove my shoes.

Even if the heel could be reattached, I never did find it, so the shoes were going in the bin. There was a mirror to my right, a full height one placed there so a person could check their appearance before leaving the house. I chose to ignore it, not wanting to see how wretched I looked.

I felt my forehead crease as I considered Alistair's question. 'He's hiding something. Given that he's in charge around here, I find it a struggle to believe that he wouldn't know if something untoward were going on. He's jolly prickly too. Refusing to answer any of my questions and basically challenging me to make him … I don't get that very often. He feels that he has the position of power.'

Alistair hadn't asked the question to make conversation I found out when he spoke again.

'Look, I don't feel that I will add much to what you are doing here. Barbie will have found something; you can let me know what it is later. I think I will make myself more useful and follow Mr Gill.'

I stopped walking. 'Are you sure, sweetie?' This wasn't what Alistair did. He would throw himself into situations for sure, always doing what he could to help. On board the ship, he would assume command and use the tools around him to get the result he needed. But the sleuthing – he left that to me.

'I'm sure,' he replied. 'This is your area of expertise, so I'm not going to try to uncover the gang behind whatever mystery shrouds George's disappearance, but if William Gill is involved in the vanishing of Lady Mary's husband, surely he will be going somewhere other than home when he leaves here tonight. I propose to follow him and find out where that is. Maybe I will be wrong but removing him from our list of suspects has value too, I guess.'

'It does,' I agreed.

I knew I had no reason to worry about him, yet that didn't stop me. I didn't want him to go, but I also knew suggesting Jermaine ought to go with him, or that he should stay with me in the house while we sent someone else would only display a lack of confidence that was unfounded.

As if reading my thoughts, he said, 'Perhaps I should take Sam. Mr Gill hasn't seen him. Sam can get close and listen if the opportunity arises. No one ever suspects him.'

Sending Sam made me worry even more, but I nodded, kissed Alistair on the cheek and said, 'That's a great idea.' He wasn't wrong that people tended to dismiss my assistant.

Barbie and the others heard us coming as we approached the study, our footsteps echoing in the quiet house. They were still where we left them more than an hour ago, but now the study was differently organised.

'Wow,' I took in the piles of paper spread across the floor.

Barbie and Sam were sat on the carpet. Jermaine was in George's writing chair typing on his own laptop.

Sam beamed up at me. 'He's been kidnapped by Shi'ite Muslims!'

Actually, Sam didn't say Shi'ite. He couldn't read the word correctly, so he said ... I'm sure you can work it out for yourself.

Barbie and Jermaine did not bother to correct him. They were too busy looking at me, their faces filling with questions they were not asking.

'I fell over,' I explained.

Barbie hitched an eyebrow. 'Patty, you look like you had energetic sex with a gorilla and a walrus at the same time.'

'Twice,' added Jermaine with a sigh I doubted I was supposed to hear. Poor Jermaine insisted on cleaning and pressing my clothes and polishing my shoes. Everything I had on was beyond saving.

'Was it good?' asked Sam, my assistant not grasping that Barbie's colourful analogy was a joke.

Feeling my face flush, I ignored Sam's question.

'I fell over,' I repeated. 'After fighting through some trees. Do I really look that bad?' I looked around for a mirror, but George's office didn't have one that I could find.

Barbie sniggered. 'Let's just say you are going to need to get changed and wash your hair before we go anywhere else today.' Shunting the joviality to one side, she brought my attention to the piles of paper spread around the carpet. 'There is definitely something screwy going on,' she told me. 'There are travel plans ...' she fished around until she found what she wanted in a notebook by her left foot. 'He was heading to Dubai. It doesn't say when, but we found money.'

Jermaine opened a desk drawer and from it removed a wad of notes secured with an elastic band.

'It's in Dirhams, the currency in Dubai,' he held it up so we could see.

I held up my hands to slow them down. 'Before we get into that, Alistair is heading out to follow someone.'

'Oooh,' Barbie's eye twinkled. 'Have you got a suspect already? That was quick, Patty.'

'Not a suspect exactly, just someone being evasive and keeping secrets.' I thought about Madison. 'He's not the only one, but it's the head keeper; the man we met outside when we first arrived.'

Jermaine's brow pinched in the middle. 'He came across as surly, madam. Should I assist the captain?'

'No need,' chipped in Alistair. 'If Sam is willing, he and I will tackle this one. It should just be a case of follow and observe to see if there is anything to report.'

Sam was already getting off the floor, his trusted magnifying glass clamped in his right hand.

'Secret spy mission time,' he grinned.

I kissed Alistair before he departed and gave Sam a hug; the two men were off to tackle our case from a different angle. I ought to be pleased to have such great help, yet I couldn't shift the feelings of doubt and worry as they made their way down the hall and out of sight.

I took a deep breath, held it for a moment, and let it go as I tried to still my heart rate.

'Madam, can I fetch you a beverage?' asked Jermaine, rising from his chair. He crossed to the hidden drinks' cabinet in the wall behind the desk, but I shook my head. I wanted to keep my brain clear for now.

Barbie was on her feet too, the nimble blonde bouncing onto her toes as if gravity were optional for her. 'Sorry, Patty. We should have asked how you got on first.'

I waved her concerns away. 'It seems like you have been making discoveries. Are you sure none of this is the plot for his next thriller?'

I got a sort of shrug from them both. 'We asked ourselves the same question. The money would seem to indicate he had genuine plans to travel though.'

'Not only Dubai, madam,' Jermaine pointed out. 'There are clues that he had a person to meet in Bolivia. We think it might be an arms dealer.'

'An arms dealer?' I stuttered, shocked at the concept.

'That's not all,' Barbie dropped her voice and twisted her head to look at my butler. 'Show her, Jermaine.'

My eyebrows rose with curiosity as the tall Jamaican man went back to the desk. There, he opened the drawer again, but instead of taking something out, he reached his hand inside as if feeling for something.

I heard a click noise as if something had been released against spring tension and the side of the desk popped out by half an inch.

My eyes popped out on stalks to match it.

'I was looking for clues or evidence in the drawer, madam,' revealed Jermaine, 'wondering if there might be something tucked at the back out of sight when my hand struck the mechanism by chance.'

Barbie spoke in a quiet voice, 'You haven't seen the half of it yet, Patty.'

Now I needed to see what was behind the secret panel. They didn't make me wait. Barbie stepped out of the way as Jermaine leaned over to lower the side of the desk. It was hinged at the bottom, so it scythed down to meet the carpet.

It was only part way there when my jaw dropped open.

The inside of the desk's secret compartment was filled with weapons and other paraphernalia. I wasn't educated enough in such things to be able to identify what they were by make and model, but they were black, sleek, modern, and deadly looking.

Barbie said, 'I know, right?' as she came to stand beside me.

I counted six handguns of various types, a large knife, and several smaller ones which looked to be designed specifically for throwing. There was money too, held in place by steel clips. It was in large bundles and clearly in several different denominations.

'Are those passports?' I gasped. I could contain myself no longer, dropping into a crouch to get a closer look at what I was seeing.

Barbie came with me, and Jermaine knelt on my left as all three of us peered inside.

I selected a passport, flipping it open to find a picture of George inside. It was a Cypriot document, listing his name as Georgios Topopolis. I couldn't tell if it was real or not, but it sure looked it.

'There are six of them,' Barbie told me. 'What does this mean, Patty?'

'We found plot lines for his books as well, madam,' Jermaine told me as he went back to his laptop. 'He appears to be working on several different stories at once, but nothing that might explain what we are seeing here.'

'I need to speak to Mary,' I murmured, shaking my head as I stood up. 'We may need to get the police back here. If he was involved in something international, we won't easily be able to follow.'

Barbie was happy to agree. 'This isn't like taking on the Godmother – we had no choice but to deal with her. This feels like we would be messing with foreign government agencies.'

The dachshunds, snuffling quietly in the corner by the study door suddenly shifted when they heard someone coming. They zipped back out into the hallway to intercept our host.

It was perfect timing on her part.

'Hello, everyone,' hallooed Lady Mary as she sashayed down the hall. 'Has there been any development?'

She had Sam's gran, Gloria, in her wake, the new member of our party sporting rosy cheeks and a wobbly smile from whatever cocktails Lady Mary had been plying her with.

I stepped into the doorway, intending to ask her about the desk, but her reaction stopped me.

'Goodness, Patricia. What happened to you? You look like you won second place in the best live scarecrow competition.'

Gloria was eyeing me suspiciously. 'There are leaves sticking out of your clothes.' It sounded like an accusation. 'What you get up to in your own time is up to you, but I don't want you leading my Sam astray.'

I exhaled a big sigh, wishing I had checked my appearance in the lobby mirror and gone to get changed before seeking out my friends.

'I fell over,' I replied as dismissively as I could. 'Don't worry, I'll tidy myself up shortly.' I stepped to the side so I could distract both ladies with the desk and its contents. 'Do you know anything about this?' I asked Lady Mary.

She had to look at it from outside in the hall and through an oblique angle but there was no mistaking what was in the desk, and no faking the shock on Lady Mary's face.

'Is that George's desk?' she asked, a little redundantly. Her feet had faltered, stopping her when she took in the surprising view, but she came forward now, fiddling nervously with the string of pearls around her neck as if they were worry beads.

Gloria said, 'Cor, look at that. Is your husband a contract killer?'

Lady Mary's nostrils flared, but she offered no response.

Ignored by the two ladies, Anna and Georgie went back to snuffling for crumbs of food and Lady Mary stepped around the piles of paper my friends had assembled to get closer to her husband's writing desk.

It was a hidden compartment that had to have been built in when he had the desk manufactured. Not only hidden but also kept secret from his wife.

'What is this?' Lady Mary breathed, gawping at the desk.

'Did George ever mention Dubai or Bolivia?' I asked her. 'Did he mention travelling to those places?'

'Dubai?' Lady Mary repeated. 'I hardly think so. George cannot abide the heat. It took hours of convincing on the part of his agent to get him to agree to some of the stops on his current tour. He insists on air conditioning everywhere he goes. And no, I don't recall him ever mentioning Bolivia or Dubai. What does this have to do with his disappearance?'

I shook my head. 'I have no idea.' I gave my friend an earnest face. 'It looks like he might have been mixed up in some kind of spy caper.'

Lady Mary burst out laughing. 'George? He's a short, balding, tubby Englishman. If there is a polar opposite to James Bond, that's what he is.'

Clearly, she found the idea preposterous. Twenty minutes ago, I would have said the same, yet here we were examining the evidence of a double life his wife had no idea about. If we wanted to find a reason for his sudden disappearance, whatever he was up to in secret sounded far more likely than a conspiracy between the zookeepers.

Gloria swayed a little as she came forward, her eyes locked on the rack of guns. They were all muzzle down, the handles ready to be grabbed and that was what Sam's gran was about to do.

Jermaine intercepted her.

'Mrs Chalk we need to touch these items as little as possible,' he politely denied her access to the dangerous weapons by blocking her way with his body.

'But they look fun,' she argued. 'There must be something around here we can use for target practice.' She held up both hands in a classic pistol pose. 'Pow, pow! Come on, let's have some fun!'

Barbie met my eyes – Gloria was a bit of a live wire with a couple of drinks in her.

'Maybe later,' I suggested, hoping that would diffuse her for now.

Barbie had a question lined up. 'Did he travel much without you, Lady Mary? Did you spend much time apart?'

I already knew they lived very separate lives.

Gloria sported a miffed look now, irked that we were spoiling her fun. I thought she was going to interrupt, but she let it go, turning her attention to the drinks' cabinet half open to show its contents.

While Sam's gran – who had already had enough to drink in my opinion - perused the bottles on offer, Lady Mary answered Barbie's question.

'George goes into a zone when he is writing. He'll spend weeks at a time locked in here. He closes the door and barely comes up for air. I learned to just let him get on with it many years ago. He was already a famous novelist when I met him, of course.'

'Don't you often travel when he is writing,' I prompted her to admit.

She nodded along, not seeing where I was leading her. 'Goodness, yes. I take a cruise most often. He always joins me when he is done ...' her voice trailed off. 'No.' she saw what the rest of us were thinking but wasn't ready to get on board. 'You can't possibly think ...'

'You cannot account for what he might be doing for weeks at a time, Mary,' I pointed out. 'Maybe he doesn't even write the books. Maybe that's just his cover. Or maybe he does write the books, but it provides the perfect cover. He could write them in half the time you think it takes and be doing ... something else,' I finished weakly which was mostly because I didn't want to say he was out doing arms deals and killing people. The contents of his desk suggested he might be doing just that.

'Oh, George,' Lady Mary fumbled for the doorframe and caught it on her second attempt. 'I need a drink,' she mumbled.

Gloria, having heard her new drinking buddy's declaration, spun around with a bottle in each hand and a big grin on her face.

64

'Cocktail?'

I had to stifle a yawn. Our day had already been full and long. This morning, I finalised my divorce paperwork and led Charlie into a trap of his own making. I'd been confident things would go my way but cannot deny the nervousness I'd felt and the recent loss of sleep to stress because of it.

I hadn't mentioned anything to Lady Mary, how could I given the circumstances? We would give it our all to find George, but it was already looking like a mammoth task that might involve getting on a plane if we could pin down where he was. Or possibly we would find ourselves attempting to negotiate with people in another country for his release.

Was he really a member of an international spy community? The question echoing in my head made me wonder if I could phone MI5 in London and ask them. I knew they wouldn't tell me, but then my memory coughed up a name I could call: Justin Metcalf-Howe.

I knew exactly one British spy, and I didn't so much have a number on which I could call him as I had a number I could text a message to. He might then appear some hours later, popping up like a magician dressed as the waiter in a restaurant, or the surgeon on call in a hospital. Or he might be hiding inside the boot of my car when I went to open it. He was like that.

As I sent him a question, my stomach gurgled its emptiness again. It was loud enough for everyone in the room to hear.

I pressed a hand to my core as my cheeks flushed. 'Excuse me.'

Lady Mary had been looking through George's passports, but now her eyes were on me.

'It is I who should be embarrassed,' she sighed. 'I am a terrible host. Here you are in my house and there is nothing for you to eat for dinner. Cook went home already, and I haven't even given you a chance to unpack or freshen yourselves.'

It was Jermaine who spoke first, 'There is no need to apologise, Lady Mary. I ought to have planned better for Mrs Fisher to travel. Our lack of preparedness is on me.'

'Nonsense,' I argued. Jermaine felt it was his role to see to my every need. I argued with him constantly about his desire to operate as my butler. We were friends and I didn't need a servant. Before we could discuss the matter any further, I said, 'Look, why don't we book a table somewhere and talk about what we know over some dinner? We all have to eat, right? I'll call Alistair and find out where he and Sam are. They can come to us.'

'Ooh, yes!' trumpeted Gloria. 'I haven't been out for dinner in years.'

I already had my phone in my hand, intending to leave no room for argument. However, when Alistair answered the phone, the plan quickly changed because we were going to him, not the other way around.

He and Sam had been successful in tailing Mr Gill when he left the zoo, and they didn't have to follow him very far because he only drove a mile before turning off into the carpark of a local pub. Alistair and Sam kept going, watching to make sure their target parked before circling back a minute later. By then, William Gill was going through the door with two other men.

Alistair claimed Mr Gill must have met them in the carpark because they were not in his car when they followed it. Alistair was in a corner of the pub now, watching carefully as Mr Gill and the two he was with met a fourth. Sam was sitting at a table close to them to see if he could hear what they were saying. My assistant was going to try to record their conversation on his phone.

According to Alistair, the men he was watching were keeping their voices low and their expressions stiff. Whatever they were discussing, it was serious business.

Those of us at the house were going to meet them just as swiftly as we could. Bags were thrown into rooms, but no thought was given to touching up makeup or changing outfits. Apart from me, that is. I looked a state.

There was a mirror by the door to my room and I had to admit that my current appearance did suggest I had been getting amorous in the undergrowth. I needed a bath, but there really wasn't time for that.

My bags and Alistair's were on the bed, still packed, though Jermaine had been good enough to place my suit carrier in the wardrobe. I stripped quickly, found a fresh outfit of jeans, boots, and a sweater. Then I balled up my ruined clothes and ran to the bathroom to do what I could with my hair.

There were bits of pine tree stuck in it. I also had mud on my legs where it had gone through my tights. On my right calf were two near perfect paw prints where Anna had climbed on me when I was on the ground. She had thought I was playing a game.

It took me five minutes longer than I wanted, most of which was picking bits of foliage from my hair and fighting it with a brush to tame it, but I was ready to go as quickly as I could be and found my friends waiting for me downstairs.

'Leaving the dogs behind?' Barbie confirmed since they were not with me.

Anna and Georgie were tucked up in their bed in a corner of my room. Their day had been busy and long too. I'd fed them some kibble and left them to sleep. I doubted they would move before I returned.

Lady Mary had a driver and a pilot on standby should we need them, and a building full of cars from which we could take our pick. She offered to drive but her personal tank was so full of high-octane gin, there was no way we were going to let her get behind the wheel.

Jermaine took the job, selecting a Bentley Continental from the line-up of cars since Alistair already had my Range Rover with him. Not that we needed to travel in luxury – the destination was barely far enough away to justify taking a car at all. In the summer, with a late evening sun providing warmth, it would be a delightful walk to the pub.

As it was, Jermaine put his foot down.

The Crooked Horse was much like any other pub in the English countryside in that its origins were probably as a coaching house where weary travellers stopped. It looked to have stood at the edge of the road – originally a dirt track cutting through a forest no doubt – for two hundred years if not perhaps three or four.

Inside, a fireplace provided an enticing smell as well as warmth for those sitting closest. The ceiling was low, as one often finds in old buildings designed when humans were shorter. Too low, it turned out as Jermaine had to duck his head to one side as he crossed the pub.

Barbie spotted Alistair almost immediately, shooting him a wave where he sat by himself in a corner. We spotted William Gill too. He had changed from his zookeeper outfit, but the casual clothes I expected him to wear after work had been subbed out for a sharp suit.

I was looking at his back though it was easy to make out who he was. He was sitting at a table with other men just as Alistair described and they were all tucking into food. Another man, sitting adjacent to Mr Gill was also in a suit which made it look like we were witnessing a business meeting of some kind. The two men across from them were in more casual clothes but the kind that made me think they had money.

I whispered to Barbie, 'Did you see any fancy cars outside?'

From the corner of her mouth, she said, 'I'll go check.'

I worked my way through the bar with Lady Mary, Sam's gran, and Jermaine. We joined Alistair and settled in next to him.

'How's Sam getting on?' I asked.

He gave a small shake of his head, making a face that showed his frustration or disappointment.

'I can't tell,' he admitted. 'I mean, I can see him. He's in no danger and he is over there with a pint of cider as you can see. He has his back to them and his phone on the table. I don't think they have any idea he is recording them.'

'Are we getting drinks?' asked Gloria, more interested in exploring the beverages on offer than getting involved in our shenanigans. Her question was echoed instantly by Lady Mary who was not only without a drink but also feeling a little discombobulated by today's events. 'This is lovely,' Gloria commented, looking around. 'The perfect place for a right old knees up. I remember going to places like this when I were but a young gal.'

'We are here following up an investigation, Gloria,' I felt I needed to point out. 'We need to remain unobtrusive and allow Sam to work.'

At the mention of his name, Gloria looked around for her grandson. Spotting him, she raised an arm and waved.

'Cooee, Sam!'

'Perhaps you would like to make a drinks selection, Mrs Chalk?' suggested Jermaine, using an arm to steer her away from our table.

Bringing her along had not been the greatest strategy. Or perhaps I could trace the potential for drama back a little further than that to the point where she started drinking with Lady Mary several hours ago. Too late now, I was glad Jermaine was wise enough to divert her before she drew too much attention to our spy.

Or it would have been if she had agreed to go. Gloria selected a chair next to me and settled in.

'So what is it we are doing here?' she asked, squinting across the room at Sam.

I had to think about my answer for a second. 'Attempting to find a corner to pick at. George is missing, but that's all we know for sure. The thing with the secret spy stuff could be a red herring ...'

'I certainly hope it is,' replied Lady Mary. 'If it isn't, he is going to get such a talking to when I catch up to him. Carrying on as a secret agent at his age?' She gasped and her eyes flared when a new thought occurred to her. 'There had better not be any hot spy women throwing themselves at him!'

I couldn't see it myself. George was lovely, but he was also tubby, balding, and short. He was not what anyone might consider a catch. The idea of saucy James Bond-esque liaisons just didn't fit.

71

'Coo, that would be so typical of a man,' said Gloria. 'My Eddie was always eyeing up the skirt. I had to give him a clip around the ear every time we went out.'

I tried to set Lady Mary's mind at rest. 'I think such things only occur in fiction thrillers. George is not the sort to stray.'

'Then where is he?' snapped my titled friend. Her worry about George's safety was now more focused on his potential infidelity. 'If he's making me worry so he can get fancy with a strumpet from the CIA or Mossad there will be hell to pay.'

Lady Mary lifted a hand and made a fist with it. Clenching her hand together tightly with a facial expression that made me wonder what she envisaged having in her hand when she squeezed.

Jermaine returned from the bar carrying a tray of drinks. There were more glasses than people at our table which might have looked odd to a casual observer. Confusion would, however, have only lasted until they saw Lady Mary select two glasses and down the first before anyone else could take one or Jermaine could place the tray on the table.

Gloria stared at Lady Mary with an open mouth. 'Wow.' Then she did the same, downing a large glass of gin in a single go.

I doubted this was a good thing for her to do.

'Do you drink gin often, Gloria?' I enquired carefully.

'Goodness, no,' she slurred. 'I only discovered it this afternoon. Lady Mary explained the subtleties and virtues of the beverage. She has quite the selection to experiment with. Pink ones, lime flavoured ones, flowery ones, strong ones … too many to list.'

Leaving Gloria in Lady Mary's care had seemed like a perfect solution when she first arrived. Seeing her rosy cheeks now, I wasn't so sure it had been. I leaned my head toward Lady Mary and hissed from the side of my mouth as Sam's gran reached for another glass.

'How much has she had?'

Lady Mary raised her glass in salute to her drinking partner before answering.

'She's been keeping pace with me all afternoon. I have to say I'm really rather impressed.'

My eyes flared with worry and a grimace found its way to my face as I watched Gloria sipping another large glass of gin and tonic.

I thought about asking Jermaine if he'd ordered strong ones, but knew it was pointless – he knew Lady Mary well enough to have the gin cut fifty-fifty with the mixer.

We were going to have to pour Sam's gran into bed if we didn't stop her soon.

Alistair coughed to interrupt our conversation and shot his eyes in the direction of William Gill and his table. Two of them were getting up.

Our attention swung their way. Were they leaving? Their meals were finished, the plates stacked to one side. As I watched, a waitress collected the dirty crockery and cutlery. The two men now standing were the ones who were more casually dressed. If I had to guess, I would assume they were business partners of some sort, and that William Gill and the other man were also partners.

The man I deduced to be with William Gill was in his thirties which made him just about young enough to be William's son. Their features were too dissimilar for that to be the case though, I judged. He was shorter by several inches, and he wore his hair longer than was the modern style, the ends curling around his shirt collar. I didn't get a good look at his face, he was looking the other way the whole time, but I saw enough to believe I would recognise him if I ever saw him again. I labelled him mentally as Gill's partner.

The other two men had a rough edge to them. I hadn't noticed it at first, but now they were standing, I could see tattoos on the hands of one. He had a beer belly protruding through his sports jacket, and a deep tan that had to be the result of many hours spent on a sun bed. His short hair was formed into a flat top – another style I hadn't seen in a while – and it was bleached almost white.

I labelled him as Ivan Drago, the famous character from *Rocky IV* played by Dolph Lungren. Okay, I admit it, I like Sylvester Stallone movies.

His partner had no hair at all. I called him Shiny because his head had to have a coat of beeswax to achieve the shine coming off it. He was taller, and more built; muscle showed on his bare forearms.

All four were still talking, William Gill and his partner making no sign they intended to get up – the body language displayed was not that which would lead me to believe anyone was leaving.

I was right I discovered a moment later when the two men standing split to go in different directions. One went to the bar for more drinks, the other to the gents' restroom in a back corner.

We all watched, no one saying anything for another minute.

'Is he a good head keeper?' I asked Lady Mary.

'William? Yes,' she confirmed. 'Invaluable, I would say.'

'That is what he claimed earlier,' I reported. I had been in two minds whether to burden Lady Mary with his attitude and behaviour earlier. She had enough on her plate without me adding staff woes to the pile. However, it was now time to delve a little deeper. 'He suggested the zoo couldn't function without him at the helm. Is that accurate?'

Lady Mary took a swig of her gin. 'I dare say he believes that. He would be hard to replace but my father taught me there is no indispensable man. If William Gill were to walk out or drop dead, the zoo would open tomorrow, and we would find someone to fill his shoes.'

'Do you have a good relationship with him?' I pressed her.

She almost choked on her drink. 'No one has a good relationship with William Gill. Not since his wife died. Even before that he was a surly character. He has always been a firm leader, but there were never any accusations of bullying. Had there been, I would have removed him myself – I cannot abide bullies.'

Alistair sucked in a breath. 'We heard what we believe was Mr Gill striking another zookeeper earlier this afternoon. We heard an argument, and then the sound of someone being punched.'

Lady Mary looked horrified. 'You think Mr Gill assaulted another member of staff?'

'We didn't see it,' I pointed out hastily. 'I could not testify to what I heard, but I share Alistair's assumption. We raced to get to see who it was but both men took off. Alistair chased Mr Gill, but he refused to talk to either one of us about the incident and then insisted we vacate the staff areas of the zoo until we had a chaperone.'

Voicing her displeasure, Lady Mary growled. 'I shall chaperone you next time. He'll not argue with me. He may run the zoo, but I own it.'

Someone touched my shoulder, and I twisted my head to find Barbie settling into a chair.

'There are several flashy cars outside, Patty. No way of knowing if the gentlemen with Mr Gill own them, not without getting closer to them.'

I had a question for her, or possibly for the group as a whole, but a different question took precedence.

'Where's Gloria?'

We had all been facing Mr Gill and his table, keeping an eye on Sam who was casually watching a TV above the bar while hopefully recording their conversation on his phone. Gloria was at the back of the table when viewed that way, and with all our heads turned away from her, had left her chair without anyone noticing.

Her absence was obvious now because Barbie was in her seat.

We didn't have to look to find her though. Her location became obvious to everyone in the pub half a second later when she started singing.

Apparently, there was a piano in the corner. Perhaps it had been there for decades and in the days before jukeboxes and piped music, happy revellers had drunkenly bashed out song after song, filling the pub with their voices.

Now Gloria was bringing the old times back but not in a good way. We were all on our feet, crossing the pub to get to her, but no one was going to get there before every eye in the building swung her way.

She could play the piano ... just about. Her rendition of *Don't Dilly-Dally* was more or less on tune so far as the notes being played went. I got the impression she used to be able to play but hadn't tinkled the ivories in years. It was the singing that was making people wince.

If you can imagine the high-pitched shriek of an eagle in flight amplified by passing the sound through a traffic cone and then add in that the eagle has its beak caught in a mangle, you might get close to what we were hearing.

Gloria was oblivious. Not only that, she was attracting company.

There were other pensioners in the pub, the type who could just about remember the war if they stretched their imagination a little.

I was weaving through tables to get to the piano, my friends all doing the same as we abandoned our table to deal with our sloshed companion.

Three more voices joined Gloria's as she shifted gear and launched her troop of willing backing vocalists into *Knees up Mother Brown*. I felt like I'd been dropped into a cockney music hall circa 1950 and found it worrying that I knew all the words and could have joined in.

Mercifully, and probably because their singing was fighting the music already playing over the speakers in the pub, a man from behind the bar – the landlord possibly – arrived just ahead of me.

'I'm sorry ladies and gentlemen, singalong night is every Tuesday. I am going to have to ask you all to finish this song and leave it until then.'

'Rubbish!' sang Gloria, tickling the piano as she ended one song and tried to start the next.

The landlord, not looking excited at the prospect of wrestling the old lady, nevertheless grabbed the piano keyboard cover and began to lower it.

Gloria punched him in the gut!

'We are having fun!' she snapped at him. 'You rotten spoil sport. Everyone loves a singalong.'

'No, we don't!' called an unseen voice from the crowd in the bar.

Others echoed his sentiment. 'You sound like a bag of cats falling from a roof,' was one comment everyone heard. It drew a laugh from over half the people present.

'It's like working on the terminal flatulence ward at the local hospice!' someone else joked.

While her elderly companions frowned and looked unhappy, Gloria was ready for a fight.

'Who said that?' she demanded to know, getting to her feet, and facing the crowd. 'Come on! Let's be having yer!'

The landlord, still holding his gut where Sam's gran sucker punched him, spotted me arriving and asked.

'Is she yours?'

'Sort of,' I admitted reluctantly.

'Well, I've never had to bar anyone from this pub, but I'm thinking about it now. I believe it is time you took her home.'

I could offer no argument.

Lady Mary volunteered, 'I'll take her. I think maybe I should have slowed her intake a while back.'

Gloria was beginning to sag, the fight going out of her as her new friends drifted away and the alcohol in her system caught up.

'Ooh, I feel a little wobbly,' she admitted. A heartbeat later, she stumbled to the side and would have fallen had Jermaine not been there to catch her.

'Perhaps I should see Mrs Chalk and Lady Mary back to the house, madam,' he suggested.

I had to nod. 'I think that might be best.'

He would come back for us in due course once the ladies were safely back in their accommodation. Lady Mary would attend to her own needs and had a butler of course. Jermaine was going to have to manage Gloria though.

As they departed to a relieved look from the landlord, Alistair nudged my arm.

'Our other friends are leaving.'

I spun around to see all four men at William Gill's table now on their feet. They were raising shot glasses – what the man must have gone to the bar to get – and were saluting/toasting something. Their body language now showed us they were done for the night.

'We need to follow them,' I stated, still wondering who they were and what they were up to. Was this a red herring? Was William Gill involved in something?

I was going to have to find out because thus far his odd behaviour was the only clue I could follow.

However, in the next second, my desire to follow the men we could see got more complicated because the two men who were not in suits sat back down again. They were staying, but William and his partner were heading for the door.

Barbie asked, 'Who do we follow, Patty?'

In a split-second decision, I said, 'See where they go,' nodding my head at the head zookeeper and his partner as they crossed the room. 'I'll stay here with Sam.'

Alistair hesitated, not wanting to leave me unguarded. After all the incidents with the Godmother's assassins I could not blame him, yet there had been no attempt on my life since we toppled her empire and sent them all to jail.

'I'll be fine,' I insisted. 'You have the car keys. Take Barbie and see what they do next. If they just go home, come back for us.'

Visibly not entirely happy, Alistair gave me a quick kiss and dashed after Barbie. I watched them go out the door, caught Sam's eye so he knew I was still with him, and went back to my table to continue observing.

It was not the right thing to do.

Sam gave me a goofy grin and a wave, lifting his pint of cider into the air and mouthing, 'Cheers,' before taking a gulp.

He would make a terrible secret agent, of course, but the two men sat at the next table were paying him no attention at all. If they thought it was odd for the man to be sitting by himself or wondered why his phone was positioned as close to their table as possible, they showed no sign. I suspected they hadn't even noticed him.

It was a truth about Sam that people didn't look his way. Possibly this was because the Downs gives him a particular look that some might find discomforting to look at. I couldn't imagine why; I just knew that it happened. Either way, his ability to blend into the background was like wearing an invisibility cloak.

The two men were discussing something in an animated way. They were not arguing but appeared to have different opinions on whatever subject held their interest.

One was using his phone, his eyes on the screen while he sent messages and talked to his partner. His thumbs would flash across the screen until a text was sent. Then a pause would occur before he received a reply and needed to answer it.

Ten minutes went by, and my stomach rumbled again. I was supposed to be here to feed myself. So were my friends yet none of us had managed to grab so much as a packet of peanuts with which to replenish our dwindling fuel supplies.

I swung my attention to the bar. I could at least get a packet of crisps or something. I had no idea how long the men might stay where they were or when Alistair might return. When my stomach made an even more insistent noise, I chose to seek sustenance from the meagre snacks on offer in an easily ingested packet. Every bar has a few to choose from.

I also needed to visit the smallest room, so with a glance in Sam's direction, rewarded with a cheeky wink, I set off to combine the tasks.

Five minutes later, feeling more comfortable and halfway to the bar, my feet stopped moving and my stomach plunged.

The two men were no longer in their chairs.

And neither was Sam!

Momentarily rooted to the spot, my breath came in terrified gasps as I looked around the bar. Telling myself not to panic, I reasoned that Sam might be in the gents' restroom. The two men could have left, and Sam, seeing no further need to stay on his post, chose to use the facilities.

The thing is I didn't believe that for one moment. There was nothing in my recent history to tell me I had no reason to panic. Quite the opposite, in fact.

I ran to the table where Sam had been sitting, grabbing the attention of a family of four at the one next to it.

'Did you see the man at this table leave?' I blurted into their faces.

I got shocked reactions. Who was this mad woman invading their conversation?

'Please,' I begged. 'Did you see him leave? Was he alone?'

They all shook their heads – they hadn't seen him at all. Sam's ability to go unnoticed was working against me now.

I tried the next table with the same result. The door to the gents' restroom swung inward – someone inside was coming out.

I held my breath, hoping it would be Sam. Or the two men - that would work almost as well, and I would blow my cover to ask them if they knew where Sam was. They'd been sitting next to him for an hour, they had to know who I was talking about.

It wasn't Sam though. Nor was it the two men he'd been spying on.

My worry cranked up another notch. I had to check for myself. I hurried to the corner of the pub, pushed the door open and leaned my head into the gents' restroom to call out, 'Sam?'

'Yeah?' came a reply.

With a relieved hand on my heart, I unthinkingly waltzed right into the blokes' toilet.

Standing at the trough urinal thingy were three men. They all had their backs to me in the peeing position and were all looking over their shoulders.

The one in the middle nudged the man to his left. 'Looks like you're in, Sam,' he sniggered.

Sam – not the one I wanted – said, 'Hold on a second, love. I'll be right with you.' It was one of those moments when Barbie would say, 'Ewwww!'

My eyes flared in horror, and I backed out the inner door.

'Where're you going?' the Sam who wasn't my Sam wanted to know.

I spun about to run back out of the outer door, but it opened inward before I could get to it and there were three more men coming in.

They were chatting about something, but leers spread across their faces as they stopped talking mid-sentence.

'Hello,' grinned the one in the lead. 'What have we here? Giving freebies away in the gents? You're a bit older than I usually go for, but I can lower my standards just this once.'

I gasped in my disgust and shoved him backward with both hands. He wasn't expecting it, my blow strong enough to make him stagger backward. He only went a foot though before he bounced off his friend.

It got worse too because the Sam that wasn't my Sam had finished his business so both he and his buddies were coming up behind me. I was sandwiched in the tiny corridor between the pub and the gents' restroom.

Had Jermaine been here, one shout from me would have resulted in bruises, torn ligaments, and loose teeth. But I was alone. Completely alone, and I was going to have to deal with this by myself. I could have asked them nicely to step out of the way and they probably would have done it. If my heart hadn't been racing with concern for Sam, that would have absolutely been my first response.

However, the inebriated young man leering at my chest chose that moment to touch what he ought not to have touched.

Pawing my right breast, he asked, 'Are these real?'

Incensed, my anger went from incendiary to volcanic in the space between heartbeats and I shot out my right hand to grab his nuts.

'Is this a slinky?' I growled as I attempted to lift him from the floor by his scrotum.

He squealed in pain and shock, grabbing for my shoulders to steady himself but not wanting to fight me in case I tightened my grip.

I growled, 'Back up,' with a squeeze to emphasise my point. This wasn't ladylike behaviour, and I did not care.

The second I was through the restroom's outer door, I let him go and started running. I bolted for the exit, creating questions as I ran because this was the second time I'd been involved in a disturbance in less than twenty minutes.

'No running,' came a shout from the bar. I believed the voice belonged to the landlord again, but I didn't turn my head to find out, I put it down and ran for the door.

Bursting through it to find myself in the darkness outside, I discovered it had also started to rain. A steady drizzle could be seen illuminated in the streetlamps erected to draw attention to the public house and provide light in the carpark.

The more important detail screaming in my head was that there was no sign of Sam, or the two men I labelled as Drago and Shiny.

I strained my hearing, becoming motionless for a second when I thought I heard voices. When I heard them again, I started running once more, around to the left of the pub. My coat was inside, which meant I was going to ruin a second outfit, but such a paltry concern never entered my head.

Getting closer, I could hear raised voices. Men's voices. I couldn't make out the words; the sound of the rain falling was drowning out the sound, making it indistinct, yet I knew I was going to find Sam pressed against a wall and hemmed in by the two men.

Jermaine had gone to Lady Mary's house, leaving me without his protection only because I was with Alistair and Barbie and in a safe place. Alistair had left me because I insisted I would be safe. Now I was running toward trouble but there was no chance I would do anything else if Sam were in danger.

I was wrong though. Wrong about Sam being hemmed in by the two men I'd sent him to spy on.

I found this out when I reached the end of the building and was immediately tackled by a different man.

'Is this her?' he asked. He had a meaty arm around my upper torso, pinning my arms to my sides.

Ahead of me the two men I was looking for had backed Sam against the boot of a large SUV. They had three other men with them which made it six on one. Six on two, I guess, if one chose to count me.

In contrast to the two men who joined William Gill for dinner, the new men were not well dressed in smart yet casual clothing. They wore heavy boots and jeans or cargo pants. None seemed to care about the rain wetting their hair.

'Yeah, that's her,' growled the one I called Drago.

I was about to start screaming blue murder, but never made a sound because the man holding me crushed my lungs like I was a scrap of paper to be scrunched up. I couldn't get any air in.

I sensed a man coming toward me and the next thing I knew, there was a bag going over my head!

Terror filled me. Not just for myself but for Sam too. There could never be a more innocent party involved in my crazy life.

'Mrs Fisher!' he called out.

I heard a slap of flesh on flesh and a small cry of pain from my assistant.

A rough voice said, 'I saw her at the zoo today. She's that investigator. She was in the warehouse and asking questions.'

Someone replied, 'Then we need to take her with us. The weird kid too,' he added cruelly, clearly meaning Sam. 'He was recording us, and I want to know why.'

'Oh, he'll tell us why, all right,' chuckled another voice as if the prospect of making Sam talk was somehow funny.

Then a new voice spoke. It was a man speaking again, but his tone of voice was entirely different than the others, his demeanour pleasant and calm, yet also rigid like steel at the same time.

'Gentlemen, I do not believe the lady and the young man wish to go with you. I propose that it is in your best interest to let them go and back away. Otherwise, I shall be forced to thrash you.'

There then passed a moment of silence. My mind filled it by racing to put a name to the voice. I was blind with the bag on my head, my senses befuddled, but my brain was insistent that the new player was someone I knew.

Drago replied, questioning the speaker's parentage in a very impolite manner, and making several suggestions about what he ought to do to himself with a poker.

Another pointed out. 'There are six of us, and only one of you. Walk away or get buried tonight.'

In the same calm tone as before, the new man said, 'Your arithmetic is off, sir. There are only four of you.'

I heard someone say, 'What?' in a confused tone. I wanted to agree that there were six of them.

However, from right next to my left ear came a sound like a tree punching someone in the side of the head and the man crushing me to his chest was suddenly no longer doing so.

I squealed in fright. Then squealed again when I felt the man hit the ground by my feet. The sound of the tree punching someone came again just as I was ripping off the bag and my eyes widened to the scene before me.

Two almost entirely black blurs were fighting the six men – already reduced to four just as predicted – and now that I could see them, the name came to match the voice.

'Tempest!' I cried in shock.

'Little busy,' came his reply.

He wasn't alone. The second blur of black in the shadows at the end of the pub was Big Ben. It couldn't be anyone else, just because of the height and girth of the shadow he cast.

The man at my feet was getting up. Driven by fear, I kicked at him, landing a blow to his ribs. It was about as effective as trying to subdue him with tickles.

Thankfully, as he got to his feet, he ran into the fight rather than tackle me again.

I ran to Sam, a terrifying proposition because it meant running between the men now throwing punches and kicks as they traded blows.

No one was winning. Except Big Ben perhaps, I conceded, as a giant leg spun through the air and one of his opponents twirled like a spinning top on his way to the rain-soaked tarmac.

I could see Tempest was flagging. He looked to be pre-injured if that is a term I can use. Favouring his right side, he was fighting, but mostly he was defending himself and keeping three men occupied as he backed away across the carpark to get them away from Sam and me.

'Sam!' I cried, grabbing his shoulders, and pulling him into a hug. 'We need to get out of here!'

He pushed me away, doing so gently, but firmly.

'I have to help,' he shouted, pulling out his magnifying glass and throwing it. It struck a man on the side of his face, distracting him just before he swung a haymaker punch at Tempest. The punch missed its target, but when I expected my paranormal detective friend to take advantage of the opportunity, he chose instead to get a little distance between him and the men surrounding him.

Before I could stop my assistant, Sam ran, getting into the fray like the brave fool he is.

Shouting and swearing are right at home in a fight, so it came as no surprise to be listening to an abundance of it now. I didn't know what to do. Part of me wanted to run back to the pub and scream for the people inside to come out. Overwhelming numbers would save the day.

Another part of me was angry and wanted a blunt weapon, a tyre iron or something I could use to deliver an effective blow. Hardly ladylike, but if there was ever a time and place for such actions then this was it.

Another part, the greater part it turned out, was frozen to the spot with indecision.

Thankfully, hidden in the shouting was an instruction to withdraw. The six men who attacked Sam and me were somehow all on their feet still though they had to be sporting an array of black eyes, fat lips, and bruised brains if the power of Big Ben's blows was as bad as it sounded. At a shout, they broke off their fight and ran for their cars.

I was standing right next to one of their vehicles, so for a split second, I thought they were all running to get me.

Petrified yet again, all I managed to do was squeal in fright and put my arms up to cover my head. Mercifully, the men running in my direction ignored me, diving into the front seats of the SUV instead as they made good their escape.

The car roared into life and the tyres screamed their protest as they rocketed across the carpark and out into the street. Two other cars followed; both large off-road vehicles. Now coated in an eerie blanket of silence, the carpark felt empty and quiet. It was a stark contrast to the violence and shouting of just a few seconds ago.

With a jolt, I regained my senses and with it my control. My pulse was still hammering like a runaway freight train, and my breaths were coming as hard gasps, but I needed to know if people were okay.

'Sam?' I blurted. 'Are you hurt?'

His voice was angry when he replied, 'I broke my magnifying glass.'

I was crossing the carpark to get to him. Sam was with Tempest who was resting against the boot of a parked car.

Big Ben was heading toward them both and we arrived at about the same time. I touched Sam's arm to get him to look at me.

'Are you all right, Sam. Did you get hurt?' In the moonlight, I caught the sight of blood on his bottom lip.

'I'm okay, Mrs Fisher,' he assured me as a big grin spread across his face. 'I hit one of them in the head.'

Tempest chipped in. 'Check his knuckles. He punched the back of someone's skull.'

Big Ben took hold of Sam's right hand, holding it up so he could inspect it in the meagre moonlight. The rain was easing, not that it made much difference now, but it did mean there was more light to be had as the clouds began to part.

'I think he's okay,' Big Ben announced. He was making Sam flex his fingers to make a fist.

'The skull is a bad place to aim a punch,' Tempest took a moment to explain to my young assistant. 'You want to aim for the soft parts like the throat. Kick to the inside of a knee, or practice grappling to get an arm bar in place. These moves are far better than striking an object that is harder than your fist. You'll just break your hand doing that.'

'Fanks,' said Sam. 'I'll remember that.'

'You doing okay?' Big Ben asked Tempest, a mild look of concern on his face. He had one eyebrow raised as if considering his smaller colleague judgementally.

Tempest levered himself upright and said, 'Ribs.' To me, he explained. 'It's an old injury I got from a klown.'

'A clown?' I questioned.

'With a K. K-L-O-W-N. You might remember there was a strange plague of them last October.'

My brain served up memories of articles on the news.

'Oh, yes. There was a battle of some kind at Rochester castle wasn't there?'

He waved a dismissive hand to move past the subject.

'Are you okay?' he wanted to know. 'What was all that about?'

I shook my head and pursed my lips. 'Honestly, I don't know. I'm fine though, thanks for asking. I could do with a change of clothes is all. What are you guys doing here? Thank you, by the way, for your most timely arrival.'

Tempest just nodded his head in acknowledgement; he wasn't the type that wanted thanks or praise.

'I'm just glad we showed up when we did. We were coming off a stake out. We have a client who reported a free floating, full torso, vaporous apparition.'

'Ooh, a ghost!' exclaimed Sam with excitement.

Tempest gave him a sorry face. 'Actually, it was some helium balloons with diodes fitted inside on top of a small drone. It didn't take us long to figure that part out. But then we had to catch the person doing it.'

Big Ben laughed as he said, 'Honestly, it was like an episode of Scooby-Doo. The client was an old couple in a cottage at a farm and the bad guy was a land developer trying to scare them into moving after they refused to accept his offer for their property.'

Tempest smiled. 'It was good to have a clean result. We caught his men in the act, and they confessed. They even agreed – after Big Ben convinced them,' I wondered, but did not ask, what method the giant man mountain might have used, 'to call him and get him to talk about it so we could record him.'

'The police are with him now,' concluded Big Ben. 'It's a shame we couldn't be there.'

I eyed him in question, wondering what he meant until Tempest sighed.

'It's not unusual for us to find someone in a costume and Big Ben has been holding out for more than a year in the hope that someone will say …' He pointed a finger at his partner to prompt him.

Big Ben grinned, licking his lips before delivering the line, 'I would have got away with it if it wasn't for you meddling kids.' It clearly tickled him because he fell into a fit of giggles as he started to yank the Velcro straps to release his Kevlar body armour.

Tempest began to remove his cumbersome outer layers too, though more slowly and favouring his right side where his ribs were giving him some trouble.

'Do you have a car here?' Tempest wanted to know.

Big Ben pulled out a key fob and the next second an oversized, extra wide utility vehicle's lights flashed.

I shook my head and patted my back pocket. My phone was still there – a mercy in itself.

'I'll call my friends. We are staying just down the road.'

'If you're sure,' Tempest seemed inclined to hang around until we were safe.

Big Ben frowned at me in question. 'Friends? Would your blonde friend be among them?'

Tempest sighed. 'Leave it be, Ben.'

'You know,' said Big Ben, ignoring his friend, 'the one with the ...' he made the universal two-handed sign for large breasts.

Sam giggled.

'You mean, Barbie,' I replied, a cutting edge to my voice.

'Yeah,' Big Ben grinned. 'Good name too. I've never had a Barbie.'

Tempest thumped him on the shoulder. 'Always thinking with your trousers. Let's pack up and get ready to go. We'll hang on until someone comes for you if that's okay.'

I was about to respond when I saw his eyes shift focus. He was looking out to the road suddenly. I twisted to see what he had spotted and caught the headlights approaching. As the car passed under a streetlight, I saw who and what it was.

'That's Alistair,' I told him with relief. 'That's my ride.' I omitted to reveal that Barbie was in the passenger seat, but Big Ben spotted her anyway.

'How do I look?' he asked Tempest.

'Like an oversized, walking penis, you big doofus,' Tempest replied with a growl. 'Let it go, she has a boyfriend.'

Big Ben chuckled. 'You mean had a boyfriend. She's about to lose all interest in him. She'll barely be able to remember his name a few minutes from now.'

'Good grief.' I couldn't stop the words escaping me. I'd met Big Ben before, so I knew he was forever stuck as a boy chasing women simply for the thrill of catching them. He was unfairly attractive but then so too was Barbie and I doubted she could be swayed by the tall, muscular man's charms.

Alistair pulled the Range Rover to a stop just a couple of yards in front of us. A deep frown ruled his brow and just as I wondered what might be troubling him, I realised he had no idea who the two men with me were. That they were dressed like special ops soldiers probably didn't help.

I didn't need to explain though because Barbie bounced out of the car in her usual exuberant manner.

'Guys!' she squealed with excitement, throwing her hands in the air, and bouncing toward them. I think she planned to give Tempest a hug –

we hadn't seen them in months, but she spotted how wet the detective was and chose instead to keep her distance.

'You all look wet,' she observed, taking in Sam and me as well.

'Is everyone okay?' asked Alistair, still eyeing the two new men sceptically.

I did the introductions, let the men shake hands, then explained, 'We got jumped.' Alistair showed his teeth – it was not news he was happy to hear. 'Tempest and Big Ben saved us. The two men William Gill met with … hold on.' As if events were only now catching up to me, it dawned on me that I didn't know what had happened to Sam. 'Did they grab you?' I asked him.

The way Sam told it the two men had known he was recording them using his phone. I guess he wasn't as careful as we all thought, or not quite so invisible as I always imagined. When they got up to leave, one picked up Sam's phone from the table and told him he could have it back if he followed them outside.

It was a ruse, of course, Sam unwittingly falling for it. The phone was gone, and with it the chance to learn what they might have been discussing.

'It had to have been something we need to know about,' stated Alistair. He was doing a good job of keeping his emotions in check, but I could see the tension in his body. Sam and I had been left unguarded and he felt a need to take responsibility for the trouble we subsequently found ourselves in.

I slid my hand into his and gave it a squeeze. He squeezed back. We could talk about it later, but I am not a piece of porcelain he can protect from every eventuality. He didn't like it, but he accepted it all the same.

Sam told us they grabbed him the moment he stepped outside. One clamped a hand over his mouth and the other got him in a bear hug from behind. In the rainy carpark with no one around, they manhandled him to the far end where their cars were parked. That was where the other men were waiting. I surmised the text messages I'd seen them sending had been about the need for backup.

'I don't want to think what might have happened if Tempest and Big Ben hadn't come along when they did.' I expressed my gratitude again.

Yet again, Tempest played it down. 'Anyone else would have jumped in too. We just happened to be the ones who were here.'

'Plus, we are heroes,' pointed out Big Ben, a goofy smile aimed at Barbie.

She giggled at him. He was making a concerted effort to flirt with her, and it wasn't the first time, yet his charms just seemed to bounce off my blonde friend.

'You're so silly,' she laughed.

Tempest blew out a breath which might have been to hide fatigue or pain; I suspected it was one or the other.

'We really shouldn't keep you any longer,' I encouraged the chaps to be on their way.

Tempest nodded his head. 'I guess you are in no danger. So yes, I think we ought to get moving.' He thumped Big Ben on the shoulder again. He took two steps then stopped as a new question occurred to him. 'Did you get the license plate for the cars the men took off in?'

I blinked. 'I did not,' I admitted.

From a pocket, he produced a small, waterproof notepad and on it he jotted down the registrations. By way of explanation, he said as he wrote, 'I've learned to memorise number plates. It's surprising how often it comes in handy.' Task complete, he held up the notepad so someone could take a photograph. Barbie got to it first.

With a final nod goodbye, Tempest pocketed his notebook and called over his shoulder as he walked toward Big Ben's big truck, 'I think I can hear the bar calling. Don't you?'

Big Ben gave Barbie a last disappointed look but capped it off with a wink – laying the foundation for another attempt later, I guess. As he jogged to catch up with his friend, his Kevlar armour hooked over one shoulder, he put his free hand to his ear. 'I dare say I do. It's beer o'clock, old boy. And I believe it is your round.'

'I'm cold,' I announced. I truly was. Winter wasn't far away, and I was drenched to my skin. Sam wouldn't be faring any better. I needed to get out of the cool late autumn air and into a hot bath. I would call ahead and have Jermaine prepare that, but there were other things on my mind.

I asked a question, 'What happened to William Gill?'

Bath Time

When Alistair and Barbie left the Crooked Horse, they had to pick between following William Gill and the man I'd labelled as his partner. Each man got into a different car and then drove in opposite directions. With no idea what either was up to or where they might be going, they flipped a mental coin and stuck with the man they knew to be keeping secrets. Annoyingly, they hadn't caught the number plate of the car they didn't follow so we had no way of finding out who the other man was.

William Gill drove directly to the zoo where a security gate prevented Barbie and Alistair from following him any farther.

Unable to tail him into the zoo without backtracking to Lady Mary's house and getting into the zoo staff areas that way, they chose to first return to fetch Sam and me. I was glad they had – I needed to warm up and get dry clothes. I also felt a powerful urge to eat something since dinner still hadn't occurred. However, the moment those tasks were attended to, I was going on the hunt. William Gill was in the grounds of the zoo at night, he was up to something – my itchy skull was certain of it, and I needed to catch him doing it.

'Any idea what this could all be about?' Barbie asked me. She was in the front passenger seat again, twisting around to look back at me.

I had to admit I was stumped. For now, at least.

'We have the head keeper involved in what appeared to be a business meeting with some men who not only wanted to keep their conversation private but were prepared to kidnap Sam and me to protect whatever secret we might have learned. They took Sam's phone, so the conversation he recorded is lost. Our only chance to overturn that barrier now is to confront Mr Gill.' I patted Sam's leg. Like any young person, his phone was a lifeline to the world, and he was upset to lose it. We would sort out a replacement as soon as we were able.

'He was disinclined to speak to us earlier,' Alistair reminded me.

He wasn't wrong and I felt certain his attitude would not have changed.

'Yes, we'll need Lady Mary to help us. She is his employer. Let us hope the threat of unemployment is sufficient to loosen his tongue.'

The remaining minute or so of the journey was conducted in silence. My cogs were whirring, trying to make sense of what I had seen so far. The problem with it was that none of it seemed to tie to George and his disappearance. He'd been gone less than twelve hours – not long enough for the police to show any concern, but quite enough time for Lady Mary to know something was amiss.

What of the clues in his study though? The spy desk, the weapons, and passports. The money and the odd suggestions of travel plans that hinted at his involvement in something either shady or secret.

What could any of that possibly have to do with what William Gill was up to?

'I'll see what I can find on the car plate numbers,' Barbie promised as Alistair parked the car right in front of Lady Mary's house. We were bailing out, and though I'd been warmed slightly in the car's interior – Alistair had been kind enough to crank the heat right up – I was instantly cold once more when I stepped outside.

Despite my desire to pursue the few clues I clung to and explore the zoo grounds looking for Mr Gill, I could not ignore my need to warm up, get some food, and change my clothes.

I hadn't messaged Jermaine – he would only have worried and blamed himself if he knew I had encountered trouble, but Barbie must have because the front door burst open as my butler raced down the front steps to get to me.

'I'm fine, Jermaine.' I was only sort of lying.

Seconds later, we were all inside and the door was closed to shut the cold air outside. Jermaine had baths running in separate bathrooms for both Sam and me, and he had prepared food, enlisting other members of the household staff to get things underway.

Lady Mary appeared in the hallway ahead of us.

'I say, that man of yours is ever so good,' she acknowledged Jermaine's skill and determination. 'I never really noticed just how slow Jeeves is until Jermaine started ordering my staff around. I dare say I need to employ someone new. I can't even find him.'

I shot her a look as I hurried to my room. 'You couldn't get rid of Jeeves, surely?'

'Goodness, no,' she conceded. 'Grandfather would turn in his grave.' She was talking as if Jermaine were not walking two paces ahead of us, but then she had grown up with servants in her house and most likely learned to … not ignore them, but pretend they were deaf perhaps.

Jermaine acted as if he heard nothing. Leading the way to my bedroom even though I knew where I was going.

'I will be down for food shortly, Jermaine,' I promised as we neared my door.

'Madam?' he was surprised I didn't plan to soak for an hour.

I needed to let Lady Mary know what had transpired and what I planned to do next. He would hear it at the same time.

'Barbie and Alistair tracked Mr Gill back to the zoo. Unless he left again, he is on the grounds somewhere. Is that usual?' I asked the owner.

'Usual?' Lady Mary echoed me. 'For the head keeper to be here at night? No, I should say not. Other keepers might be; the veterinary staff too when occasion demands because we get sick animals or expectant mothers. Esme the tiger isn't due for at least another week, so I doubt he is here because of that.'

My door barked, the Dachshunds on the other side getting uppity now that they could hear and smell me. I turned the handle, letting them out. They jammed their heads through the gap as it widened, forcing their way through it before it was really big enough and both doing so at the same time. The result was that Anna, with her greater mass and strength got through the gap first. However, Georgie, not to be outdone, chose to launch herself upwards and onto her mother's back.

'That's not something you see every day,' remarked Lady Mary as Georgie came through the door riding on Anna's back like they were a circus act double-decker Dachshund.

I started tugging at my cold wet clothes. 'Anyway, I'll be down for food soon. I am almost more hungry than I am cold, but as soon as I have eaten, we need to check out the zoo grounds. If your head keeper is here, it's because he is up to something.'

Lady Mary pulled a grumpy face. 'In direct contrast to George then.' When I hitched an eyebrow because I wasn't sure what she was saying, she clarified, 'George isn't here because he is up to something.'

The secret agent thing again. I was having a lot of trouble convincing myself but had to question whether that was a mark of just how good he was. If George was a secret agent with a double life and wanted no one to ever suspect him, he'd gone the right way about it.

I repeated my promise to be down soon and shut the world outside as I closed the door and started to strip. The Dachshunds trotted happily after me. I would have given them a gravy bone if I knew where they were.

I pulled my wet sweater off my shoulders and dropped it on the tile as I walked into the steamy, inviting warmth of the en suite bathroom. My shoes were already discarded, and soon to follow them would be my sodden jeans.

Just as I unsnapped the top button of my jeans, a hand came from behind and clamped over my mouth.

What Hides in the Steam?

I tensed to scream but the hand over my mouth prevented me from filling my lungs to do so.

'Shhh, Mrs Fisher,' soothed Justin Metcalf-Howe.

He let me go, removing the hand from my mouth and stepping back a pace to get clear of my arm as I swiped at him. My cheeks flushed. I was half naked and it was only serendipity, and the fact that I felt a desperate need to get out of my rain-soaked jeans, that meant my bra was still on.

Justin was in his thirties, handsome and athletic in a very British way, but even though he was standing in front of me in my bathroom looking at me in my undressed state, his eyes never drifted downward from my face.

'You have a question for me?' he asked.

'I already sent it to you,' I pointed out, now curious why he had come here rather than just send me an answer.

'Yes. It confused me, dear lady. I was in London – just a short hop to get to you …'

'Hold on …' I interrupted him. 'I didn't tell you where I was.'

I got a cocked eyebrow in reply – I was being silly. Men like Justin do not need to be told things.

'Since I did not wish to send messages back and forth – the more one transmits, the easier it is for the transmission to be interrupted – I chose to visit in person.'

I wanted to ask how he got in, but that would have been a silly question too. Justin Metcalf-Howe, suave British super spy, went where he willed without concern for security systems, locked doors, or security guards.

'Is he then?' I prompted an answer. 'Can you even tell me? If you can't, can you at least tell me that I should stop looking for him?'

Justin frowned a little. 'You're serious then. This is why I came. You believe the bestselling thriller novelist who writes about spies and international intrigue is using that as a cover because he is, in fact, a spy involved in international intrigue?'

It felt silly now that he said it like that.

'Well ...' I started to defend myself.

Justin sighed and sat on the edge of my bath. 'He wouldn't be the first.'

'Wait, what? You think George might be a spy?'

'I didn't say that,' he tried to clarify his position on the matter. 'However ...' he gave me an earnest look, 'if he is, then he is not one of ours.'

'What!'

'George Brown is not a British spy. I almost dismissed your question as foolish when I first read it, but then I remembered there was a Russian spy in the eighties who toured the world as a chess grandmaster. No one had any idea until the cold war ended. Then there was a Chinese woman a few years ago. She got caught sneaking out of the Pentagon. She was an American citizen, or so everyone thought, and she played an on-screen spy. It was literally the dumbest cover ever, and yet it worked.'

My mind was reeling, the solid tiles under my feet feeling as if they were in motion. Not only could it be true that George was involved in espionage or arms dealing or something equally criminal and shady, but if he was, then he wasn't on our side.

The term *sleeper agent* popped into my head. 'If he isn't working for the British, then who is controlling his movements?' I half murmured the question.

'That I could not say,' replied the British spy currently invading my bathroom.

I came to my senses a heartbeat later. I was still in my bra with my jeans undone at the top. That the attractive man in my bathroom seemed not to have noticed, or showed no interest if he had, was mildly concerning. Not that I want to be ogled, but his utter indifference was like a negative vote, and I thought I looked pretty good for a woman in her fifties.

Regardless, I still needed to get clean and dressed, and though the steam in my bathroom was nice and warm, I was still shivering for the cold had penetrated to my core.

It was time to get rid of my visitor.

'Thank you, Justin, for coming in person. I find myself in your debt yet again.'

He bowed his head a touch to acknowledge my thanks. 'Think nothing of it, Mrs Fisher. This country remains in your debt, and I am pleased to see to it that you are safe. I will reach out to my colleagues around the world. If anyone knows anything about George Brown, I will know it within twenty-four hours.'

He slipped from my bathroom, closing the door behind him as he bade me a final goodbye and good luck.

Feeling yet further pushed for time, since I claimed I would be down for food shortly and wanted to get out to find William Gill, I tore off my bra and shucked my sopping wet jeans. They were a fight to get off, the denim gripping my skin and refusing to move. In a way this was of benefit – by the time I got them off, I was almost out of breath and warming from the exertion.

The door opened again. Justin had been gone for a scant few seconds and must have remembered something. Of course, now all I had on was a pair of damp knickers.

I squealed and reached for a towel.

'Justin, I'm not decent!'

Alistair poked his head around the doorframe. 'Everything all right, darling?' he asked.

I breathed a sigh of relief and hooked the towel back over the rail I'd snatched it from.

'Yes,' I replied, sagging to sit on the edge of the bath. My heart was made to race far too often. 'I just need to get a bath and warm up. I'll be down shortly.'

In contrast to Justin, Alistair was very aware that I was naked and made no attempt to keep his eyes on my face.

I pushed myself upright, stood on tiptoes to kiss him, then turned about and slid my knickers down in a seductive manner. As they hit the floor, I looked back over my shoulder, winked at my lover, whose eyes were already starting to dilate, and said, 'Get out.'

I heard disappointed muttering – all in jest – as he left me to finally get in the bath.

Just as I stepped over the side, the door opened yet again – it was beginning to feel like the turnstile at Kings Cross Station.

Alistair was eyeing me with a frown.

'Who's Justin?'

True to my word, I stayed in the bath just long enough to warm through, got clean and ran through my room as I got dressed and applied a swipe of makeup – I needed it to take the fatigue out of my face.

You'll call it unnecessary, and it is, but I habitually wear earrings and felt just a little underdressed going out without them. Putting them in wouldn't cost any time; I could do it while walking downstairs to find everyone else.

However, they were not where I left them ten minutes ago when I arrived in my room and started to strip. Looking at the spot I would swear I had placed them, I frowned and pursed my lips. Was this the early signs of dementia?

I felt my earlobes, confirming I wasn't going doolally and still had them in. I checked my jewellery box. Jermaine had set my things out in front of the mirror as he always does, but they were not there either.

Perplexed, but unwilling to spend any more time looking for them, I stuffed my phone into a back pocket – I chose to wear jeans and a stretchy top with a mid-calf boot again. My hope was that I could make it to the end of the day without trashing yet another set of clothing. The Blue Moon boys wore what looked like army boots, rip-stop fabric clothing, and Kevlar. They were hardly the items I wished to be seen in, yet there was a certain attraction that came with not ruining one's favourite outfits all the time.

My friends were gathered in Lady Mary's kitchen. Gloria had gone to bed – probably been put to bed I suspected though I did not ask. However, everyone else was there and waiting for me. Dinner had been hastily prepared - steaks and game chips. The house cook had gone home for the night but that probably worked in our favour as my loyal Butler, Jermaine, found what he needed to produce a sumptuous, yet fast and filling meal.

I was the last one to eat, Jermaine serving the steak freshly sliced into bite-sized pieces on a thick slice of granary bread topped with honey and mustard dressing.

Ravenous, I took a bite, then had to chew fast because I wanted to speak.

'Has anyone seen my earrings?' I asked.

'The diamond ones?' Barbie sought to confirm. She was sitting at one end of a central island in the big kitchen and half hidden behind her laptop.

I wore them more than any other. They were one of the very few things Charlie gave me during our thirty years of marriage that I chose to keep. Others might have discarded or sold them, willing to be rid of the reminder, yet they gave me a sense of … balance perhaps. Charlie was long behind me and fading from sight in my rear-view mirror. The ink on our divorce paperwork was still drying, yet to me it was as if our marriage was a lifetime ago. Getting rid of a beautiful, and favourite, pair of earrings would harm no one but myself.

I nodded my reply around my next mouthful, swallowing quickly so I could say, 'I swear I put them on the side in my room.'

A sigh from Lady Mary drew our eyes and ears.

'I'm sorry,' she apologised. 'I should have warned you. This is another problem I need to tackle.' She huffed an annoyed breath. 'One of the house staff has light fingers. Had I recently taken on someone new, I would have an obvious target for my suspicions, but the most recent employment was more than five years ago.'

I waved a dismissive hand, not wanting to make more of it than necessary.

'It's not important.'

'I disagree,' Lady Mary countered. 'Your possessions have been stolen while you are in my house attempting to help me. Things are going from bad to worse. I thought I was inviting you to help me find George, but now we have my head keeper up to something shady, George possibly involved in international espionage, and to top it all off, I can no longer ignore the theft occurring in my house because it has affected you, Patricia.'

Alistair asked, 'What else has been stolen?'

Lady Mary huffed again. 'Just a few jewels so far. It only happens when I put something down. I took a ring off because I noticed the stone was coming loose, but before I could get it to the jewellers for repair, it had vanished. That was from the sideboard in the drawing room. George had some diamond cufflinks go, and there have been other items. At first, I put it down to the two us being forgetful and just misplacing things, but that's not it and had there been any doubt left in my mind, your missing earrings would eradicate it. No,' she sighed with great disappointment and frustration, 'I have a thief in my house.'

I swallowed the last bite of my food, gratefully accepted a napkin from Jermaine to dab my lips and clapped my hands together to get things moving along.

'It's just a pair of earrings,' I insisted. I didn't really mean it, but in the big scheme of things, I knew it was true. 'We'll look into who might be stealing from you when we get to the bottom of the other events.' I shot Lady Mary an encouraging smile.

'What's the plan, Patty?' Barbie wanted to know. 'I've been trying to track the registration numbers we got from Tempest. It just takes a while. It would be easier if I were able to do it in person.' By which my blonde friend meant one smile from her would probably be enough to get a man at the DVLA to take a few moments to look up the information she wanted. Like bank accounts and other sensitive personal information, car ownership details were not easy to come by on the web.

'Do you want to stay on it?' I asked her, making it clear from my tone that I considered it to be a good use of her time. 'They are shady and no mistake.'

Mr Gill might confess when we corner him and Lady Mary asks the questions, but then again, that might depend just how shady his secret activities were.

Barbie said, 'Sure. Maybe Sam can help me,' she suggested.

Sam wasn't great with computers, truth be told. He could work a games system just fine, but as a research assistant to Barbie, he would be next to useless. However, Barbie was trying to give him a reason to stay inside after his soaking earlier and I grasped it.

'Yes,' I aimed my eyes at Sam. 'Can you do that?'

'Yes, Mrs Fisher,' he replied dutifully, shucking the coat he had over his shoulders in preparedness for going out again.

I sucked in a deep breath through my nose and started toward the kitchen door. 'The rest of us will try to find Mr Gill. If he is still here, then like Lady Mary said, he must be up to something. Let's find out what it is. Maybe then we will get some idea as to what is going on.'

It would have been safer to travel as one team, but the vastness of the zoo dictated we split up. Much to Jermaine's disgruntlement, I asked him to drive Lady Mary – I was going to be safe enough with Alistair I assured him. We were only looking for signs of activity after all. If one of us found something, we would call the other pair and rendezvous.

Lady Mary tried calling the number for her head keeper of course. He wasn't answering, the phone switching to voicemail when it finally timed out each time. It had been like that since we returned to the house with news of our attack.

Heading out into the cold air again, I felt at least that we were getting somewhere. I still had no idea where George had gotten to – the original purpose for our visit – but I was yet to be entirely sold on the concept that he was a spy or secret agent. I thought it more likely we were going to find whatever Mr Gill was up to had something to do with why George had vanished.

Lady Mary, however, was becoming ever more convinced that her husband had a secret double life involving guns, girls, and gangsters.

'You know this explains all those times he would vanish while we were away together. I lost him for almost an hour in Barcelona once. I bet he was carrying out an assassination.' Her face was a disgruntled grimace as she mentally pummelled her husband. It was as if she'd already caught him cheating. The worry she felt over his disappearance earlier was long gone. 'Then there was that time in Bangkok when he said his tummy had gone all wobbly. He went to the restrooms but was gone for over forty minutes. Now I think about it, we were right next to a giant electronics firm's national HQ. He picked where we were going to eat. I bet he snuck in there to steal some cutting-edge technology for his masters.' She gasped. 'That would explain why he was so sweaty when he came back to the table and didn't want his food. I bet he had to fight his way out and left a trail of bodies in his wake!'

As we got to the cars outside, I wanted to argue that George had probably been sweating because Bangkok is hot and humid, and he had a dicky tummy. His forty-minute absence most likely had a less exciting explanation that involved a goodly amount of toilet paper.

I didn't wish to dwell on it, and I chose to keep my mouth shut as Jermaine held her door so she could get into her Bentley. All the while she continued to regale him with anecdotes about their trips and times when George was – in her opinion – probably off killing people and stealing secrets.

Alistair drove my Range Rover, the headlights doing their best to pierce the gloom. There were no streetlights to illuminate the roads and tracks at the back of the zoo which meant, out here in the countryside, when the sun went down, it got truly dark.

Jermaine followed behind for half a mile until we reached a junction. At that point, we split; there was a lot of territory to cover. If we could just find someone working, they would probably have a radio and could be used to surreptitiously find out where the head keeper was. That was the rough plan anyway.

I felt we were against the clock. Had I not been so cold and utterly soaked when we left The Crooked Horse, I would have championed looking for Mr Gill straight away. At the time, my need to get warm had overridden my desire to stay in the hunt. Now I was regretting it and wishing I had pushed myself harder.

There was no sign of activity in the zoo. None at all. Alistair drove us around the back areas of the zoo and up to gates that led through the visitor area. We didn't have keys to get through but could see no sign of life beyond the gates either. I knew I could have it wrong, but I believed whatever William Gill was up to had to be something that was taking place in the back areas where only staff went.

Glowing eyes appeared spookily in the darkness beyond the fences. Under the night sky I had no idea what sort of animal might be looking at me. It could be an antelope, a hippo, an emu, or almost any other creature on the planet. The zoo had plenty to pick from and they were all just as dangerous as each other. Even the herbivores could kill – they were wild animals after all.

As the idle thought crossed my mind, another voice added that it might not be the animals I needed to worry about. The most dangerous creatures in Lady Mary's zoo might be the humans behind whatever was going on.

If only I could have caught up with the man I chased this afternoon. His altercation with the head keeper was bound to throw light on my quest for knowledge. If nothing else, knowing who Mr Gill's fight was with would give me a small steer.

For that matter I could moan about losing Sam's phone and the recording of the conversation that took place in the pub. I could complain about a dozen things that had not gone my way so far, yet doing so would waste time and achieve nothing. I focused on what we could do.

'Let's go back to the warehouse,' I suggested.

Alistair twitched his eyes in my direction. 'The one we were in earlier with all the feed?'

I nodded. 'Yes. That was a hub of activity earlier and Mr Gill was there. He was very defensive and very insistent we vacate the premises. I think we should have another look at what was in it.'

I called Lady Mary.

'Any luck?'

She tutted loudly. 'No, there is no one here, no sign of life at all.'

'We found the same.'

She tutted again. 'I guess we missed him.'

I let her know my intention to head back to the feed store and she agreed to meet us there.

Neither of us had the slightest inkling of the horror we were going to find there. Nor did we know we were being watched.

Empty Shelves

Approaching the warehouse, my heart thumped hard in my chest when headlights suddenly filled our windscreen. Someone was coming toward us in the dark. A second later, my brain kicked in, telling me it was almost certainly the Bentley I could see.

When it turned away and the lights shut off, I could see the large feed warehouse looming like a giant square block of black behind it. It filled the night sky as we approached, our own headlights picking up the dark form of Jermaine as he scooted around the car to let Lady Mary out.

He had an umbrella – very John Steed – hooked over his left elbow in case the rain returned, but no bowler hat tonight.

'Do you have a key?' I asked the zoo owner as she stepped from her car.

Alistair had swung the Range Rover around in a large circle before parking to place my door next to hers with the cars pointing in opposite directions.

She shook her head. 'It would be unusual for it to be locked in my experience. Not that I can remember the last time I felt a need to come to any of the behind-the-scenes buildings after dark. I dare say we can break in if it is. It's my building after all.'

She made a fair point.

Maybe the building was locked and maybe it wasn't. The side door we came to was and the probability that others would be too was sufficient to stop us bothering to check. The door had a glass panel in it from waist height upward. Not for long though.

Jermaine found a handy rock which made short work of the reinforced glass. Taking care not to catch his suit on the jagged edges, my butler reached in to flick the handle on the inside, and we were in.

The warehouse was dark, as one might expect. Our footfalls sounded loud as they echoed in the silence of the huge chamber.

When I spoke, my voice echoed too. 'Anyone inside?' I called out. I didn't expect a response. We were coming through the threshold and down a short corridor which opened out into the warehouse. It was a different door to the one I entered through last time but brought me into the same space.

My phone was on, casting light from the torch function as were Alistair's and Jermaine's.

'Anyone see a light switch?' asked Alistair.

Lady Mary found them first. She might have known where they were; I didn't bother to ask. Blinking in the sudden harsh light as dozens of overhead lights came to life above our heads, my eyes were immediately drawn to a stand of empty shelves.

Pointing across the warehouse, I stated, 'They were full earlier.' I didn't make my claim with a high degree of certainty, questioning whether I was remembering things right or not. Looking about to orientate myself, I had to move around to work out where I had been standing earlier.

The doughy bald man and then the small crowd of annoying people questioning my identity had been in my face and distracting me, that much I knew. I picked a spot on the floor and walked to it, turning around until the memory in my head matched what I could see.

Alistair, Jermaine, and Lady Mary were all watching to see what I might do or say next.

I nodded to myself. 'Those shelves were full.' This time I was more sure of myself.

'Of what, madam?' asked Jermaine.

I shook my head; I didn't know. What I could tell them was, 'It was boxes.'

Looking around the warehouse, I wasn't seeing many other boxes. We were all walking across the warehouse floor, all going in the same direction as we went to the one empty area of shelving. All around us, in every direction we could look, the shelves were stacked with sacks of feed. There were other areas stacked up with pallets containing feed of a different kind. There were massive bales of hay and no doubt there were other areas where meat for the carnivores would be stored – most likely this required some refrigeration.

It was all background details to be filed away because none of it meant anything yet. All I had were some empty shelves that had been full earlier if my brain could be trusted. Looking along them now, there was nothing to indicate what might have been in the boxes.

'Were they all the same?' Lady Mary asked.

I consulted the image in my head.

'I can't be sure, but no, I don't think they were.'

'Were there any markings on the outside, sweetie?' she persisted, attempting to jog my memory.

'There were,' I conceded. 'I just wasn't close enough to notice what they were.

We all got busy inspecting the shelves for any clue as to what might have been in the now absent boxes. We split up to go down both sides. There was about forty yards of it in all and there were four levels of shelves, the top two above my head. Jermaine ascended the steel frame to walk along the very top but reported the same negative result we all found.

It could be nothing, but a persistent itch at the back of my skull wanted me to believe the empty shelves meant something important.

We looked around some more and Lady Mary helped us find the office where the manifests for the deliveries were logged and filed. The four of us – Lady Mary managing without a cocktail in her hand – spent over an hour trawling through paperwork in binders and on the computers without finding anything that might help us to identify what it was that might have been in the boxes.

When I saw a yawn split Alistair's face, I followed suit, so too Lady Mary's. Only Jermaine, his ninja skills helping him no doubt, was able to resist the inevitable chain reaction.

'It's getting late,' I managed around another yawn. 'I think we should call it quits for now. In the morning, we need to get here early and quiz some of the warehouse workers. Someone drove the forklift truck to move the boxes. Someone supervised the boxes leaving here.'

Lady Mary had something to add. 'And I need to speak with Mr Gill. He can tell me exactly what is going on or he can tell the police. I shall be calling that chief inspector fellow again if I do not like the answers Mr Gill gives me.'

'Could it be drugs?' asked Alistair. When we looked his way, he expanded his statement. 'There is a warehouse in the middle of nowhere with stuff coming in and out all the time. How often do the police come here?'

'Never,' replied Lady Mary.

'And we are close to the coast. If,' Alistair aimed careful eyes at Lady Mary, 'George stumbled upon them when he went to visit the tiger earlier today ...'

Lady Mary's eyes were wide with horror.

'You did come home unexpectedly,' I pointed out. 'Alistair makes a good point. It might not be drugs.' I racked my brains for something less startling. 'It could be stolen antiques or artwork or ...' I was struggling to come up with alternatives that might be less terrifying than finding out the zoo was the epicentre of a giant drug smuggling ring.

'It could be human trafficking,' Jermaine suggested, his voice quiet and respectful.

He was trying to help as I floundered, but from the look on Lady Mary's face, she would clearly rather it was drugs.

'Oh, my,' she gasped, putting out a hand to grab a filing cabinet for support. 'I feel I might need a rather stiff gin and tonic. Are we about done here?'

As if on cue, my phone rang. Barbie's name was displayed.

Putting Lady Mary's question on hold, I pressed the green button to answer the phone and the speaker button so everyone would hear.

'Barbie, how are you getting along?'

'I'm striking out,' she let us know. 'I'll have to sweet talk someone tomorrow. Could we ask Mike Atwell?' she asked, naming the friendly detective sergeant from my home village.

'I should have thought of that already,' I admitted. 'I'll send him a message when we get back to the house. I think we are about done looking for Mr Gill.'

'I take it you haven't found him.'

'No. No sign of anyone,' I let her know. 'It's a bust our end too.'

I got a small laugh from her. 'At least you didn't find a body,' she joked. When I failed to say anything in the next couple of seconds, she blurted, 'You didn't, did you?'

'No,' I snorted a sad chuckle of my own. 'Thankfully not on this occasion.'

I let her go with a promise to be back shortly and the suggestion she and Sam get themselves to bed rather than wait for us.

With the call ended, I thought again about Lady Mary's question: she wanted to know if we were done. We were not, but that was only because we had failed to find anything of worth. If anything, our excursion had created more questions than answers. There was no doubt in anyone's mind that there was something decidedly fishy occurring at the zoo. The staff, at least some of them, were engaged in something extracurricular. That it would prove to be illegal was very possible. Whether it tied into George's disappearance remained to be seen, but whatever it was, we were unlikely to achieve anything further tonight.

Had we been able to uncover a single piece of evidence, either of the zoo staff's activities or to tell us what might have happened to George, I would be calling the police right now. Instead, I was accepting temporary defeat and heading back to the house to get some rest.

We would attack this again before the sun was up, but sleep would do us all good.

Yeah, that didn't happen.

Everyone Knows Blood When They See It

We turned off the lights in the office, Jermaine powering down the computers and leaving them as they had been found before we made our way back toward the cars.

In the lead as we filed down the short corridor toward the exit, Jermaine froze when he opened the door.

The message to stop didn't reach my feet in time to prevent me bumping into his back, but he put his arms out to stop me going around him as he partially blocked the exit with his body.

'There is blood here, madam,' he warned me.

Startled by his news, I jerked forward, grabbing the sleeve of his jacket and peering around his arm so I could see what he was seeing. All I could find was the wet tarmac where it was raining yet again.

Lady Mary and Alistair hurried to get a look too.

Sensing that we couldn't see what he had seen, he urged us to back up.

'The light from the door,' he explained. We hugged the walls, letting the light inside cut a swathe where sure as anything, there was a large pool of deep red blood. There was no question we were seeing something else.

A question formed on my lips, but before I could ask if it had been there when we first arrived, I shot my eyes to the linoleum floor we were standing on. Right there, unnoticed in the mud and rainwater we traipsed in from outside was the same red blood. We had all walked through it to get inside and no one noticed it when we arrived because it was dark – we turned the lights on only when we got into the main part of the warehouse.

Jermaine was already moving, popping up his umbrella when Alistair said, 'We need to try to preserve it.'

The rain was a steady drizzle, so even with Jermaine holding an umbrella above it, the blood was slowly being washed away and diluted. It didn't help that all four of us had walked through it.

Whoever the blood belonged to, there was enough of it on the ground for me to believe that person was in deep trouble. Not only that, we had been inside for over an hour. We were lucky the rain had left off for a while or there would have been no trace left to find.

Alistair was on his knees on the far side of the red pool now illuminated in the light from the door.

'I need something to go around it. Something absorbent,' he called out hopefully. 'It will be gone in minutes if the rain picks up.'

I rushed into the warehouse again, shouting over my shoulder, 'I'll be back in a minute. Someone call the police!'

It took me five minutes to find the area with all the health and safety equipment in it. I knew there would be one; there always is. The absorbent snake-looking thingy I wanted turned out to have a label on it displaying the trade name: absorbent snake. I guess that made it easy to remember and refer to.

Conscious Alistair and Jermaine were fighting a battle against the rain they stood no chance of winning, I ran back to the door, arriving out of breath but jubilant with the snake in my hands.

I tore it from the packet to answer the curious looks and had a water blockade around the blood pool five seconds later. Alistair stood up and twisted in place to free off the kinks in his back. Just like I had been earlier, he was soaked, only it was his back half, backside, and lower legs that bore the brunt. His front half had been facing down and thus protected from the rain.

Lady Mary was holding the umbrella, I noted. My butler was nowhere in sight.

'That should give us a bit longer,' he commented. 'The rain was winning but maybe there will be enough left for the police to analyse.'

'I spoke with them,' Lady Mary announced. 'They will have someone with us shortly but will have a devil of a time finding our location without a guide.

I felt sure she was correct, but asked, 'Where's Jermaine?'

Alistair answered, 'He went to see if there were any other signs of a struggle. There is a big pool of blood here, but a fast search didn't turn up any more in the near vicinity.'

The sound of footsteps muffled by the rain reached our ears in the next second as Jermaine came around the corner of the building at a steady jog.

'I could find no further trace of any blood,' he stated with certainty. 'Given how much of it we found here, and how long ago it must have happened, the wounded person is either in hospital or in a serious condition somewhere.' He was stating what we all knew, but there was something nobody had said yet.

'This was an attack,' I stated boldly.

Alistair nodded his head and blew out a hard breath. 'Probably, yes.'

I pointed to the area around the pool of blood. 'Barring that the person was out here practicing their chainsaw juggling, there is nothing here for them to hurt themselves on.' The door was five feet away but had the person cut themselves on that somehow – I couldn't picture how – there would be blood on it, or closer to it.

'Who else was here tonight?' Jermaine voiced a question as if lifting it from my head. It was rhetorical, obviously because we had no way of knowing who might have been here.

'I'm calling Mr Gill again,' snapped Lady Mary with an annoyed timbre. She got the same result as all the other times she'd called him this evening.

That the blood could be his was undeniable. He had been inside the zoo grounds. However, I felt it more likely the blood belonged to someone else, and Mr Gill was the one who inflicted the wound. I based my assumption on nothing but gut feel, but it rarely steered me wrong.

Until we found him, we couldn't know one way or the other.

Lady Mary checked her watch, then said, 'I should head to the gate to make sure the police officers do not drive all over the zoo attempting to find me.'

'I'll go with you,' volunteered Alistair. 'I could do with warming up a little,' he admitted as he started toward the car.

They would return soon, I felt confident. For now, I felt quite safe with Jermaine here to protect me. He had done so many times in the past and would again if given the slightest opportunity to do so. Had I been alone, the environment would have seemed creepy and foreboding. Instead, it was nice to spend time alone with Jermaine.

I tucked in under the umbrella he had reclaimed from Lady Mary as she left, and we talked about returning to the ship.

'Are you looking forward to moving in with the captain, madam?' he asked me.

Rather than answer, I asked, 'When I do, will you finally give in and start calling me Patricia?'

My question elicited a wry smile. 'I may be able to relax enough to address you as Mrs Fisher, madam. I will still be employed on the ship as a butler though. The level of decorum demanded of me is high, as you already know. If you and I were to relax at all, it could not be in public.'

His answer saddened me. He took his role seriously; few knew that better than I, and I would never insist he compromise himself to make me feel more comfortable. I considered the tall Jamaican to be one of the closest, if not *the* closest, friends I had ever had. I regularly doubted I was worthy.

'I think I am going to struggle,' I admitted, returning to his original question. 'The opulent surroundings of the Windsor Suite are a wonder to behold, but I do not need them. Living with Alistair will be nice, yet I fear I will never be truly happy wherever I am because I will miss your company.'

A tear rolled down my left cheek and Jermaine placed an arm around my shoulders.

'I feel the same, madam. Perhaps there will be periods when the Windsor Suite is not occupied, and I will be permitted to assist you with whatever case you might be pursuing.'

'That sounds nice,' I mumbled quietly. Somehow, I felt close to wretched. I was looking forward to getting back to the ship for many reasons. Travelling the world this year had opened my eyes to all that our planet had to offer and there was still so much to explore. I had barely scraped the surface of what I was yet to discover, yet doing it without Jermaine around, even if I did get to be with Alistair … it just didn't fill me with the same amount of joy.

I love Alistair, don't get me wrong. I could even envisage me changing my policy on maybe one day marrying again which was something I didn't think I would even consider. Not that he had asked, and I harboured no desire for him to do so. Alistair was everything I felt a man should be. Or perhaps he was everything I wanted him to be. Either way, we fit together hand in glove, but shedding the husband I had - let's not forget I only signed the divorce paperwork this morning – had imbued me with a fiercely independent streak and moving into the captain's quarters not only felt a little sudden but also too big of a step in our fledgling relationship.

This was not the first time I had raised these thoughts and discussed them with myself. I'd even had a chat or two with Barbie on the subject but whatever decision I made had to be my own. At this time, I had no alternative to the plan to which I was already committed.

Whichever way I tried to look at the situation, Jermaine would be employed all hours of the day for whoever was staying in the royal suite, and I would be engaged in making sure any crimes committed on board were quickly resolved. It would leave little time for socialising together.

Honestly, I worried I might hardly see Jermaine at all.

Headlights coming over the hill heralded the return of Lady Mary and Alistair. They had a pair of police cars behind them.

I patted Jermaine's chest where my right hand had come to rest when I relaxed my weight into him and pushed myself away once more to receive the police.

Nothing to Report

I found my nerves jittery as the police cars approached and I knew why – I expected to find Chief Inspector Quinn among the officers arriving and really didn't feel like having another heated face off.

When I first met the man, he'd been polite and helpful. That attitude didn't last long once I started solving crimes he was actively pursuing. He saw me as a poacher, stealing his collars even though I habitually turned them over to the police.

I am an investigator; I don't arrest people. Although technically I could restrain a person if I knew they were guilty of a crime and could justify doing so for fear they would either abscond or commit further crimes, there were very few instances when I had.

Even then, it wasn't me who did the restraining. I'm a petite woman in her mid-fifties and I have a six-foot four-inch ninja butler in my shadow most of the time.

However, my concerns were for naught. Chief Inspector Quinn did not grace us with his presence. A squad car pulled to a halt a few yards away next to Lady Mary's Bentley and they had an unmarked car behind them. What they really needed was a forensic van, but for all I knew that could be on its way.

When the squad car's engine shut off and the doors opened on either side, the light inside came on to illuminate the cops getting out. I recognised them both.

A beaming smile filled my face. It was out of place given the circumstances by which we were caused to meet again, but I couldn't hide the relief I felt to see friendly faces.

'Hey, Mrs Fisher,' called Constable Brad Hardacre, a smile crossing his face too. I met him a few months ago when he and a colleague responded to a call for help. It's a long story, but he helped me bring down a psychotic cult attempting to raise a demigod through human sacrifice. It was kind of a strange night.

I gave him a wave, then spotted who he was with.

'Yo, Patricia!' yelled Constable Patience Woods. Patience is sassy, loud, and a whole lot of caramel-skinned woman stuffed into a police uniform. I was not surprised to see the last bite of a doughnut vanish into her mouth as she sashayed across the tarmac with a coffee cup in her other hand.

Brad rolled his eyes and turned to face the two men getting out of the other car.

'It's right across here,' indicated Lady Mary unnecessarily. There was no way anyone with eyes could miss the area Jermaine and I were trying to protect from the elements.

The two detectives were young men, by which I mean they were in their thirties. Personally, I like my detectives to be a little more seasoned which is probably why I got on so well with Mike Atwell.

'DS Atwell not available?' I enquired of Patience as the two men in cheap suits inspected the pool of blood.

'Mike? I think he is taking some time off,' Patience frowned as she made a face and tried to recall what she knew. 'It might be his mum died, or his sister is sick. I don't remember which, but it was something like that.'

I crossed off any plans to contact my detective sergeant friend. I had called on him plenty for help in the past weeks anyway. Making a mental note to send him a message wishing him well, I watched the plain-clothes officers working.

Something howled in the distance. To be fair, animal noise was a constant at the zoo, the various bird calls, predator growls and snarls, and many any other noises filling the air like a chorus. It became background quickly – something to be ignored like the music they play over the tannoy system at the shopping mall.

However, Patience did not agree.

'What was that?' she spat, her eyes bugging out as she looked around for a deadly creature about to swoop.

Lady Mary cocked an ear. 'Hoolock Gibbon, I think.'

'Is it dangerous?' Patience asked, a hand moving to the telescopic baton on her belt.

Lady Mary eyed the police officer with disdain. 'Dangerous? Yes, quite so.' Patience's eyes shot out another half inch and she twisted around to face the howl as it rang through the night again. 'If you are a mango,' Lady Mary added. 'Hoolock Gibbons are the size of a domestic cat and are vegetarians.'

'The animals are in their cages and enclosures, Patience,' I tried to reassure her. 'We can hear them, but we are quite safe.'

Brad frowned at his partner. 'Get a grip, Patience.'

'You get a grip!' she snapped back. 'You don't have to worry. If a lion gets loose and wants to eat someone, it won't pick you, will it, skinny white boy. Not when there are tasty brown sugar treats like me to be had.' She was gabbling, nervousness causing words to tumble from her mouth.

Mercifully, the detectives were out of their car and Patience chose to clam up even though her eyes remained on stalks. They introduced themselves as Detective Constable Drummond and Detective Sergeant Henwick, skipped over any pleasantries, and started asking questions. They used a kit to take a sample of the blood and expressed that it might not be of much use since we had walked through it, and it was being diluted by the rain. Despite our best efforts, it had all but washed it away.

'What were you doing down here at this time of night?' the one called Drummond asked. He had light brown almost blonde hair cut in a style that made me think he must have modelled it on a popular footballer. He clearly put a lot of effort into it and stuck it together with product because the rain was having no impact on it at all.

His question was easy to answer. I told him about Lady Mary's missing husband, the strange behaviour of her head keeper, and the general suspicion that something criminal might be occurring.

His superior began to take notice at that point. Until I filled in a few of the blanks for them and told them Chief Inspector Quinn had already been to the property that morning, they acted as if ready to dismiss our call.

I understood why - there was no crime that they could see. A pool of blood is not a murder victim. It could be a fox taking down a hedgehog. Okay, there was far too much blood for it to be that, but without a body, they had nothing to investigate.

DS Henwick asked to see inside the warehouse, so we all traipsed inside again and looked at the empty shelves.

They asked lots of pertinent questions, such as what we thought might have happened to George and what crime we believed might be behind it all. They asked who we suspected and wanted details.

We didn't have anything to give them. There was no way I was going to tell them about George's desk and the worrying contents behind the secret panel. Nor did I wish to reveal the attack at the pub tonight. Doing so might help to identify the men who tried to grab Sam, but then I would have to explain how we got away and that would drag Tempest and Big Ben into things. It was a hassle they didn't need.

Not only that, I couldn't see any advantage to be gained from involving the police at this time. Quinn would hear about this latest report in the morning, read that all we had was a pool of blood, and divert his resources to investigate other crimes.

Until I had something solid to tell them, there was no point in attempting to keep them around.

They did, however, arrange for a squad car to go to William Gill's house. That happened while we were showing them around the warehouse. He wasn't there.

'Actually, what we can report is that he is not answering his door,' clarified DS Henwick. 'We have no reason to force entry. He may simply be asleep.'

I flicked my wrist to check my watch and found it was coming up on midnight.

'There's nothing here,' we all heard DS Henwick comment to his junior partner. Turning to face Lady Mary, he said, 'I will file a report and follow this up in the morning, ma'am. Please call if there are any further developments.' He produced a card from an inside pocket, handing it to the zoo owner before bidding us all a good night.

The cops led a procession back toward the exit – the same one we'd been using all evening, and headed back to their car.

Patience paused in the doorway to put her hat back on.

Brad Hardacre asked her, 'Feeling brave enough to go back outside? What if there is something out there?'

DS Henwick overheard him. 'Why would there be something out there?' He glanced at Lady Mary. 'There are no animals on the loose, are there?'

'Of course not,' I answered for my friend, getting in quickly before she could reveal how strange Constable Woods had been acting. I didn't want to cause her any problems.

Constable Hardacre chose to embarrass her anyway.

'Patience is afraid of the noises.'

'Am not,' she snapped indignantly. Stuffing her hat back on her head, she went outside in a show of nonchalance.

DS Henwick, the senior officer in attendance, eyed her sceptically.

Patience did her best to hide her fear. Until something roared in the darkness. It genuinely didn't sound like it was all that far away.

Patience squealed. 'Waaaah!'

'Leopard,' supplied Lady Mary, confidently naming the creature responsible. 'They like to hunt at night.'

It was the wrong thing to say to Patience.

'Waaaaahhhh!' She ran to the squad car, grabbing the door handle on the passenger's side and yanking on it.

Next to me, Brad Hardacre let slip an evil chuckle. The car was locked.

Patience yanked again, rocking the car and making me question whether she might rip the door off if he didn't use the plipped to open it soon.

'Is she all right?' DS Henwick wanted to know, his lip curled in question.

Brad chuckled again. 'Compared to what?' He hit the button on the key fob and we all got to watch as Patience tore the door open, dived inside and slammed it shut again.

The senior detective viewed the odd scene in wonder. 'If noises in the dark scare her, how does she manage when she has to face down a six foot six criminal shot up with drugs and wielding a knife?'

Brad snorted another laugh. 'Generally she kicks them in the nuts and makes them beg for their mumma. She's actually a pretty good cop. She just has a few … personality quirks,' he chose his words carefully.

Turning to walk backwards to his car, he asked me, 'You guys all right?'

I gave him a half shrug. 'Probably. I think there is something screwy going on here. I just don't know what it is yet.'

He nodded his understanding, Patience hitting the horn in the squad car to make him hurry up. His radio burst into life before he could say anything else – they had another call to which they needed to respond.

'I'll keep my ears to the ground,' He promised as he backed away. 'If I hear anyone matching Mr Gill's description turns up, or I hear anything about this place at all, I'll let you know.'

I gave him a wave of thanks as he ducked into his squad car. The rooflights came on, the brightness hurting my eyes until I turned away.

137

Seconds later, we were alone again.

I spent the night tucked into Alistair. It was a comfortable place to be, but his warmth and reassuring presence made me feel worse for Lady Mary who was sleeping alone.

The mystery of George's whereabouts plagued my dreams, waking me with a start several times. Was it his blood we found on the ground outside the warehouse? Where had he been all day? Was he even in the country?

In my dreams, I was scared to look behind me, convinced Justin Metcalf-Howe or some other secret agent would be standing there waiting to scare me.

Fearing I was robbing Alistair of sleep with my fitfulness, I slid out from under his arm just before six in the morning and stole silently across the carpet gathering clothes as I went. Once I had the door open, I beckoned to the two dachshunds eyeing me suspiciously from their bed in the corner of the room.

However, urgent gestures to come with me did nothing to convince them to leave their warm spot and when I grew insistent, they burrowed back under their blanket to vanish once more.

I guess they felt no need to go outside just yet.

Backing out of the door and doing my best to not disturb Alistair as I left him to sleep, I closed the door quietly, turned around, and almost wet myself.

Looking right at me was the damned Ostrich. Quite how a person shares their house with such a giant bird, or any creature of that size, I couldn't fathom. Its beady eyes were locked on mine, or so I told myself, and my feet were frozen to the spot.

Logic dictated that the bird was most likely friendly – it was allowed to live in the house after all.

'Hello,' I tried in a friendly voice. The way I wanted to go was blocked by the bird. I could hug the wall and squeeze by, but my feet didn't like the way the bird was looking at me and they refused to move when I told them to.

'Are you going to peck me if I get too close?' I asked.

Octavia – I remembered her name, turned her head to one side. Now only one beady eyeball stared at me. It was hardly an improvement.

Wondering whether I should just go back inside my room and give it a few minutes before trying again, I convinced my feet to take a step back. Octavia chose that moment to fluff out her feathers, spreading her stubby wings to each side and fluttering them – the Ostrich version of limbering up perhaps.

My stomach tightened as my brain told me the giant bird was about to charge me, but just as I was about to bolt back through my door, the bird turned around and walked away.

I slumped against the door, letting my heartbeat return to something close to its normal pace. Once the stupid big bird was out of sight at the end of the corridor, I blew out a sigh of relief and hurried toward the stairs.

'Where does it even poop?' I wondered aloud. Could an Ostrich be house trained? Who managed that?

In the kitchen, my search for coffee led me to a machine that belonged on the Starship Enterprise. I poked it a couple of times and moved a lever, but it looked like it ought to have an instruction manual that would take a week to read.

Mercifully, I found instant coffee in a nearby cupboard with which I made a strong cup to beat back the fatigue hanging around my neck. I yawned deeply, my face splitting in two to force my eyes shut.

When I opened them again, I squealed in shock to find Barbie standing in front of me.

She was dressed for a run with an added layer of fabric over the top in deference to the cool air outside. The run was clearly something she had already completed for there was steam rising from her shoulders and water droplets on her hair where the cool air must have condensed.

'Hey, Patty,' she flipped me a wave as she raided the fridge for a carton of milk and proceeded to drink the whole thing.

I sipped at my coffee, cradling the mug with both hands, and enjoying the warmth.

Once the carton was drained, Barbie gave me her attention once more. 'What time did you guys get back last night? I went to bed, but it took me a while to drop off and I didn't hear you returning.'

I let her know about the pool of blood we found.

'You think someone was murdered?' she asked with a grimace.

'I think it's pointless to speculate. As soon as the zoo staff start to arrive, I am going to be in William Gill's face and Lady Mary will be with me. He has some explaining to do. For a start, I want to know the names of the men he was with last night. Taking Sam's phone and attempting to take Sam must be to cover up whatever they are doing. I don't know if that has anything to do with George, but I'm going to find out.'

Barbie wriggled her lips around as she pondered the problem.

'What if George is a foreign agent, Patty? What if the missing boxes from the warehouse are because you stumbled across George shipping weapons or something highly dangerous?'

Until she said it, the idea that Lady Mary's husband might be involved in the warehouse shenanigans had never once occurred to me. Her question had merit, and it fit the situation ... almost. *Our presence in the warehouse yesterday made people nervous so they shifted the gear in case we came back.* I nodded my head at my own conclusion.

Then I shook it again.

'George wasn't supposed to be here,' I reminded Barbie. 'He was booked for a publicity tour in the States.'

'But they flew back because he hurt his foot,' she met my eyes with a piercing gaze, 'then he walked down to see the tiger.'

My eyes flared as I sucked in a breath. Every time I dismissed the notion that George could be involved in anything remotely to do with international espionage or crime, another detail cropped up to put the concept back on the table.

Her voice quiet, Barbie asked, 'What if George faked his injury and came back because he had to? What if William Gill works directly for George and there is something massively illegal going on under Lady Mary's nose?'

It was a terrifying thought. Not because it couldn't happen or because it meant we were dealing with a high level of criminal who would stop at nothing to protect their secrets and investments, but because of the potential impact on a good friend of mine. I didn't want Lady Mary to have to go through the horror of finding out her husband was nothing close to the man she thought he was. I had to wonder what that might do to her.

It couldn't drive her to drink, she was already sloshed by lunchtime most days.

'I need to ask her about George and his foot,' I stated, putting my coffee cup down with the intention of heading upstairs to wake her – this couldn't wait.

It turned out I didn't need to.

'What about George's foot?' Lady Mary asked, drifting into the kitchen wearing a cream chiffon robe over a nightdress. It had a fluffy faux fur collar and cuffs that matched the pair of mules on her feet.

Before I could gather my thoughts to pose a question that wouldn't startle her this early in the day, she opened the fridge and took out an empty jug.

'Always keep the jug cold, that's the secret to a good bloody Mary,' she informed anyone who might be listening.

As she reached back in for tomato juice and a bottle of vodka I hadn't even noticed when I looked inside, I started talking.

'George hurt his foot,' I reminded her. 'That's why you returned.'

'Yes, that's right,' she agreed, pouring equal measures of tomato juice and vodka.

'How did he then walk down to see Esme the tiger?' I challenged her.

From the refrigerator, Lady Mary removed a head of celery, tore off two sticks and put the rest back. A heavy-handed dash of Worcestershire sauce got stirred with the celery before she bit a chunk off the end. Her face told me she was contemplating my question.

'I don't know,' she concluded once she cleared her mouth. 'He was limping something terrible when we got home. I remember him saying he was going to check on Esme, but I don't recall anything after that. I was in the kitchen fixing us a brunch.' I remembered her telling us this part already. 'He would have gone out through the side door via the wet room where we keep our boots. I wouldn't have seen whether he was limping or not even if I had been facing out of a window.'

Lady Mary could not explain her husband's sudden ability to walk. It was yet another mysterious clue, so many of which pointed to the very real possibility that George was indeed involved in shady dealings of the kind that get people killed.

I came here hoping to quickly resolve his disappearance and return him home. Less than a day later, I couldn't decide if I was more likely or better off to find him dead. The alternative was to discover and prove he was a deadly criminal.

Was it his blood on the ground last night? Or was he responsible for putting it there?

As the sound of other people moving about filtered down through the house, we three ladies looked at each other and worried.

One thing was for certain – I had a busy day ahead.

Room Service

Jermaine appeared first, dressed for the day in an elegant navy-blue suit with tan shoes and belt, and a black shirt and tie. Immediately upon arriving in the kitchen, he doffed his jacket and produced a pinafore which he tied around his waist.

'Your breakfast wishes, ladies?' he enquired.

'Cook will be along at eight,' Lady Mary replied, sounding as if her concern was that her staff member's nose would be severely out of joint to find someone else doing the cooking.

I stepped in to smooth things over. 'I think we need to be moving long before eight o'clock, Mary.'

She shrugged her indifference. 'Very well. How about an omelette Arnold Bennett?'

It sounded like the gauntlet being thrown down – was Jermaine good enough to just grab ingredients and make one?

'Ooh, that sounds good,' Barbie cooed encouragingly at Jermaine.

My butler took one step to his right, opened the refrigerator door, and peered inside. Moments later, eggs, fish and other ingredients appeared on the countertop as my man got busy.

I've never been all that comfortable having a servant. It just doesn't sit well with me, but Jermaine loves his role and gains a quiet self-satisfaction from showing off his skills in the kitchen when the opportunity presents.

The dish is not a fast one to present. Not unless one cuts corners, which Jermaine never would. By the time the individual trays came out of the oven, Sam and Alistair had joined us, so too Gloria who looked none the worse for wear despite her overindulgence the previous evening.

I would like to say we ate in respectful silence but nothing of the sort occurred. We were like a rabble – how I imagined a large family might be in the panic to get everyone out of the door and to school or work on time.

The discussion was all about George, William Gill, the warehouse, the mysteriously empty shelves, and what we were going to do about all of it.

It was the sort of case that I might silently wish I had never started. Under the circumstances, there was really no option other than to see it through to the end – we had to find George, or at least solve the mystery of his disappearance. Part of me wanted to drag it out, because when we found George, and caught Mr Gill in the act of doing whatever it was he was doing, the case would end and with it my reason for remaining in England.

Alistair was already itching to get back to the ship. I could tell even though he hadn't said anything. The Aurelia was his home and his love. Our time away from it had been good for both of us, but I couldn't keep him to myself forever. Then there was my new post on board to consider.

I was to be the ship's detective and the role was waiting for my return. I was excited to get started, excited to return to the floating palace I too was beginning to think of as home, yet I could not deny the reluctance I also felt each time I looked at Jermaine. Ending this case and going back to the ship meant an end to our time together.

It might not normally be possible to love two men, but in this case my affections for both Jermaine and Alistair were very real and very different. What Jermaine and I felt for each other was entirely platonic and always would be.

My thoughts on the subject were broken when Barbie nudged my arm.

'Hey, Patty.'

'Huh?' I showed everyone my intellect.

She sniggered at me. 'I've been talking to you for the last minute. You didn't get any of it, did you?'

I swallowed my last mouthful of delectable omelette. 'No, sorry. I was thinking about something else.'

'I asked if I should still try to find out about the cars,' she offered me an open expression waiting for my response.

'The cars?' I questioned, still in the dark having missed the last chunk of conversation.

I got more laughter from her. 'We got the registrations from the cars last night, remember? I was going to sweet talk a man at the DMV and see if I could find out who owns them.'

My brain finally got up to speed.

'Righto, yes. I think that is a good idea. You mean the DVLA, of course,' I corrected her.

'What's the DVLA?' she wanted to know.

'The Driver and Vehicle Licensing Agency,' I explained.

She nodded her understanding. 'Same thing.'

'You might as well see if you get a result,' I told her. 'There's no good us going after Mr Gill mobhanded. If he is as guilty as I am starting to think, I doubt he will admit to anything anyway. If he thinks we are onto him, he might even have already gone into hiding and that's why the police got no answer at his house last night.'

'There's one way to find out, madam,' Jermaine commented, his voice hard and forceful as he cleared the plates. 'We get back into the staff areas of the zoo and start asking hard questions.'

His suggestion silenced everyone around the table. It was precisely what we were going to do. Someone knew something and we were going to continue poking our noses into places they were not wanted until we started getting answers.

Alistair pushed his chair back from the breakfast table and stood up.

'Right, who needs to do what before we get going?'

Barbie hopped off her chair and stretched in place. 'I need to get a shower, but I am heading into the local town to find the DVLA.' She paused to think before asking a question. 'What is the local town?'

'Canterbury,' Lady Mary and I both replied at the same time.

'Will it be easy to find?' Barbie enquired, getting to her feet.

We gave her directions and assigned Sam to go with her. Alistair, Lady Mary, Jermaine, and I were going to rattle some cages down in the zoo and see what fruit fell. I was mixing metaphors in my head again, but I knew what I meant.

Getting up from the table myself, somewhat slower than Barbie who always moved as if her limbs were spring-loaded, I said, 'I need to get dressed and I need to walk the dogs. I don't think taking them around the zoo today is a good idea.'

'I can walk them,' volunteered Gloria. 'I take it they don't need to go far, not with their little legs.'

In truth a dachshund will happily walk quite a distance but are just as often happy to run to the edge of the lawn and back. Especially if it is raining.

The sky outside was dark, the threat of rain there but holding off for now.

Sam bounced to his feet. 'I'll go with you, gran. I should have brought Skull Biter with me.'

'Skull Biter?' I needed to get moving but couldn't help but ask him to clarify who or what that was.

I got a goofy grin in response. 'That's what I call Ringo now. I think it is more fun and he seems to like it too.'

Sam's gran just rolled her eyes.

A while back – it literally felt like a lifetime ago – Anna came into season when she was in the vicinity of the Queen's corgis. We were in Zangrabar at the time and my mind was on things other than my dog's chastity. Things like staying alive primarily. Anyway, four puppies arrived a few weeks later which I then named John, Paul, Ringo, and Georgie. I kept Georgie, the little girl in the litter, and let the boys go. Sam wanted one but it never occurred to me he might rename it.

'Skull Biter,' I repeated, trying the name on for size as I made my way back up to my room to fetch the dogs. Sam trailed after me to save me coming all the way back down again.

Approaching my door, the sound of the girls growling and wrestling reached my ears. They were awake (for once) and playing by the sound of it. They would want some kibble and then exercise.

'Good morning, ladies,' I called out as I swung the door wide.

The next thing I said was completely unprintable.

My expectation was that the silly sausages would be chasing each other around the room and playing a bit of rough and tumble. I did not expect them to be annoying a large snake.

The colourful banded serpent was in the middle of the carpet in my room, hissing and striking at the two dogs who were either side of it and staying out of reach.

The snake appeared to have a wound – I wanted to say on its tail, but where the heck does a snake's tail start and where does its body end? There's probably a joke in there about it being just behind its knees. Whatever the case, one of the dogs had already tagged it.

I bellowed for them to stop. 'Anna! Georgie! Come to mummy!' They completely ignored me, their expressions focused entirely on dealing with the threat to their front.

I took a pace forward, desperate to grab one of the dogs, but the snake looked at me and I changed my mind.

Sam was peering around the doorframe too.

'Cor, a snake,' he observed. 'Is it yours, Mrs Fisher?'

I said something else that couldn't make it into print. The shorter version of my reply would be, 'No,'

'Mary!' I screeched. 'Mary! Your snake is in my room, Mary!'

Feet were already thundering up the stairs, more than one pair of them, so everyone was coming my way.

Anna darted in again, snapping her teeth at the snake and zipping back before it could bite her. I squealed with fright when the snake's fangs came within a quarter inch of her tail and again a second later because Georgie made a run from the other side.

The snake was three feet long and the width of my wrist. I had no idea what kind of snake it was – Lady Mary had told us when we arrived, but I hadn't thought to memorise the information.

Whatever it was, it was mean, nasty, and ready to eat one of my dogs for breakfast.

I felt faint.

Barbie got to me first because she was already upstairs and faster on her feet than anyone else I had ever met.

I guess she saw how wide my eyes were or how little colour there was in my face because she grabbed hold of me to keep me upright. I wasn't actually going to keel over, but I was starting to wonder if I might be sick.

'Patty, what is i ...' she saw the snake and uttered more or less the same thing I had when I first opened the door.

Jermaine exploded into the corridor as he cleared the top of the stairs. He was ready to kill but seeing me safe, if a little unsteady on my feet, he relaxed.

Falling back into his butler's reserved manner, he enquired. 'How may I be of assistance, madam?'

Barbie screamed at him. 'There's a snake and it's going to kill Anna and Georgie!'

Alistair arrived, both men peering around me to see the battle still raging in my room.

'Lady Mary's snake got loose. I'm sure it's not normally dangerous but the dogs have riled it up now,' I gasped, hoping someone was going to know how to pick up the horrible reptile.

'Um, that's not Lady Mary's snake,' stated Alistair with authority. 'Lady Mary has a Boa Constrictor. That's a coral snake.'

'How do you know?' I begged, my question coming out as a squeak.

Alistair went around me and into the room. 'I met the Boa yesterday. It's in a vivarium downstairs. No one in their right mind would keep a coral snake as a pet,' he advised us, still sounding like he knew what he was talking about.

Jermaine went into my room too, and around to the head of the bed where he selected a pillow and removed it from the case.

'Whyever not?' asked Barbie.

Lady Mary, the slowest and least fit of any of us, reached the top of the stairs.

'I swear there were fewer steps when I was younger,' she wheezed her way along the hallway.

Alistair's attention was on the snake, his eyes never leaving it as he began to crouch. I couldn't draw a breath and my heart was thumping so hard in my chest I was shocked people couldn't see my ribs move.

Just as I was about to beg him to not try anything silly, his right arm flashed out. The snake was in the process of striking at Anna again and thus facing away from Alistair when he grabbed it two inches below its head.

I squealed in fright for him, but as the serpent wrapped its long body around his arm, it was clear he had it under control.

The dogs were climbing his legs, pawing at him to get to the snake he now held.

Jermaine moved into position with the pillowcase, and I saw then what it was for.

Lady Mary arrived between me and Barbie.

'That is not my snake,' she stated. 'That's a coral snake.'

'So we heard already,' I gasped between laboured breaths.

Alistair dropped Stripey the snake carefully into the pillowcase before looking up. 'And jolly deadly they are too.'

My jaw fell open again. 'What?'

'Oh, yes,' agreed Lady Mary. 'One bite would kill a man stone dead. What was it doing in your room?'

'You're asking me?' I gasped. 'Mary, your house is a menagerie! Do you even know what creatures live here?'

She frowned at my impertinent question. 'Yes, thank you. A coral snake is not one of them.'

My heart still thumping away in my chest, I fell to my knees to scoop my dogs. They rewarded me with kisses, their excitement too much for them to contain. It had all been a great game to them.

With the snake safely secured in the makeshift bag, which Jermaine took away, I allowed myself to relax slightly. I needed a minute to get myself under control because my legs felt wobbly and weak. I tottered to the bed, getting a hand from Alistair when he saw how unsteady I looked.

Once sitting, I let the dogs go. They were still hyped up and wanted to play.

'Can you feed them, please?' I begged.

Moments later, they were crunching on kibble and I was able to tell myself the danger had now passed. It left a serious question to be addressed though.

'Where did the snake come from and how did it get to be in my room? Why my room?' I wailed.

Alistair sat by my side, an arm around me for support. He had no answer for me.

Nor did Lady Mary. Not really. 'My guess would be that it is part of our reptile collection.'

'How did it get to the house?' asked Alistair.

Her advice on the subject was chilling. 'It's too cold for it to have made the journey by itself. Someone had to have brought it here.'

The terrifying conclusion then was that the same someone put it in my room with the sole intention of getting me bitten. Or Alistair. Or possibly just the dogs with the hope I would be so distracted dealing with them, or too upset because they died, to continue with my investigation.

It was Barbie who was the first to vocalise it.

'Someone is trying to stop us.'

'Or put barriers in our way,' said Alistair.

Sam chipped in. 'That means we are onto something. Doesn't it?' he questioned.

I nodded, shuddering at the memory of the snake as I forced myself to get up onto my feet again.

'Yes, Sam, that's right. We might not yet know the rules of this game, or even what game we are playing. That makes it hard to win, but you can be sure we are playing it all the same, whether we want to or not.'

Alistair took my right hand, clasping it in both of his.

'We're going to have to be extra vigilant,' he stared into my eyes, questioning whether continuing with the case was something I really wanted to do.

It both was and it wasn't. Running away and never coming back sounded like a great idea, but there was no chance I could accept things as they were. I needed closure on the mystery we had stumbled across and I wanted to know the truth about George.

One way or another, I was going to get to the bottom of both things. Only once I got there would I know if they were connected or not.

Barbie appeared in the doorway again. She was dressed now, a pencil skirt and matching heels showing off her toned legs. Above it she wore a blouse with a button 'accidentally' undone. It was no accident, of course, and would probably shoot off across the room if she were to manage to fasten it over the push up bra doing wonders for her ample chest. Her outfit showed off the assets she planned to use to elicit information from whomever she managed to sweet talk at the DVLA.

She was a drop-dead bombshell with blonde hair, blue eyes, and a natural tan.

'Come on, Sam,' she beckoned with her right hand. 'Let's go get some information.' Sam grabbed her hand and let her pull him through the door.

We got a wave goodbye and a fast, 'Good luck,' as they set off into town.

Adrenalin was draining from my system, leaving me feeling a little spent. The dogs were dancing by the door, ready to go outside now they had eaten, and I still needed to get dressed for the day.

Alistair checked our room for further diabolic creatures that might jump out on me, declared it safe, and took the dogs down to let them out.

Lady Mary took herself away to get dressed also, which left me to get on with the task of making myself presentable.

I still had the toothbrush in my mouth when I heard the scream.

I was in my underwear, multi-tasking to get ready swiftly. Partly this was because I felt an urgent need to be actively in the pursuit of answers, and partly it was because the room now gave me the heebies and I needed to be somewhere else.

Regardless of that, the scream got me running.

I ripped a robe from the back of the bathroom door and spat my toothbrush into the sink as I tore from the room barefoot.

Running was beginning to feel like the flavour of this trip. Running and abject terror.

I didn't know who had screamed, the walls muffled the sound, making it too indistinct to tell if it was Lady Mary or someone else. I knew it was a woman though.

Thundering along the hallway to the stairs, I made a mental note to switch out my bra for something with more support. I was back in the habit of buying and wearing nice underwear now that I had a sex life again and I was getting more jiggle than I was comfortable with when I ran.

There had been no further screams, but I had to get downstairs to find out why that was.

At the bottom of the stairs, voices led me around to the left and back toward the kitchen at the rear of the house. Much like my own place, the pure vastness of Lady Mary's mansion made it hard to pinpoint where sounds were coming from.

It took me half a minute to locate them and coming closer I was able to make out what was being said.

'By 'eck, I thought that were a demon the way it came out of the bushes at me,' said Gloria.

The robe was around my shoulders but still not done up as I got to them in the kitchen. I paused just outside the door to tie it, then strode in already asking a question.

'What happened?'

Gloria was sitting on a chair near the door, a large balloon glass that might have once held brandy nestled in her hands which were resting on her lap.

Alistair was attending to her.

'The peacock,' he gave me the short answer. 'It went for the dogs again.'

'Where are they?' I looked around since there was no sign of them.

'They ran off. Jermaine is out trying to find them now.'

It was just one thing after another today, delay after delay. How were we to ever progress if we couldn't get two minutes peace to organise ourselves? Perhaps that was the intent of the persons involved.

My head itched, that familiar feeling that I had just hit upon something. This is something to do with George and Lady Mary returning early, I thought to myself. The itch came again. They came home unexpectedly and interrupted something. Another itch.

It begged a new question: What was it that they interrupted?

Jermaine came back past the windows before I could go looking for him. I had nothing on my feet so going outside to help find the dogs was not a happy proposition.

Mr Reliable had, of course, already caught them both.

'They are suitably ready to return to the house,' he announced, letting them both off their leads. It was butler talk to say they had both pooped.

'Did you kill the peacock?' I enquired, genuinely curious.

'Goodness, no, madam.' Jermaine was surprised by my question and might have been more so if he'd known I felt disappointed. 'It ran away when I pursued the dogs, madam.'

Anna and Georgie whizzed around the kitchen floor, running to find the water bowl in the corner. I peered at it, curious to make sure Lady Mary didn't have a small dolphin or something living in it. The dogs were none the worse for their second encounter with the peacock, but it still struck me as ridiculous that they would befriend a tiger, attempt to tackle a deadly venomous snake, yet run from a colourful bird.

Mr Peacock was outside right now, making his distinctive squawk somewhere hidden in the early morning mist.

In her chair still, Gloria held the glass up to be refilled.

'I shall need another of those, deary. You could put it in a strong coffee if you like.'

Alistair collected the glass from Gloria's hand.

'As you wish, Mrs Chalk.'

'Oh, you can call me Gloria, deary. Everyone else does.'

I left the kitchen, heading back to my room for yet another attempt at getting myself dressed for the day. The dogs followed me when I called for them. They were naturally quite lazy so would most likely enjoy being left alone to sleep in my room for the next few hours.

I'm not sure what triggered it, but heading back up the stairs, a sense of hope, or perhaps you could call it positivity, settled over me. We were going to get in peoples' faces this morning, get some answers, and bring the whole thing down on the people responsible. If that included George because he was at the centre of this mess, then so be it. I would be here to shore Lady Mary up.

I heard the front doorbell chime when I got upstairs. Jermaine would answer it, I thought idly to myself before remembering this house had its own butler. Jeeves then. Either way, the caller was unlikely to be of interest to me.

I was wrong.

It was almost eight o'clock by the time I got back downstairs. Finally dressed for the day, I felt imbued with a need for justice to prevail and the desire to get on with it.

There were voices drifting through the house: Alistair's and Lady Mary's for a start, but then someone else spoke, and I felt the skin around my eyes tighten as my expression pinched with displeasure.

'Chief Inspector Quinn,' I identified the source of my irritation as I strode into the drawing room. 'Good morning.' I wanted to quiz him about the reason for his visit, but this was not my house, and my host was already here. Besides, I knew why he was here. The report of blood spilled last night on top of the still missing George Brown was sufficient to trigger his interest.

'Good morning, Mrs Fisher,' he rose like a gentleman to greet me, shaking my hand lightly. He was a consummate politician and perhaps that was why he had risen in the ranks and would continue to do so. He could be insulted one moment and smile for the cameras the next. 'I was just discussing the incident last night; I read about it in this morning's reports. Do you have anything to add.'

I thought for a moment about the vague suspicions I had creeping around my head and what they could mean.

He waited patiently, his eyes searching mine as he wondered why I hadn't yet answered.

'I believe we overreacted,' I stated with an apologetic sigh.

Alistair and Lady Mary both looked at me with confusion on their faces, then exchanged a glance to see if the other had any idea what I was doing.

'Yes, sorry about the wasted manpower,' I continued. 'It was most likely an animal kill; there are plenty of wild predators in the English countryside.'

CI Quinn blinked. Just once. He was not used to hearing me back down or withdraw a statement. I was going to have to play this carefully or I might tip my hand, make him suspicious, and that in turn might get me the opposite result to the one I sought.

'DS Henwick reported missing inventory from a warehouse in his report. Is that not the case?'

I wanted to defer to Lady Mary but there was no time to explain my play.

'Probably not, no. What we showed your officers last night was some empty shelves. Again, on reflection, it seems likely the warehouse manager moved the goods before closing down for the day. It is a feed storage warehouse, so goods are constantly coming in and out. There will be a simple explanation.' I did my best to look embarrassed.

'What about Mr Gill?' asked Lady Mary, failing to play along. 'What about the attack in the carpark, Patricia?'

Chief Inspector Quinn twisted his torso to look at the lady of the house before looking back at me, one eyebrow cocked in question.

'Carpark?' he invited me to expand.

'It was a disagreement about cars, nothing more, Chief Inspector,' I lied dismissively. 'When we left the pub last night, the car next to mine

162

had a scratch to its flank. The driver insisted it wasn't there beforehand. Things got a little heated, but it was not worth reporting.'

Now Lady Mary wore a deep frown. My lies were confusing her. Alistair most likely felt the same, but he knew well enough to back me up.

Getting to his feet, he said, 'Yes, the persons involved were rather unpleasant, but the scratch was not a new one. When we argued, they accepted defeat.'

Quinn pursed his lips and studied my face. I think he knew I was lying but wasn't yet prepared to call me out.

'And what of Mr Brown?' he asked, switching subjects. 'Has there been any contact from him?'

I shook my head sadly. 'Nothing. We are quite worried, Chief Inspector.'

'Very worried,' echoed Lady Mary. My pulse spiked as worry set in. Was she about to reveal the secret contents of his desk and the unbelievable concept that he might be something other than a famous thriller novelist? I breathed a sigh of relief, when she said, 'This is so unlike him. He's not very good at fending for himself.'

The senior police officer, visiting only because he sniffed a case that might make the news and was thus worth leading, let his gaze rove from me to Alistair and on to Lady Mary. We all met his eyes with the same guileless look.

After a second or two, he sniffed in a breath, let it go and changed his expression.

'Very well. I thank you for your time. I will ensure all my officers are aware to be on the lookout for Mr Brown. If he does not reappear or make contact by the end of today, I will step things up and call for a press conference.' I knew he loved getting his face on the TV. 'We took the details of his credit and debit cards yesterday and can report that he has not used them at any point thus far. If he does, I will let you know. Until I call again, please keep me informed of any changes.'

Pulling his hat from beneath his left arm where it had been tucked, the chief inspector dipped his head to bid us good day and left the room.

Jeeves appeared in the hallway outside as if by magic.

I made my friends wait until the old butler got the chief inspector to the door and watched out of the window to make sure he had left before I turned to them.

'Patricia, sweetie, what was that all about?' Lady Mary wanted to know.

Alistair had already guessed. 'You don't want the police here, do you?'

I gave a short shake of my head. 'No.' I knew they were both going to ask why so I just kept on talking. 'For a start, if we tell them anything about George, they will look in his desk, find the weapons, money, travel plans and everything else and then tear this house apart looking for more of the same.'

Lady Mary put a hand to her mouth in horror.

'That's not the real reason though. I think something is about to happen. Your unexpected return home threw a spanner in the works for something that your zoo staff, or some members of the zoo staff at least, are involved in. William Gill may or may not be at the head of it, I cannot yet say. Nor can I tell you what 'it' is. However, the altercation we overheard yesterday between Mr Gill and another zookeeper was due to their plan falling apart. Whatever it is they have up their sleeves, I think it is going to play out soon. If the police are here snooping around, they will either get nervous and shut it all down, in which case the trail might go cold, or they might go the other way and resort to violence. The blood we found last night was no animal kill.'

'What does this have to do with George?' Lady Mary wailed.

I could offer her nothing but an apologetic look. 'I wish I knew.' I crossed the space between us, taking her hands in mine. 'Mary, I want you to consider that George might be right in the middle of this.'

'But we were supposed to be away,' she argued.

'Yes, but it looks like he might have faked an injury to come back here.'

'Why?' she wanted to know.

I still didn't have a good answer for her, but I did have a guess. 'If he is at the helm, and planned to be away, he might have caught a whiff of something going south, or someone trying to double cross him. I could waste a day on conjecture, but I'd rather get out there and find some answers. What do you say? Shall we ask Mr Gill some uncomfortable questions?'

A determined look, one chipped out of flint, stole across her face.

'Yes, Patricia. Let's do exactly that.'

Mr Gill wasn't in his office. Lady Mary took us straight to it. For once, possibly for the first time since I'd met her, she was completely sober. I did not feel a need to comment on it but had to wonder if she were just too distracted to drink or making a conscious decision to keep her mind sharp.

'I haven't seen him this morning,' explained the lady employed to handle his diary and affairs. She was in her twenties and curvy in an attractive way. An abundance of lustrous dark brown hair had been pushed up in a style reminiscent of the sixty's beehive hairdo. 'He is usually in by now,' she added, trying to cover for her boss. 'I know he had been working some very late hours recently.'

We already knew the last part, but I doubted the hours he clocked at the pub for his meeting last night, were anything to do with official zoo business.

'We need to see his office,' I spoke aloud as I left the woman at her desk. Some yards farther down the corridor from her was a door labelled 'Head Keeper'.

'Oh, I, ah,' William Gill's PA started to get flustered. He probably didn't like having people mess with his office. I found the door to be locked but that wasn't going to be much of a barrier.

'The key, please,' demanded Lady Mary in a tone that held no chance for discussion.

We were in the zoo's headquarters, a set of offices behind the visitor centre at the main guest entrance. Somewhere on the other side of the wall, happy families or couples, or perhaps school groups on a day trip would be paying the entry fee and making their way through the turnstile to explore the wonders Lady Mary's ancestors collected. Of course, the creatures now within the fences were the descendants of those originally introduced, but the attraction was as lucrative and popular now as it had ever been.

The curvy young woman, blushing crimson as she bustled to produce a key to the door, hurried along the corridor. We were attracting the attention of other members of staff working in the HQ building. There was perhaps a dozen of them, most opting to stay in their seats though they were craning their necks to peer around their computer monitors to see what was going on.

A few felt they had need to involve themselves.

'Can I be of assistance, Lady Mary?' asked a swarthy man in his early fifties.

I judged him to be of African heritage, but mixed race somewhere deep in his past for he had twinkling blue eyes that sparkled against the backdrop of coffee-coloured skin. His hair was greying around the temples but cut short so it barely showed.

Lady Mary gave him a kindly smile. 'No, thank you, Richard. It's family business.'

It seemed that was all she had to say. Richard held his hands up at chest height in mock surrender as he backed away.

The curvy woman, now getting flustered at her attempts to find the right key, finally got the door open.

'If I may, madam,' requested Jermaine, slipping around the curvy lady as she retreated so he could enter the office first.

I guess he was checking to see if there was anything inside I might not wish to see – such as William Gill's body. There was nothing.

Having prudently checked the interior with the door mostly closed, Jermaine now swung it wide so the rest of us could follow him in.

'Where is Mr Gill?' Lady Mary asked. She wasn't expecting an answer, just voicing her thoughts.

'Gone to ground would be my guess,' I let her know what was in my head. 'His business partners – whoever or whatever the men he met for dinner last night were – must have tipped him off that we were following and attempting to record him.'

Last one in, Alistair closed the door behind him. 'Shall we check his drawers?'

We did just that, three of us rifling through his filing cabinet, desk drawers, and the notes on his desk. Nothing we found provided any clue.

Feeling frustrated again, I exhaled slowly to settle myself and focus my thoughts.

'We need to widen our search,' I announced. It was a statement without meaning until I added, 'All the other members of staff … someone has to know what he is up to.' Then a thought occurred to me. 'When George first went missing, who did you report it to?' My question was aimed at Lady Mary.

On the spot, she looked panicked for a half second, before saying, 'It was Mr Gill. He promised me he would alert all the staff to be on the lookout.'

I had the office door open less than a heartbeat later.

'Who here knows that George Brown, Lady Mary's husband, has gone missing?' My shout was loud enough to get the attention of everyone in the offices in my vicinity and the reaction on every face told me all I needed to know.

Richard, the man Lady Mary spoke to on our way in, was out of his chair and coming my way. He was not the only one.

The central hub of the zoo business, where the administration, accountancy, decision making and suchlike took place, was filled with middle and senior management in smart office wear. I had no idea what kind of environment it was to work in, but the people I could see looked at ease in their surroundings; happy with the job they were employed to do.

To my mind, that made them invested in the success of the business so the worried, concerned, or just plain startled looks I could now see were entirely in place.

'George is missing?' Richard repeated my words as if genuinely questioning them.

I posed another question rather than answer as he joined me in the hallway and other members of staff formed up behind him. 'No one told you?'

He looked to his left, saying, 'I heard nothing about it. Did anyone hear about George?'

The murmurings and mutterings that formed his reply were unanimous: No one had passed on the information.

Lady Mary came to stand beside me. 'You are sure Mr Gill did not announce that my husband vanished on his way to visit Esme yesterday? He promised he would tell everyone.'

I turned through forty-five degrees to face the zoo owner and leaned in so I could whisper.

'I found the same yesterday when I visited the tiger enclosure. The tiger keeper had no idea.'

Yesterday, I figured it was an oversight; George's disappearance was still in question and only a few hours old. I allowed myself to believe the passage of information simply hadn't filtered that far at that time. That wasn't it though. William Gill hadn't told anyone.

Whispering still, I asked Lady Mary, 'Of all the people here, who would you trust with your life?'

She shifted away a little so she could show me her incredulous expression – what on earth was I asking?

'With my life?' she replied quietly. 'I don't know any of them that well, but if I had to pick one, it would be Richard. He's been here for years.'

I wasted no time discussing the subject further, straightening up to look the man in the face.

'Might I beg a few moments of your time?' I enquired politely, stepping back into Mr Gill's office as a gesture that he should follow me.

Richard's eyes showed bewilderment, but he came. The other staff in the hallway all watched with curiosity and then disappointment as I closed the door on their faces.

'What is this about?' Richard wanted to know before any of us had a chance to speak.

I noted that he had naturally gravitated to the centre of the room, which meant that we now surrounded him. I had not intended to present such an aggressive stance, but this was not the time to change it.

'What is Mr Gill up to?' I demanded to know.

Richard reacted as if I had accused him of something, backing away a step as I came forward.

'What? No, I have, no … What do you mean?'

'He is not here when he should be. Lady Mary's husband is missing, and Mr Gill failed to pass on that vital piece of information. Have you seen George spending time with Mr Gill?'

Richard's eyes were going wild, flitting from my face to Lady Mary's and then to either Alistair or Jermaine who both remained silent and impassive like deadly sentinels waiting for the order to strike.

'It's a simple question,' I barked, tired of my usual softly, softly approach. I had no reason to believe Richard was involved, but also no patience to spare on his feelings.

'No. No, I don't think so,' Richard stammered. 'Look what is this about?'

'Has Mr Gill been displaying unusual behaviour?' I posed a different question. 'Has he been working late? Has he been preoccupied with matters or in any way acting as if he has something secret or private he has been working on?'

We all saw Richard open his mouth to say, 'No,' but the word never left his mouth.

'What is it?' I implored, closing the distance between us, and grabbing his arms. 'Please, the clock is ticking, and we need answers.'

Richard's direction of focus shifted. We were in William Gill's private office with the door shut, but Richard's eyes left my face to look at the wall and it took me a second to realise he was visualising something he would be able to see on the other side.

'He's been working with Heath Martin.' Richard had a faraway look as if he were adding things up in his head. Snapping back to reality with a jolt, his eyes came back to mine and then shifted to look at Lady Mary. 'We were all surprised when William suddenly promoted Heath. He's a great guy, and all, but he's not been with us for long. William seemed to invent a new post – Head of Developmental Projects – and put Heath in it. None of us really know what he does. The two of them have been working on something together for a while though.'

'Where is he?' I demanded urgently.

Richard moved toward the door. 'At his desk in the main office.'

Alistair ripped the door open so we could bundle out again. Richard was the second one through it, his right arm rising to point out the man we needed to speak to.

It got about halfway up before it faltered. Through the glass that started halfway up the wall, we could see through into the pool of desks. The heads of those seated at their computers or working on something in pairs or threes at a breakout table were all turned our way again.

'He was right there a moment ago,' Richard frowned in confusion. When he reached the door to the main office, he called out so everyone would hear. 'Where's Heath?'

No one answered. They looked around and at each other but drew a collective blank. Mostly they looked surprised to not find him sitting at his desk.

Jermaine drew the obvious conclusion first. 'We spooked him, and he took off, madam.' Jermaine was already heading for the exit, going outside to see if the man might still be there.

We all ran after him, Richard included. He was now the one asking questions.

'What is this about, Lady Mary?' he begged to know. 'Is Heath doing something he shouldn't be? Is it something to do with George going missing?' As we burst into the sunlight outside, Richard gasped, 'His car's gone!'

Lady Mary had been mostly quiet thus far, but she had something to say now.

'Richard, I don't get involved in the operation and daily running of the zoo very often. In fact, these days it would be fair to say that I do little other than chair the annual Board meeting.' She faced him, demanding his full attention when she said, 'I want every member of staff to be on the lookout for Heath and William. If they are seen, I want them detained.'

Richard's eyes flared – it was a startling request to place upon the staff.

Lady Mary held up a hand to stop him from speaking. 'I don't care if they have to borrow the tranquiliser gun from the vets. William Gill needs to answer some questions. If he shows his face anywhere within the zoo grounds, or if anyone knows where he is, I want to know about it.'

Expected to respond, Richard mumbled, 'Okay. I'll make sure everyone is informed.' He turned about, heading back inside to do as he promised. It left the four of us in the staff carpark outside.

'What next?' asked Lady Mary.

Champagne

We were not finished in the office. If Heath was working on something secret, then there had to be something on his desk, or in his computer that would tell us what it was.

The office and the people in it looked to have been flash frozen. It was how I remembered seeing the unfolding drama of the 911 attacks in America – people had just been staring at the TV screen unable to process what they were seeing.

This was just like that. The owner's husband was missing, now too the head keeper who might just be up to something and Heath, who was possibly his partner in crime, had just absconded.

Not only that, the owner, who by her own admission never got involved in the daily operation of the zoo, was in the office and asking questions.

Our return to their environment broke the spell. Richard, who must have just finished telling them to call around the zoo and have everyone on the lookout for William and Heath, spun around to face us again as we approached. His stunned office of people went back to their desks. They were jabbering, picking up phones, and shooting questions at each other in disbelief.

'Which desk is Heath's?' I asked, scanning around for one that was empty.

Richard began backing away immediately. 'It's over here,' he jerked a thumb.

'I want to see what he has been working on,' I told him as I followed close behind.

There was a thin snake of us crossing the office, weaving between the desks to get to one in the corner. It had been positioned facing into the room so Heath's back was to the window. No one would be able to look over his shoulder without him seeing them coming. Perfect if he needed to keep what was on his screen a secret.

'Patricia,' Alistair nudged my arm as we got to the desk and pointed to a framed photograph standing to the left of the computer monitor.

I saw why as soon as my eyes locked onto the picture. The subject of the photograph was a man. He was in his thirties and had hair grown longer than was the modern style. It curled over the collar of his shirt. He was on a beach somewhere tropical with a girl on each arm. Smiling for the camera, he looked happy, but neither the location, the girls, nor his mood were of interest.

Alistair pointed out the photograph because he was the man we saw with William Gill last night. His business partner, or so we assumed at the time, was also a member of staff - the so-called Head of Developmental Projects.

'This is Heath Martin?' I asked Richard to confirm.

Richard was tapping the mouse, bringing the computer to life. He looked at the photograph.

'Yes, that's him. I'm just trying to get into his files. Oh,' he curled his top lip. 'There's a password.' Richard slid into the chair and started to poke in drawers and under notebooks, looking for a slip of paper that might have the password on it.

When he drew a blank, he pushed himself up from the chair to look over the top of the monitor.

'Does anyone know Heath's password?' he called optimistically.

He got a lot of nos and several head shakes. It was as I expected. If the man was doing something illegal, which my itchy skull insisted he was, then he would have made it as difficult as possible for anyone to uncover it. We would do what we could to get around the password and access his files, but I was not going to be surprised when I discovered there was nothing incriminating in them.

'Jermaine, can you get around it?' I asked.

My butler puffed out his cheeks. 'With time, madam, yes.'

Richard butted in before I could speak again.

'I can get the IT support firm to unlock it.'

'You can?' I sounded surprised because I was now wondering why he hadn't already done that.

'Sure. It's just one phone call.' He was looking up at me from the chair like he was waiting for me to give him permission to do it.

I shot my eyes at the phone on the desk. 'Please do so,' I prompted.

Leaving him to make the call, I stepped back a pace to give him some space. I had no idea how long this would take but moving back, my eye caught sight of something under the desk.

'Is that a bag?' I asked.

Jermaine saw where I was looking, which was on the other side of Richard from where I stood. To get to it would be a complicated do-si-do because there were four of us crammed in behind the chair.

Jermaine crouched, slid a hand under the desk and came up with a small blue backpack in his hands.

'There is something heavy in it, madam,' he announced.

We could all see it. The object inside was a foot long, bulky, and heavy enough to pull the back pack's material to one side. Immediately, my head filled with a singular thought – my wild guess about the arms dealing was right on the money and Jermaine was about to unzip the pack to have a small machine gun fall out.

I couldn't get the words out fast enough to stop Jermaine, but as panic gripped me, the now open top of the pack shifted, and I saw what was inside.

It wasn't a deadly weapon at all. It was a bottle of champagne.

'Planning to celebrate,' murmured Alistair.

Jermaine lifted the bottle out, placing it on the desk with the label toward us as he rummaged inside the backpack to confirm there was nothing else with it.

I blinked, my mouth forming an O as I stared at the bottle. I blinked again, the back of my skull itching like mad until I worked out what I was seeing.

'I need to go back to the house.' I was talking to myself, my voice a whisper as the big fat clue on the desk demanded all my attention.

'What was that, darling?' asked Alistair, leaning closer so he might catch what I was saying.

I tapped my pockets to make sure I had all my things with me. 'I need to check something,' I murmured, still consulting my memory to see if I could recall the information accurately enough to avoid making the trip.

Richard chose that moment to put the phone down. 'I'm in,' he announced triumphantly. The screen, which had been showing a picture of mountains under a blue sky dissolved to reveal a standard desktop image with the usual icons one might expect to find.

Richard turned to face me with a grimace. 'It might take a while to find what you are looking for.'

I sucked the inside of my cheek for a second and made a decision.

'I need to go back to the house.' This time I said it loudly enough for my friends to hear. I held my hand out to Jermaine. 'Do you have the keys, sweetie. I'll be right back.'

My promise to return directly wasn't good enough though.

'I will accompany you, madam,'

'Someone needs to go through this,' I pointed to the computer. 'I want to check I am right about something, but even if I am, it won't tell us what is going on.'

Alistair interlaced his fingers and cracked his knuckles meaningfully. 'I can dissect the files on a computer, darling. Lady Mary and I will see what we can find. He stepped forward to replace Richard who was standing up to vacate the chair. Alistair stopped to touch my shoulder before he sat down. 'Now, you do promise to come right back?'

I lifted my right arm, three fingers held upright at shoulder height as I made the Girl Guide salute.

'I promise.'

He rolled his eyes and plonked into the chair.

'Please be sure that you do, Patricia. If you get any crazy ideas and shoot off to apprehend someone, I shall be most displeased.'

Alistair was teasing me, but he also meant it; I gave him cause to worry far too often.

Jermaine hefted the keys to the Range Rover, and I picked up the bottle of champagne.

It was time to see if I had just found a corner of the puzzle.

Evidence. But what of?

Jermaine and I raced through Lady Mary's house, startling a housemaid performing cleaning tasks as we ran to my room. I kept a wary eye out for Octavia and any other exotic house inhabitants but made it to my room without needing to evade an angry bird.

Outside my window, on the lawn below, I could hear Stretch the peacock's shrill calls.

Anna and Georgie leapt from their bed as we burst through the door, excited back ends wagging madly.

'Yes, yes, hello girls,' I cooed to them as I started rifling through the handbag I carried yesterday.

'What are we looking for, madam?' Jermaine enquired. On the short hop back to the house, he had remained in his usual silent butler mode. He rarely asked questions, deeming such behaviour to be impertinent, but he couldn't help me if I didn't include him.

'An invoice,' I revealed. 'It's slightly smaller than A4 size and scraggly looking because I dug it out of a patch of nettles. I folded it carefully and put it in my handbag ...' I was mentally running through my movements. It definitely went into my bag. What did I do when I got back to the room?

'Is this it, madam?' asked Jermaine, stooping to retrieve something from the waste bin in the corner.

As he straightened, he had the invoice, still folded, between the index and middle fingers of his right hand.

My eyes lit up.

When he handed it to me, I placed it carefully on the surface of the desk. It had dried overnight but the previously soggy paper was now inflexible and threatening to tear as I attempted to unfold it.

Jermaine could see me grimacing as I wrestled with it.

'If I may, madam?'

He took the invoice and went through the door to the bathroom where he turned on the hot tap at the basin. When steam began to billow a few seconds later, he held the paper over it and gently allowed the moist air to do what I had been unable to.

In less than a minute, the page was flat again.

'You are a genius, Jermaine. Where did you learn that?'

'I am a butler, madam. Removing creases is part of my role.' I shot him a sceptical eye. His cheeks coloured slightly, and he came clean. 'I saw it on television.'

'What show?' I prompted while I fetched the champagne bottle from the bed.

Now my butler looked distinctly uncomfortable. A smile broke out on my face.

'What show was it?' I teased.

He put his head down and mumbled, 'Hong Kong Phooey.'

I spat out a laugh but pushed the amusing moment to one side to focus on the task at hand.

'I knew it!' I punched the air – a most unladylike action I had unintentionally picked up from Barbie.

Jermaine came in close to see what had gotten me so excited.

'The champagne,' I pointed to the entry on the invoice. 'I found this invoice in some weeds down by the tiger enclosure yesterday. I only kept it because I saw the label of the champagne. This is Hartfield and Champettier vintage Champagne.' Jermaine did not need to be told what that meant. It is high end stuff and costs an eye watering amount per bottle. 'There are twelve cases on this invoice.'

Jermaine wore a deep frown as he tried to unpick what this meant.

'Is Mr Martin planning a party?' he wondered aloud. 'Why would that be something he needed to keep secret?'

I had no idea, but I did plan to find out. The number for the wholesalers was right under their name on the invoice. My phone was in my hand the next second but ringing before I could start to dial their number.

The name displayed on the screen was Alistair so of course I answered it.

'Hi, Alistair. Did you find something?'

I got a cryptic response. 'Sort of. There doesn't look to be anything much in his files, but we looked in his browser history and he has been looking at flights. All his searches appear to be for two seats in first class going to the Bahamas.'

'Does it show dates?' I asked, biting my fingernails as I waited for the answer. We were getting somewhere finally.

I heard the mouse being clicked. 'It looks like he was going this week. The dates are all for two days from now. There's something else you need to know, Patricia.' I held my breath. 'The flights are all one way.'

'He wasn't coming back.' I blurted the logical explanation and tried to fit that into what else we knew. 'Is Mary there?' I asked.

'Here, sweetie,' her voice came back immediately. 'Feeling rather parched, but still with you.'

'Mary, I found an invoice for twelve cases of champagne and a list of other drinks and things. It was by the tiger enclosure. I didn't say anything before because I thought maybe it was just your weekly shop,' I found time to make a joke.

'Very droll,' Lady Mary replied with frost in her tone.

I dropped the humour. 'Can I assume it is not yours and you do not have a party planned for the near future? The supplier is Brenchley Premier Goods, is that someone you use?'

'No,' she replied. 'I've never heard of them and we have no parties planned. We are not supposed to be here if you remember.'

I remembered. That was part of this, my itchy skull insisted. I got Alistair to perform a document search for any containing the words champagne or Brenchley, but he drew a blank. Heath Martin was doing something secret with the zoo's head keeper. William Gill had appointed Heath to work on an unnamed project no one else knew about and both men had vanished now that they knew we were on to them.

Whatever it was involved a lot of high-end champagne and then a flight to the Bahamas. On top of all that, George was somehow also involved. Was he the instigator? Was he the financier? Was he really leading a double life as a secret agent? If so, how did that fit in?

We had uncovered a few clues, but so far all we had done was stir up the already muddy water.

I tapped the side of the champagne bottle with a manicured fingernail.

'We're coming back to you,' I announced. 'I think it's time we had another look at that warehouse. Someone must have been driving the forklift or checking inventory. I'm willing to bet the empty shelves we found held the delivery from Brenchley Premier Goods. If we find out where it went ...'

Jermaine started toward the door, the dachshunds dancing along at his feet. They wanted to go out again.

I huffed a sigh. It would be easier and faster to move freely without them, but I was a dog owner, and it came with responsibilities.

I promised Alistair we would be back in a few minutes, picked up the dog leads and followed them from the room.

I should have left them behind. It would have saved me a lot of heartache. Of course, I had no idea what was about to happen.

Another Clue Without Meaning

We were moving at a slower pace on our way back out of the house. Jeeves stopped us before we got to the door so he could ask about our lunch plans. Just like that, most of the morning was already gone.

I had no advice for him on the subject but promised to speak with Lady Mary.

'Are you returning to her now, Mrs Fisher?' Jeeves enquired.

'Yes. She is in the offices behind the visitor centre. I shall pass on your message. I am sure she will call you if she deems it necessary.'

Jeeves dipped his head, politely acknowledging my answer, and opened the front door for us to leave.

Outside, I checked for the peacock before I let the sausages off their leads. They scampered happily across the gravel drive and onto the immaculate lawn bordering it. They needed to exercise themselves and do their business, but I was content to let them take their time because the pressure to get to the next point had lessened. Only slightly, but getting to the warehouse five minutes later probably wouldn't matter.

When the dogs were ready, I called them to the car where I loaded them into the passenger footwell by my feet.

Jermaine closed my door, diligent as always, and walked at his butler's pace to get to the driver's side.

The grounds of the zoo are set on the rolling hills of the North Downs. It's a series of humps ranging across a good portion of Kent. It made the landscape of the zoo a little more dramatic as one would crest a hill and discover elephants in the woods to one's front. They were inside an enclosure, of course, but free to roam around it, nevertheless.

Our route took us back the way we had come, wending through the countryside captured inside the grounds of the zoo.

My phone rang again, this time displaying Barbie's name on the screen. I thumbed the button to answer it and then the one for the speaker.

'Hi, Barbie, how did you get along? Did your 'assets' do the trick?' I asked with a snigger because they always did. Men are such simple creatures.

'No, they didn't,' she replied grumpily. 'The whole stupid office is staffed by women. There wasn't a man in the place.'

I gritted my teeth, disappointed to hear that her morning had produced even less than mine.

'However,' she interrupted my annoyed thoughts, 'having Sam with me worked out a treat.'

Jermaine took his eyes off the road for a moment to cock an eyebrow at my phone. 'It did?' he asked.

'Yeah,' Sam laughed through the phone. 'The ladies thought I was wonderful. They told us everything.'

Barbie sniggered. 'He was an instant hit. They loved his magnifying glass. I think the duct tape holding it together added a certain vulnerable charm. Anyway, Tempest gave us three vehicle registrations and I have the names of the people who own them. We'll need someone in law enforcement to help us work out if they are criminals or not, but I can do some basic searches when I get back to the house. I should be able to dig out addresses and employment history, that sort of thing. How have you guys got on?'

I told her that William Gill was still in the wind and about Heath Martin, who I believed was up to his neck in whatever the head keeper was keeping secret. The champagne confused her as much as it did me, the flights too.

'It sounds like they are planning to do something and then escape with a plan to never return,' she observed. 'Surely to do that a person has to have a pot of money.'

My eyes flared instantly. 'Missing jewels!' I blurted. 'Lady Mary said she was missing a ring and maybe some other bits. My earrings were worth a few thousand – imagine what Lady Mary's jewellery must be worth.'

'You think they have been stealing it, madam?' Jermaine questioned.

I scrunched my face with the effort of trying to make it all fit.

'What's the champagne for then?' Barbie wanted to know.

'Maybe they are stealing the jewels and there is something else going on. The jewellery could be a little extra on top,' I hazarded. How were they getting into the house to steal it though? Surely Jeeves and the other members of staff would notice members of the zoo staff roaming the halls.

Barbie changed the subject when she asked what sounded like a random question.

'Have you ever been to an auction, Patty?'

'An auction?' I repeated, wondering why she would ask. 'No. I mean, I went to a few charity ones at the church, but I doubt that is the same thing you have in your head.'

I could almost hear Barbie's cogs turning before she said. 'One of the cars from last night was registered to Rivingtons in London.

'Rivingtons?' I was a regular echo today. It was impossible to not know the name; they were arguably the biggest and most famous auction house in the world. If you had a Picasso to sell, they were who you called.

'Yeah, do you think maybe the champagne is for a big auction? Did Lady Mary say anything about that?'

I shook my head, the gesture meant for me not anyone else. 'An auction,' I repeated yet again. If I connected the world's biggest auction house to Lady Mary's zoo and threw in a whole load of top-quality champagne and cocktails, what did I get?

'They're planning an auction,' I concluded. 'That's the big secret they are trying to protect.' I was nodding along as I talked. 'Barbie, I have to go, I need to call Lady Mary and Alistair.'

'Okay, Patty. We are just outside the DVLA now. We're on our way to the car. I'll call when we get to the house and you can tell us where you are then.'

We said goodbye and disconnected.

Jermaine had a question on his lips, but he didn't get to ask it because he saw the expression on my face. My mouth was widening into a scream of terror because I could see what he could not.

We were sweeping down a decline into one of the dips of land, trees on both sides as we passed through the thick woodland to get back to the guest centre.

We were not going to get there. Twenty yards in front of us, a tree was falling to block our path.

I remember the crash as something horrendous. It didn't happen in slow motion and there was no time to react. I read somewhere that the thing to do if you are going to crash is just relax. If your body is floppy, you are less likely to hurt yourself.

Yeah, whoever said that is an idiot.

Every muscle in my body went tense at the sight of the tree. The human brain is a marvellous thing – mine needed less than a second to calculate distance and speed. We were going to hit the tree and there was nothing anyone could do to change that.

Jermaine braked hard. He'd seen the look on my face and was moving his foot before his head and eyes could get around to see the mammoth object falling into our path.

The car slowed, but the amount by which our speed decreased was so little as to be insignificant and we hit the tree at what had to be close to fifty miles per hour.

The front end of the Range Rover crumpled as I'm sure it is supposed to. I recall squealing my fear for the dogs who were still by my feet and having my cry of horror cut off by an airbag to the face.

The car stopped. I've been in a couple of minor road traffic accidents. Who hasn't? One car misjudges the distance or doesn't look properly and pulls out in front of someone. There is a squeal of tyres, a bump or a bash, and it's annoying but no big deal.

This wasn't like that at all.

Driving into the tree was like going off a cliff and hitting the ground below – it didn't give at all. All that equal and opposite reaction guff just got laughed at by the massive chunk of wood. We stopped dead, and were thrown forward by the inertia to then be held in place by the seatbelt and the airbag. It felt as if my organs carried on going.

Was everything inside me still attached?

Before the noise of the impact had even died away, the airbag was already going down, fading from view as the car's engine protested and died.

'Madam?' asked Jermaine. He sounded groggy, like he wasn't really with it. I turned my head to look across at him, my neck protesting at being moved and my head reacting by splitting in two down the centre of my skull. I paused to see if that was what had really occurred, waiting for blood to begin pouring from the wound.

Nothing happened.

I managed to turn my head the rest of the way and that was when I saw the tree trunk. The stump left in the ground had been sawn through.

It should have been obvious that this was no accident, but my brain hadn't yet connected the dots.

'Madam, I suggest we vacate this area,' Jermaine mumbled. He was fiddling with his seatbelt, the catch refusing to work for him. 'Madam, I appear to have some injuries. Please leave me here, I suspect this was a deliberate act.'

The news that Jermaine was hurt, delivered oh so calmly, was enough to jolt me into action.

Ignoring the crushing pain in my head and the reports of bruising and torn muscles coming in from all over my body, I fumbled for the door handle and kicked the door open.

Anna and Georgie bolted.

'Girls!' I bellowed as the traumatised dogs leapt to the ground and vanished into the undergrowth. I regretted raising my voice instantly. Doing so was much like how I imagined pushing an aubergine through an eye socket so it touched to the back of my skull would feel.

Regardless, I put my hands on my head to prevent it from exploding and called for my dogs to return again.

The undergrowth was completely still in every direction. Anna and Georgie were gone. It terrified me, but losing them in the woodland inside Lady Mary's enormous estate was the least of my concerns.

Steam hissed out around the sides of the crumpled bonnet and liquids dribbled out from beneath the engine. The car was a wreck, completely undriveable. Using it for support, I made my way around the back of the car and to Jermaine's door.

I got it open, grateful that the car was tough enough to absorb such a terrible collision without the doors jamming shut.

'Jermaine,' I started to examine him. 'Sweetie, can you walk? How bad is it?' I found the button for his seat belt and fought it until it popped free.

I didn't get an answer from my butler. He was hurt, that was for sure, but he was also getting out of the ruined car, forcing me to one side as he set his face with an angry grimace.

While I was trying to free his seatbelt, he'd been looking over my shoulder which meant he saw the men coming out of the woods.

'I told you your timing was off,' said one man to another, his tone amused.

His partner smiled in reply. 'Yeah, fair dos. I could have dropped it right on them if I'd let it go when you said. 'That would have been something.'

They were both wearing zookeeper uniform, cementing my belief that the head keeper was up to something nefarious and criminal. They had just tried to kill us and were laughing about it. Not only that, as they came closer, I realised I had seen their faces before.

One had a split lip and colour around his left eye where Big Ben had punched him. The other also had a black eye and steri-strip stitches holding cuts closed in three separate places on his face. They were among the men who jumped Sam and me in the pub carpark last night.

Now they were back to finish their work.

Jermaine nudged me to one side, placing his body between me and the pair of advancing killers.

'What are you going to do?' asked the one on the left, humour in his tone. 'You look like you can barely stand, mate. Don't worry. You'll be lying down soon.'

He was close enough now that I could read his name badge.

'David, you don't want to do this,' I insisted.

His colleague, whose name badge displayed 'Jeff' took a knife from his belt.

'You're in the way, that's all,' Jeff said, as if apologising.

Jermaine took a step toward them, stumbling slightly. His arms were not hanging correctly, that was what I noticed. Had he broken them? He'd been gripping the steering wheel when he hit the tree I remembered.

'That's close enough, gentlemen,' he warned.

They just kept on coming, stepping out of the woodland and onto the road. They were sporting grins.

'Isn't it about time some of you rich folk let someone else have a turn at the trough?' asked Dave, pulling a knife of his own from a leather holder on his belt.

Jermaine, still looking wobbly on his feet, flicked out a long right leg, spinning on the spot to sweep it around in a wide arc. It connected with the left side of Dave's face to fell him like a ... well, like a tree.

Jeff couldn't believe his eyes.

Jermaine staggered again as he came back to stand on both feet. I rushed to his side, grabbing his arm and back for fear he was just going to fall over.

Eyes widening in panic, Jeff thrust his knife at Jermaine's chest.

My ninja butler, even injured, was too fast for the zookeeper to touch him. I was too close; the reward for keeping Jermaine upright a shunt backward to slam me into the side of the car.

I needed my phone. Why hadn't I thought of that until now? I should have called for help the moment we hit the tree.

Too terrified to question where my phone was, I could do nothing but watch as Jermaine trapped the next thrust under his left armpit and twisted his body to send the knife skittering under the car.

He wasn't using his hands at all, confirming that they or perhaps his arms were both injured.

Now disarmed, Jeff looked distinctly less confident. His opponent was swaying in the breeze but was clearly still outclassing him for fighting skill.

He could have gone for Dave's knife; it was on the ground near the fallen man's hand, but Jeff picked a different option.

He ran.

Ripping the radio from his belt, he started yelling an urgent message as he sprinted for the trees again.

'Send back up! This is Jeff! They just took out Dave and disarmed me!'

I heard the crackle as he let go of the button but didn't hear the reply; Jeff was already twenty yards away and increasing the distance by the second.

Neither Jermaine nor I were in any shape to do anything about it.

Jermaine swayed again, then began to crumple. I was close enough that I was able to step in and support him, getting my hands around his waist and then my head under his right arm.

With some effort, because he is jolly heavy, I pulled him back to the car where he could lean against it. We were both out of breath and in worse shape than I could ever remember.

Just what had we interrupted?

At that precise moment, flames suddenly shot out from under the bonnet. Where it had crumpled, it was folded upward in the middle to form a hump. Flames were licking out from both sides, foul black smoke rising into the air.

The smoke would attract attention soon enough, but Jeff's call for backup meant there were more people involved yet and they were going to get to us before anyone else could.

Something went pop under the bonnet, and the flames, which were worrying a second ago, were now five times the size and spreading. Burning liquid hit the ground under the car and started to spread.

I needed my phone, but I wasn't going to get it now. I grabbed a handful of Jermaine's jacket and tugged him after me as I staggered to the trees.

'We can't stay here!' I wailed. The heat from the burning car was pushing us away, and the danger it might explode drove me to get some distance between us. Once inside the treeline, I pushed my butler and protector up against a tree, so we had that as a shield, and started to root through his pockets for his phone.

'Shoulders,' he rasped. 'I appear to have dislocated them both, madam. Terribly sorry for the inconvenience.'

'Jermaine, you are ridiculous,' I sighed. 'Without you, I'd have been dead months ago. Plus, you just beat off two men with your shoulders dislocated. I think it's about time I took care of you.' My head was pounding, and I knew we needed to get farther away from the car before Jeff's buddies could get to us, but I wanted to call for help first.

I just couldn't find Jermaine's phone and was running out of pockets. The only ones left were on his trousers and, quite frankly, I felt a little odd about putting my hands in them for a rummage.

'Sweetie, where is your phone?' I begged.

He twitched his head backward.

'In the car, madam.'

I said a colourful word.

A noise and the sense of movement brought my head and eyes around. Dave was getting back to his feet. He gave his head a shake, his brains undoubtedly rattled by the blow Jermaine delivered.

I tensed, questioning what he might do, but when he saw the two of us behind a tree and no sign of his partner, he chose to pick up his knife and run away too.

Yet again, I saw the opportunity I'd missed as he grabbed the radio from his belt and began jabbering into it.

'We have to go,' I insisted. 'It can't be more than a mile back to the house if we go in a straight line. It's time to call the police. They can just arrest everyone and work out what is happening from there.'

Jermaine resisted me when I attempted to get my head back under his arm.

'You should go, madam. You will be much faster without me to slow you down. They will come here first, attempting to pick up your trail. I will hold them here.'

'Oh, no you won't,' I snapped in his face. Angry that he would try to sacrifice himself for me, I grabbed his lapels and yanked him away from the tree. 'We're doing this together and we are going to survive. Alistair and Lady Mary will be questioning where we have got to already. They will have a search party out for us before you know it.' I was forming a plan in my head as I started to march through the woods with Jermaine's body leaning heavily against mine.

'We'll stay in the woods until we see someone we know to be friendly. It won't take long to get back to the house.' We were heading up a steep incline and going slow. Not long was likely to be half an hour or more. I was out of breath and we had only covered ten yards. I sucked in a fresh lungful of air so I could speak again. 'Barbie and Sam are probably already back. You'll see. This will be the case cracked. All we need to do is get back to the house.'

I willed my legs to keep moving. My thighs were burning before we had covered the first hundred yards, and our pace was dictated as much by my breathlessness as it was anything else.

Jermaine tried once again to convince me to go on ahead. He felt I could send help back to collect him, but I wasn't willing to leave him behind, and the argument soon stopped when we heard quad bikes on the road behind us.

The foliage was too dense for me to be able to see who it was; there was a chance it was the good guys coming to investigate the fire, or even people Lady Mary had sent to look for us when we failed to arrive at her location.

However, I surmised that were that the case, they would be shouting for us to make ourselves visible. Since they were not, I was glad we could hide from them.

I was worried about my dogs – how could I not be? Sausage dogs are hardy little things but hardly designed to survive in the wild. They would not fair well when the sun fell in a few hours. They would be left to face down owls and foxes and other predators who would consider them to be snack size.

I tried to not think about it, forcing my legs to take the next step and then the next one.

Back on the road below us, the quad bikes were idling and the sound of raised voices as the riders shouted to be heard drifted through the trees. I couldn't hear what they were saying, but my guess was they were trying to work out which way we went.

Had we left tracks in the mud at the edge of the road? I had not thought to conceal our route into the woods. I would have held my breath if I could have; honestly, I was worried they would be able to hear my panting and gasping.

When the engines revved again, two or more of them, and they drove off once more, I could only breathe a mental sigh of relief – I had no air in my lungs for anything else.

It was a little lift of hope. Exactly what I needed to propel me onward. We were going to make it back to the house, and once there we would bring the police crashing down on this place. It would make the news and be embarrassing for Lady Mary, but everyone would get to come out of it alive.

Heck, we might even uncover the truth about George.

Digging in with my toes, I took the next step. It was slow going, but with each step we came closer to the top of the slope. Jermaine was sweating profusely. I didn't ask him how he felt; it would be a stupid question. Instead, I kept going, onward and upward until the land began to flatten out.

If the map in my head was even close to accurate, the house was now directly in front of us and no more than a hundred yards away once we reached the edge of the trees. It took another ten or more minutes before I started to see light patches ahead of us, and with each step, fewer and fewer branches blocked our view.

I didn't catch sight of the house until we were almost clear of the woods. I had been off with my trajectory, but not too badly. The topography helped. Had it been flat, I might have wandered off course, but guided by the steep incline of the hill, we emerged to a surge of hope.

'It's just there, sweetie,' I gasped between laboured breaths.

Jermaine managed to grunt, 'Very good, madam.'

I paused before we came out from between the last few trees. I was being cautious; watching and listening for anyone who might be there. If I saw someone at the house, I would shout and get them to come to us. However, I was also looking for the quad bikes.

Even straining my ears and holding my breath, there was nothing to suggest they were anywhere near us.

'Last push, sweetie,' I said as much for my benefit as Jermaine's. Rushing to Lady Mary's house yesterday, I expected to clear up her mystery and find George squirrelled away writing somewhere having suffered a sudden bout of inspiration. We would have drunk gin and had a few laughs.

Instead, our visit had been a nightmare since the start. I felt like I had been hit by a freight train, my feet were bleeding from the effort of trudging up the hill in boots designed for looking good in, and my head still felt like it was splitting in two.

But we were nearly there.

With gritted teeth, I adjusted my hold on Jermaine and stepped out of the treeline. Jermaine winced and sucked in a gasp of air. He needed medical treatment urgently.

With each stride, my confidence grew.

However, twenty yards out of the woods – just far enough that we couldn't easily duck back in, the sound of the quad bikes starting filled the air.

Fear ripped my head around to face the noise just as they rounded the trees to our right. They'd been hiding out of sight. Whether it was a good guess that we would make our way back to the house, or if they had a dozen teams covering all possibilities, it didn't matter.

We were caught.

'Jermaine,' I squeaked fearfully.

The house was right there, less than a hundred yards away. But as the quad bikes bore down on us, it might as well have been on the moon.

They were coming right for us, helmets covering their faces which just made them look emotionless and inhuman.

Yet again, I was frozen to the spot, my feet refusing to move. There was no safe direction I could choose to go in even if they would respond, but when my brain insisted I was about to get run over, I was suddenly moving through the air.

Jermaine screamed, the sound painful to my ears as he roared with pain in defiance of his injuries. He'd lifted me from the grass, tossing me to the side like a ragdoll.

I could have complained about being thrown around, but he was being Jermaine again – trying to sacrifice himself to save me.

As I fell to the ground, I got to see him take two fast strides and leap into the air. The lead quad bike was going too fast and was too close to get out of the way. With his visor down, the rider's face was hidden but I could imagine the expression he must have pulled just before my butler's feet connected with his chest.

There was another grunt of pain from Jermaine as he bounced off and spun sideways to sprawl in the grass.

The second quad bike, right on the tail of the first, turned hard to avoid running over his colleague. Too hard, it turned out, as the bike turned broadside, and the wheels dug in. Despite the low centre of gravity, the quad bike flipped, sending the rider to the ground where he slammed in face first.

Jermaine was wheezing from the pain he felt, lying on his back, and trying to get up without the use of his arms.

Both quad bike riders were down, but neither was out.

My breaths were coming in heaving gulps. I needed to do something, but was I going to try to beat our attackers into submission? Did I run to the house and try to raise the alarm?

A shout from the direction of Lady Mary's residence brought my head around to see where it came from, and a tearful cry of joy escaped my lips.

The geriatric old butler, Jeeves, was hurrying in my direction. He had a gun of some kind in his arms – it looked like a rifle to my untrained eyes, but slow as he was, I could tell he was going to get to us soon enough to save the day.

I forced myself off the scrubby grass and onto my feet. Stumbling forward, aches, pains, and protests reporting in from all over my body, I felt an upwelling of triumph that bore me onward.

'Jermaine needs an ambulance,' I cried in desperation. 'Have you called the police?'

'Yes, yes, not to worry,' replied Jeeves, ambling as fast as his old frame would allow. His voice and demeanour were remarkably calm, even for a butler.

One of the quad bike riders was getting to his feet behind me, I heard him grunting and swearing and would have panicked if Jeeves hadn't been raising the business end of the rifle he carried. I expected the old man to shout a warning but instead he pulled the trigger.

Only when I felt the shot hit my stomach did I notice the rifle was pointing straight at me.

I staggered back a pace, looking down at my core to find a dart sticking out from my clothing.

I'd been shot with a tranquiliser dart!

I looked up again, questions firing in my head. Jeeves was no longer pointing the weapon at me. I felt a little foggy, my senses numbing as my knees voted for a few hours off.

The old man reloaded the rifle and fired again, this time hitting Jermaine as he struggled to his knees.

I wanted to ask what was happening. Confusion ruled as I sank to the grass. I put out a hand to steady myself but when it touched the grass, I couldn't feel it.

My arm collapsed, sending me to the ground where I lay looking up at the sky. I was losing consciousness, but when Jeeves came to stand above me, looking down with the rifle cradled in his arms, I managed to whisper a single word.

'Why?'

The light was fading, dancing lights clouding my vision as the darkness claimed me. Just before the blackness came, I heard the old man cackle.

'Because it's time someone else had a turn at the trough.'

A voice invaded my unconscious mind. 'Madam.'

I knew that voice. Why did I know that voice?

'Madam.' It was being insistent.

There were hands on me, touching my shoulders, shaking me. They were big hands. They felt strong.

'Madam.'

My eyes fluttered open, but I couldn't see anything. I heard a sigh of relief from the voice, and it took me a second for the information being gathered by my brain to filter down.

'Jermaine,' I murmured. 'Why can't I see anything?'

'It is night, madam. Or late evening, at least. And we are inside a small den.'

'A den?' My confusion was absolute, but memories were flooding back to me. I tried to sit up but felt a hand on my chest holding me down.

'The ceiling is very low, madam.'

I reached up with my left arm, finding a solid surface before my arm was at full stretch.

'What are we doing in a den?' I asked, curling my legs around so I could get off the hard floor and into a crouched, kneeling position. It wasn't much of an improvement.

The sudden sound of something snuffling, air being drawn into a large animal's nose, made me jump.

'What was that?' I squealed.

'One of the hyenas, madam.'

I choked, 'Hyenas!'

'I believe so, madam.' Jermaine's voice remained calm – no trace of the panic I felt.

My eyesight was starting to adjust. It was beyond dark in the small, cramped space we inhabited so even as my eyes tried to pick up shapes, there was almost no light by which to do it. The snuffle came again, this time followed by the sound of a paw scraping against wood.

Then a chittering of a recognisable hyenas laughing bark arose, answered by more of the same. It was a chilling sound to hear.

Jermaine placed a hand on my shoulder. 'I surmise we have been unconscious for some hours, madam. Fortunately, I came to just as the keepers were locking us in. The hyenas were gaining confidence and might have attacked had it taken me a moment longer to get my limbs working.'

'You pulled me to safety? How are your shoulders?'

'The right arm appears to have gone back into the socket. It is sore, but functioning. I need to get the left arm back in too if we are to escape.'

'Let's not do anything in a hurry,' I suggested, not wanting him to do more damage. 'Surely there is a way out of the den that doesn't put us in the enclosure again.'

Jermaine sighed. 'That was my expectation, madam. Alas, in the dark, I failed to observe that the den does not connect to the keeper access point. The only way out is back through the hyenas. The fence will, however, be difficult to scale.'

Especially with a ravenous pack of hyenas trying to eat us.

'They planned for us to get eaten,' I said the words in stark disbelief. Then, a thought hit me like a punch to the gut. 'Where are the others!'

Jermaine's hand squeezed my shoulder. It was all he could do. We were trapped by our own circumstances, but safe inside the den we could wait until someone less murderous found us tomorrow. Our friends though ... Alistair, Barbie, Sam, and Lady Mary; since we had been tranquilised and nothing had been done about it, I felt it safe to assume my friends were in much the same predicament.

Had they already been eaten? There were lions here, and huge African pigs. Crocodiles, wolves, and goodness knows what else that might happily eat a person and leave almost no trace.

'We have to help them,' I cried in desperation. When Lady Mary asked for my help, it never once occurred to me to say no, and my friends all followed me without a second thought. Were they all to be eaten now? What would I say to Sam's parents?

Feelings of misery and helplessness filled me. I still hadn't worked out who was behind the crime or why. Or even what the crime was. Clearly, Jeeves was involved, so too William Gill. If I could find a way to survive this, I could bring them to justice, but I wanted to stop them now, not later.

Focusing my efforts on working out the why and how of the auction I suspected to be occurring would do nothing to improve my current situation. I needed to work out how to escape the hyena enclosure. That was task number one.

With a deep breath in and then out, I closed my eyes, snapped them open and decided it was time to turn the tables.

'You said you saw the keepers leaving?' I asked Jermaine to confirm.

'Yes, madam. They appeared to be in quite a hurry. They did not notice when I started moving and were gone when I carried you away from the advancing hyenas.'

It was a safe guess that they had somewhere else to be and no desire to watch us be devoured. Maybe they planned to return later to clear up the mess.

'We need to get out, Jermaine. There must be something in the enclosure we can use for a weapon. If we can keep the hyenas back, we can look for a weak spot or a way to get over the fence. The enclosure was built to keep four-legged creatures inside.'

In truth, I thought I was being more than a little hopeful and brave. Was I going to turn myself into a hyena chew toy? The prospect turned my stomach, yet I refused to stay where I was and run the risk that my friends might die because I was too scared to try to save them.

Jermaine moved across the den, the information coming to my ears, not through my eyes in the absolute blackness. The hyenas heard him too, their chittering barks growing in excitement as if someone had rung their dinner bell.

'I shall endeavour to push them back so you can exit, madam.' He made the comment in the same tone as he might if telling me that tea was served.

A shaft of slightly less than absolute darkness appeared the next second as Jermaine pushed a door to one side. I call it less than absolute darkness because it wasn't exactly light. The moon was doing its best, but there was no artificial light to be had.

Jermaine roared like a bear as he untucked himself from our cubby hole and thrust out into the darkness.

His bellowed growls were answered by startled yaps and yips, the hyenas darting back to get a little space. I reminded myself they were not true wild animals. This was not Africa, and they were not used to bringing down their own prey. The zookeepers brought them their meals, yet thousands of years of instinct would take over again if we hung around too long.

I slid out through the same hole, following hard on Jermaine's heels. Terror gripped me, and the aches and pains inflicted by the car crash earlier had not gone away. I questioned if I had ever been in a worse situation.

Coming to stand in a crouch behind Jermaine, I scanned around to find something I could use to fend the animals off with.

The moon caught on something white – or whitish might be more accurate. I stooped to grab it, grasping it with both hands so it felt like weapon. I realised instantly that what I was holding was a bone. It would be leftovers from a previous meal not yet cleared away by the keepers, but hopefully hard enough to use as a club if they came close enough.

Jermaine was reaching behind to get my hand. He was big enough and scary enough to convince the hyenas to keep their distance, but I think we both knew that wasn't going to last long. It helped that we had the den behind us so they couldn't come from our rear. Getting to the fence to find a way we could escape was going to be far more challenging.

As I hoisted my bone club above my head and showed the hyenas my teeth, something slid down the bone to clatter against my knuckles. It was hard like steel, and when curiosity forced me to twitch my eyes away from the growling pack of animals, I screamed.

The bone club flew ten feet as I had a small heart attack and then threw up.

'Madam?' Jermaine sounded a little desperate now. He needed me to be ready to help him. The hyenas were circling and getting braver. Soon, one would make a dash to nip at either him or me, but though I knew we were in dire straits, there was nothing I could do to help him right now.

'Gill,' I wheezed, my stomach retching still. 'That was William Gill's watch!'

I'd picked up his forearm. The hyenas had picked his bones clean but eaten around the watch. He might have been dead when they put him in the enclosure, or he might have been just like us. The blood we found last night at the warehouse … right now I was willing to bet it was his.

'Madam, we need to move,' hissed Jermaine, tugging at my arm to get me moving.

I threw up again, the feeling of William Gill's bone in my hands too much to rid myself of.

A snarling snap from a hyena broke through my terror when it almost got Jermaine's other arm. He swung a kick at it and missed, the animal darting back before he could get to it.

They were getting braver and pressing in on all sides. We were not going to get to the fence.

Jermaine roared again, the sound loud and terrifying, but not enough to dissuade the hyenas. They cringed, crouching when Jermaine bellowed, but they did not retreat as they had earlier.

Was this how it had gone for William Gill?

'We need to get back into the den!' I wailed. I didn't want to accept defeat. I felt sick from my need to find my friends, but we were not going to win against a pack of hyenas, and I knew it.

However, when I twitched my head to glance back at the den, I gasped in horror to find hyenas standing on top of it. They couldn't get behind us – there wasn't enough room, but they could if they went upward!

Their teeth were bared, snarling threats of imminent violence, and I think it fair to say that I had never been more scared or more certain I was about to die than at that precise moment.

I squeezed Jermaine's hand, terror stopping my voice from making a sound.

The hyenas were going to strike.

The sound of Lady Mary's voice echoed through the night.

'Come here, my sweeties. Come to Mary.' It was almost singsong, the words presented at a higher pitch than she usually spoke, and they sounded childlike in their delivery. 'That's it, come to Mary. There's my good hyenas.'

Incredibly, the pack of animals, ready to tear us to shreds a moment ago, were now loping across the moonlit scrubby grass toward the other side of their paddock. The two behind us jumped down from the top of the den, one brushing by my hand as it trotted to catch up with its pack.

A gasp of air filled my lungs – I hadn't thought to bother breathing for the last few seconds.

'Mary?' I called into the dark.

'Patty?' Barbie called out. Her voice came from our left. We were looking at the departing pack of hyenas which placed Lady Mary dead ahead. 'Patty, are you okay? Is Jermaine there with you?'

We moved out of the shadows, carefully sidestepping to our left. As the moon caught us, I heard Barbie squeal with delight. I could see her too for she was standing in a rare patch of moonlight sifting down between the trees. She had Sam with her. They both looked to be in one piece, and they were smiling.

'Jeeves shot us with a tranquiliser gun when we got back to the house,' blurted my blonde friend. 'That lovely old man is not very nice at all.'

A snort of laughter left me at her choice of words, but a quiet yet insistent call from Alistair got my attention.

214

'Patricia,' he called out to get my attention. 'Can you and Jermaine both make your way slowly toward me, please?'

He was behind us somewhere, the darkness in the zoo making it impossible to spot his exact location. Barbie met my eyes as she took Sam's hand and started to move around the outside of the enclosure. She was going to meet us on the other side.

Jermaine still had hold of my hand, using his good arm to draw me toward Alistair's voice. I saw the open door a heartbeat later. The surge of hope almost overwhelmed me, making my head spin even as Jermaine broke into a jog and tugged me along in his wake.

The door clanged shut a nanosecond after we came through it, the noise like the voices of angels singing to my ears. Alistair swept me into an embrace, his strong arms holding me tight, and I clung to him, unwilling, or possibly unable, to let go until he pushed me away so he could check me for injuries.

'I'm fine,' I assured him. If I ignored the aches and bruises, it was true. Looking at him properly now, my forehead creased. 'How come you are dressed as a zookeeper?' I wanted to know.

'How do you think I came by a set of keys to let you out, darling?' he shot back. 'Lady Mary and I have been trying to find you for some time. Had it not been for your shout and Jermaine's roaring, we might have passed right by. Our next guess was the crocodiles. We happened across a pair of keepers a while back. They are auctioning off the exotic animals.'

There it was. Like a bolt from the blue, I saw it all. They had waited for Lady Mary and George to leave the country and were going to rob them blind before they returned. However, the owners came back early and ruined it all which was why, within hours of getting off the plane, George had gone missing.

It must have been quite a shock for Jeeves and whoever else was involved to suddenly have the owner and her husband in the way. How close had they been to grabbing Lady Mary too? It must have been close, but the police turned up because she told them he'd been kidnapped and then I showed up with a team of friends.

The memory of William Gill trying to send us away and asking what our business was flooded back. It happened seconds after we arrived; one of the men I suspected to be at the centre of the conspiracy turning up as if he had been watching the house – which William Gill probably had.

He was dead now. At least I believed he was. A watch on a bone is not irrefutable evidence of the victim's identity, yet somehow I knew William Gill was dead. Had he been betrayed?

They needed to get rid of us – that was the conclusion I came to - but that was easier said than done. How many were involved? It couldn't be many of the keepers, how would they ever cover it up? Yet it had to be enough to allow them to pull this off.

My head filled with questions, and some answers, but Barbie arrived with Sam and checking they were okay had to take priority over everything else.

'We almost got eaten, Mrs Fisher,' laughed Sam. 'There was a big lion.'

He thought it was funny, but my heart hurt from the stress of knowing he had come so close to death.

Barbie was hugging Jermaine, but when he winced, she pushed away to get a better look at him much as Alistair had with me. Her hand went to her face.

'Oh, my gosh. Is your shoulder dislocated? How did that happen?'

Her question prompted an explanation from me about our run in with the tree and our slog uphill through the woods only to be captured when we had the house in sight. All the while I was talking, Barbie was getting Jermaine to stand still while she moved his left arm around. It popped back into the socket with a sound that made me want to vomit again.

Alistair had to step in to steady Jermaine as he almost fainted. Barbie and Sam were there too, all helping him. He needed a second to recover but claimed his arm felt better now.

'You'll be going to hospital the first chance we get, sweetie,' Barbie promised/threatened him.

'How did you get out?' I begged to know.

Barbie appeared next to me as soon as I got finished with Sam. I thought she was going to pull me into a hug, but instead she held out her hand.

I looked down at it, not sure what her open palm was meant to convey.

'Where's my twenty?' she demanded.

'Huh?'

A faux angry grin split her face. 'I bet you twenty we would get shot at, Patty. And oh, by the way, don't you think it would be helpful to have a couple of the ship's security team with us right about now?'

She did have a point.

I hung my head. 'Yes, Barbie. Schneider and Pippin would be fine friends to have at our side tonight. I do believe, however,' I met her eyes again with a wry smile, 'that our bet was whether we would get shot at by the end of the first day. And we did not.'

Barbie laughed and wrapped her arms around me.

'Patricia Fisher, you are a slippery one.' After a two count, she released me. 'You asked how we got out. Lady Mary pulled her crazy animal mojo thing with the lions.'

Right on cue, Lady Mary appeared at the gate so Alistair could let her out.

'I know all the animals personally,' she explained to my confused face.

I shook my head with disbelief. 'But you always talk about how you don't have anything to do with the zoo. You told me it was boring.'

'Running it is boring, Patricia dear. Running it. It's a lot of staff meetings and visits to the bank and listening to the accountants and project managers. I handed all that over the first chance I got. But the zoo itself, the animals … well, they are my pets. I hand-reared some of them. I grew up here, let's not forget.'

'So … what, you told the lions to leave Barbie and Sam alone and they just did it?'

'Yes,' she replied. 'Just like I did with the hyenas.'

Alistair cut in, 'She had to convince the warthogs first.'

Warthogs. I'd noted a scent of something on the ship's captain but hadn't felt it was worth bringing up. I doubted I smelled great.

'Oh, the warthogs were the easiest of them,' bragged Lady Mary. 'They are kept well fed.'

'Nevertheless,' argued Alistair. 'Had you not woken when you did, I would have been unable to stop them snacking on your toes.'

Seeing that his statement required at least a little expansion, Alistair took a few seconds to explain how they received word that Jermaine and I had gone directly to the warehouse because William and Heath were there.

They tried to call me – undoubtedly when my phone was melting inside the burning Range Rover – got no answer and demanded a car. The car was flagged down by two zookeepers and they were shot with tranquilisers before they knew what was happening.

Lady Mary listened, staying quiet until Alistair finished his story with an explanation about how they escaped – the warthog enclosure has a tree Lady Mary used to use to get in and out when she was a child. The fence is designed to keep four-legged pig things in, not humans and the keepers failed to take that into account. When he fell silent, she said, 'I rather think we ought to be getting back to my house. I understand from Barbie that my butler has been rather naughty.'

'Yes,' I agreed. 'He shot me with a tranquiliser dart.'

'Us too,' chipped in Sam.

'Shouldn't we call the police first?' I questioned.

'No phones, Patty,' said Barbie. 'We all got stripped of anything useful. I am counting myself as lucky I still have my clothes on for once.'

'What about the keepers?' I asked.

Alistair shook his head. 'Neither was carrying a phone.'

219

'That's standard procedure,' Lady Mary explained. 'Too many of the animals would eat something that size. The keepers never carry anything loose that might cause harm if eaten.'

'What did you do with them?' I enquired.

Alistair grinned at Lady Mary, who confessed, 'We stripped them and used one set of clothing to tie them up. They are in the back of the warthog enclosure.'

Jermaine raised a pertinent point, 'Didn't they have a vehicle with them?'

Alistair tutted at himself. 'Yes. The keys got dropped inside the warthog enclosure when I tackled the keepers.'

Lady Mary said, 'I went back in to look for them, but it's a big area.'

'Back to the house then?' I suggested. We were going on foot, but it wasn't all that far.

'There's going to be a lot of people there,' warned Alistair. 'If they are holding an auction, that's got to be where it is.'

It made perfect sense. Invite people with money to a grand property in the countryside and ply them with alcohol – hence the champagne and cocktails – then sell them exotic animals that belong to someone else and probably artwork and other easily moved goods from the house.

I shook my head, disappointed with myself for not figuring it out sooner.

'Heath Martin was going to make a killing and then board a plane,' I lamented. 'He must have planned the whole thing with William Gill and then double crossed him at the last moment.'

'Hmm? Double crossed?' Barbie voiced the question everyone but Jermaine needed an answer to.

Jermaine let them know, 'It would seem Mr Gill was fed to the hyenas last night. We found remains that are probably his.'

My stomach rolled again at the memory.

Alistair made the connection. 'Then it was his blood we found last night.'

'Maybe,' I replied. We had no way to know for sure. That they were auctioning off the exotic animals had been bugging me ever since I found out. My skull was itching, telling me there was something I needed to remember, and it hit me just as a set of headlights appeared in the distance.

We had been walking quickly, going in the direction of the house, but we all froze to the spot. The headlights belonged to a Land Rover, another of the zoo's off-road vehicles. It was coming down the hill from the house on a different route from the one Jermaine and I took. It reached the edge of the enclosures and turned down between two of them.

'It's heading for the tigers,' Lady Mary told us.

I pushed to the front and headed the same direction. 'Good. That's where we need to go.'

'We do?' questioned Barbie.

'It's Esme,' I pointed out. 'I should have seen this straight away.'

'What about Esme?' asked Lady Mary.

I didn't stop moving but turned slightly so I could look back at the people following me.

'No one believed the immaculate conception thing, did they,' I pointed out. 'So Esme had to have either met a Mr Tiger, or they artificially inseminated her. I think the latter is more likely, but that means a veterinarian has to also be involved.' I got questioning eyeballs in response to my statements. 'Okay, you're a billionaire or whatever and you want to buy something you cannot buy anywhere else. Then this auction comes up. I can only guess at how they might have advertised it, but they have a stack of bidders coming to the house and probably more online. You are going to spend a pile of money on a rhino or something, then you want a vet to promise you it is in mint condition and not about to drop dead.'

Barbie interrupted, 'Why would someone want to buy a rhino, Patty?'

I didn't answer straight away. I was looking at my group of friends and trying to work out why my brain believed something was missing. The group was complete; everyone was here. So why did I feel that I had forgotten someone? It was the absence of the dogs, I told myself. Before I could give it any further thought, Barbie asked her question again.

'Philanthropy?' I suggested. 'I doubt anyone knows the animals are being sold without the owner's permission. The buyer might think they are saving it. Maybe they plan to release it or start a breeding program.'

'Maybe they plan to have a big game hunt,' argued Alistair. The thought had occurred to me, but I'd chosen not to voice it.

'Whatever the case,' I continued. 'The vet is necessary. Doubly so because what could possibly be more valuable than a super rare Caspian tiger?' The question was posed to everyone, and they all got it at the same time.

'One with a baby.' Lady Mary rubbed her head and cursed. 'I should have known there was something criminal going on. How else could it be that Esme's vet and keepers had no idea how she got pregnant. My goodness, I have been thick headed.'

'Nevermind that now.' We were nearing the tiger enclosure and I wanted everyone to focus again. 'My guess is they are here to collect the auction's top attraction – the biggest draw will be the final lot, and we need to be the ones to deliver it.'

We could hear two keepers talking - they were both men. It would not have mattered who they were; this farce needed to come to an end.

I stopped in a shadow on the far side of the tiger building. The Land Rover was parked around the corner, just a few yards away. Putting my arms out, I encouraged everyone into a huddle like we were about to engage in a game against a rival team and this was my pep talk.

I had a rough plan of action in my head, but it got derailed when an animal noise came from the tiger cage.

It wasn't a roar or any noise a tiger would make and from the look on the faces of all my friends, I hadn't imagined it.

Drunken Old Bag

Barbie said it first. 'Where are your dogs, Patty?'

Until two seconds ago, I would have said they were lost in the woods. Now I had to go with, 'In the cage with Esme the tiger.'

I was part racked with terror for my dogs, and part wanting to swat their back ends with a rolled-up newspaper for making me worry so. However, I just knew I was going to find them curled up with the pregnant tiger and in no danger at all. I'd seen Esme looking at them yesterday and it was curiosity – like a little girl staring at teddy bears – not hunger in her eyes.

Putting the dogs and their plight to one side for a moment, I explained what I thought we should do, and we broke the huddle.

'That was cute, wasn't it,' said a man pointing a shotgun in our general direction.

His partner, standing two feet to his left, was holding a tranquiliser rifle in a way that made me believe he was ready to use it, cracked a grin. 'It really was. Kind of like they are getting ready to play a game.'

I recognised them both. It was Dave and Jeff, the two who tried to kill me with a tree a few hours ago. This time, they'd come armed, and they had the drop on us in the truest sense. The distance between us was too great for us to cover. If we chose to charge them, they could shoot us all before we got anywhere near them.

Even my ninja butler, had he been in his best form and not the broken shadow his injuries reduced him to, could not have changed our fate.

A shadow of motion caught my eye right before a noise like a lump of wood striking a skull reached my ears. The sharp crack came right before

Dave dropped his shotgun. His eyes rolled upward, and he started to slump.

Jeff spun inward to see what had happened to his colleague and thus caught the next swing full in the face.

As he dropped too, the moonlight shone through where they'd been standing to show us our saviour. A terrified Hewitt had a handy piece of branch gripped in both hands. His eyes were wild with fear, flitting down to the two men he'd just felled and back up to stare at the six of us and then at his hands and the piece of wood as if it could not have possibly been his actions that resulted in the two bodies at his feet.

Alistair ran, darting forward to get to the weapons.

'Well done, young man,' he cheered, disarming both men and handing a weapon backward so someone would take it. That turned out to be Sam, who Barbie thankfully disarmed no sooner than he got his hands on the tranquiliser gun.

I love Sam to bits and would defend him to the end if anyone ever suggested he couldn't do something. However, I had to draw the line at projectile weapons. In the same way that my wonderful assistant will never drive, there are simply some things he is not safe to attempt.

Even though he had come to our rescue, Hewitt was borderline wigging out.

'What's going on?' he wanted to know. He was stuttering and shaking from the adrenalin in his body. 'There're hundreds of people at the house and Mr Martin seems to be selling the animals.' He stopped midway through telling us what he'd seen at the house because Barbie stepped out of a shadow. We all got to see his mouth grind to a halt. 'Wow, who's that?' he mumbled, sounding like he didn't even know he had said it.

Barbie looked a mess, which is to say her outfit was dirty and her hair had leaf-litter and such in it. There was mud or dirt on her hands and her face, yet she was still an absolute knockout.

I sighed and clicked my fingers in front of Hewitt's face. It broke the spell, his eyes blinking and coming back to look at me.

'You were telling us about events at the house,' I reminded him.

'I was going to ask someone about it but then I noticed that all the zookeepers were armed – some of them with shotguns. That's not normal, and I heard them talking about Lady Mary getting eaten by her own warthogs. I guess that didn't happen because there she is.' His eyes focused on the zoo owner for a second. 'What's going on?' he repeated his first question.

'I'm being robbed,' growled Lady Mary. 'Some of the keepers and some of my staff, I shall find out who, have chosen to relieve me of my possessions. That I can accept with a degree of stoicism. Selling the animals though ...' Lady Mary's expression was murderous.

Alistair was back on his feet the shotgun hooked into the crook of his right arm.

'We need to secure these two and gag them,' he said, looking around for something we might use.

I countered his suggestion. 'We need to get into the tiger house and rescue my dogs.'

Accepting that I was right, Alistair said, 'I'll keep an eye on these two. They won't go anywhere.'

'Have they got phones?' asked Barbie, holding her gun to one side as she knelt to start patting their pockets.

They didn't have phones; what Lady Mary said about the keepers not carrying them in the zoo holding true. They had radios instead. It gave us the option to listen in, or possibly to employ them for our own needs perhaps. There was no chatter over the airwaves currently, but I expected that would change when Dave and Jeff failed to return.

'What should I do?' asked Hewitt. The young man looked bewildered by recent events. I wanted to trust him, but caution made me quiz him first.

'How did you come to be here after the zoo closed today?' I pinned him to the spot with my eyes.

He swallowed hard, glancing around at the six dishevelled people surrounding him.

Unable to avoid our collective gaze, Hewitt started talking. 'I, um. I saw guys zipping around on the quad bikes this afternoon. They were acting odd, and when I asked one about it, he told me to mind my own business. So since working here is my business, that is what I am doing.' He stopped talking, watching my face intently to see how I would react to his statement. I remained deliberately quiet so he would feel the need to fill the silence with more words.

He swallowed hard again before adding, 'I watched them set up the marquee. Mr Martin is there; he's acting as if he is in charge. The keepers are working for him, I guess; they are doing what he says anyway, and they have been taking animals in cages up to the marquee for the people there to bid on.'

'How many people?' asked Alistair.

Hewitt shrugged. 'Lots. More than a hundred. They are dressed nice. Like it's a cocktail party or something.' He glanced down at Dave again

227

when he groaned. I tensed, waiting to see if the keeper was about to come around, but there were no other signs that he was regaining consciousness.

Looking back up, Hewitt revealed, 'I overheard Dave and Jeff say something about the Tiger, so I followed them down here and that's when I saw all of you.'

Voices echoed out from inside the tiger house to my left, prompting me to address my most pressing issue: my dogs.

'I need to rescue Anna and Georgie. Even if Esme intends them no harm, the keepers won't be pleased to find them with her.'

Lady Mary, just ahead of me as I turned toward the tiger house, raised a hand. Pointing a finger at Hewitt, she said, 'You are currently the only member of staff here that I believe I can trust, young man.'

Unsure what to say, Hewitt, mumbled, 'Okay.'

'You are now the stand in head keeper of my zoo, Hewitt. I believe I will have need of you this night.'

Hewitt's cheeks coloured, startled by the sudden promotion, even if it were temporary.

'What about Mr Gill?' he asked.

'Mr Gill got eaten by the hyenas,' Alistair told him. 'I believe the position is what you might call open.'

I could spend no more time discussing the matter. We left Alistair and Hewitt to guard the unconscious men and slipped inside the tiger enclosure. We were entering from the rear, following where the keepers had already gone.

It was a functional part of the enclosure where the tigers would sleep at night and could be manoeuvred or handled into a cage for transport. That was exactly what the keepers were trying to attempt now.

We came into the corridor behind them, our feet silent on the concrete floor. They had prepared a cage for transport, but Esme was not cooperating. Watching them from her cage, she twitched her tail idly but wasn't moving.

Against the wall a few yards behind them, their weapons were abandoned – they needed their hands for the task.

I got to listen to them as they argued, and I knew instantly who I was hearing even before I saw her face.

'You can't tranquilise her, dummy,' snapped Madison. 'She's pregnant for a start but she also weighs half a ton. How do you propose to move her once she is unconscious?'

'I dunno, do I?' snapped the man with her. 'I look after the reptiles, don't I. When Jeeves wanted a deadly snake at the house this morning, they didn't call on you, did they? No, they called the reptile guy. I told Heath we needed more than one big cat expert on the team.'

'And what did he tell you?' asked Madison in a mocking tone.

Grumpily, her colleague said, 'That every new person involved spreads the likelihood that someone talks and diminishes the share of the money taken.'

'Exactly. That's why there are so few of us. It's hard but we are going to make a fortune selling the drunken old bag's animals.'

I felt Lady Mary stiffen. 'Unless the drunken old bag goes sober and catches you!' she snarled.

Madison and her partner spun around on the spot to face us, their jaws dropping open in shock. Madison reached for her radio.

'I wouldn't,' advised Barbie, pointing the tranquiliser gun at her. 'This would not be my first time using a gun.'

Jermaine went forward with Sam on his heels, collecting knives and radios. Jermaine kicked into their knees from behind, applying minimum force, yet sufficient to drop them to the concrete. They stayed there, on their knees with their hands up.

Esme the tiger was visible in her sleeping area, a bed of straw around her for comfort. The majestic creature observed me as I came up to the bars. Where were Anna and Georgie? I'd heard them for certain, but there was no sign of them now.

Until I got really close, that is. Both dogs were cuddled against the tiger's ample belly, all three sharing their body heat and mutual comfort. When the car crashed, the dogs ran off to find somewhere safe.

I couldn't think of anywhere safer.

'Anna, Georgie,' I cooed.

Both dogs popped their heads up and their tails began to wag with excitement when they spotted me.

Ignoring the pain I was sure he still felt, Jermaine grabbed the two zookeepers under their arms. 'Let's get these two outside with the others.'

They came back to their feet, looking around nervously as Jermaine frogmarched them outside. Barbie and Sam went with them.

I was on my knees, fussing the dogs who were small enough to squeeze between the bars of the cage. I stroked, hugged, and kissed my dogs, happy to find them at all, let alone unharmed.

Lady Mary came to the edge of the tiger cage as I stepped away. I had a dog under each arm, hugging them to my bosom to carry them outside. I found my friends there. Barbie and Alistair were still holding their guns on the four zookeepers we now held captive.

'We need to tie them up and gag them,' Alistair insisted. This was not his first rodeo.

However, Barbie had a better idea.

'Let's strip them.'

'Sorry, what?' asked Madison.

Her plan wasn't cruel or unnecessary. Butt naked, they were far less likely to create further problems for us and we got to use their clothes to tie them up. A sock went into each mouth and Sam found a roll of duct tape in the back of the zoo vehicle.

Just as we were securing all four of them to the bars that formed the outer wall of the tiger enclosure, Lady Mary exited the building.

Esme padded out after her.

I have to tell you, the full effect of seeing a tiger up close is not to be easily dismissed. I, for one, uttered a particularly rude word and found my feet taking a pace backward without me asking them to.

My friends all did more or less the same. The zookeepers, now completely devoid of clothing, acted as though they believed we had tied them up so the tiger could eat them. They bucked and thrashed and yelled. The gags muffled their voices, and we all ignored them because Lady Mary was walking between us like a magical person from a fairy tale.

'Um, where are you going, Mary?' I posed a question as she strolled by. She was moving slowly, the lady tiger at her side heavily pregnant and waddling a little, but her strides had purpose and direction.

'I am going to kick some people off my property,' she announced in a nonchalant manner, her tone that of someone telling a friend what filling they planned to put in a sandwich. 'They are expecting Esme, and that is what I am going to give them.' She continued onward, adding over her shoulder, 'plus a few of my other friends.'

'Friends?' Alistair questioned.

'Shouldn't we find a phone and call the police now?' questioned Barbie. 'Surely, it's time to call in reinforcements.'

I couldn't agree more.

Sam put his hand in his pocket, pulling it out a moment later to hold a phone aloft. 'I found my phone in the Land Rover,' he announced with his usual goofy grin. 'Can you use that?'

Barbie, nearest to Sam, grabbed it from him. 'We have a phone now,' called out Barbie. 'Lady Mary we can call the police!'

Lady Mary held up a hand. 'No. If you do that, the police arrive and cause even greater confusion. My animals are at the house. What will happen if the police storm it? Either they will get hurt or they will hurt my animals. Or both things will happen. My creatures may be dangerous, but not to me. Like Patricia so often says - I have a plan. You might think it a little whacky, but I am going to do it anyway.'

Rampage

We had to convince Lady Mary to slow down for a second. I loved that she had a plan, but we needed to know what it was. I also wanted to call the police as a precaution. They would take a while to get an armed response team to our location anyway, so the call was made by Jermaine while Lady Mary outlined what she wanted to do.

I will admit that some of the ideas I have come up with to lure out a criminal or trick them into revealing themselves have been a tad bonkers. Lady Mary made them all look boring and mundane. Of course, I'd never had access to a zoo full of creatures.

'I spoke with Chief Inspector Quinn,' Jermaine informed us all as he slid the commandeered phone into a pocket. 'He was … dubious about my information. I believe he had a hard time believing the parts about …' Jermaine puffed out his cheeks and wrinkled his brow. 'No, I guess he didn't believe any of it. The chief inspector actually said I had to be making it up.'

'What did you say to that?' asked Barbie.

'I informed the chief inspector that he has a chin like a baboon's scrotum and that his mother spends her evenings in alleyways with lumberjacks. I then invited him to come and get me. I believe, from the shouting I heard just before I cut him off, that he will be here as soon as possible.'

There followed a few seconds of stunned silence as we all stared at my elegant butler. Then I jolly near spat out my teeth when I roared with laughter. Everyone joined in, even Jermaine relaxing his posture enough to allow a wicked grin to cross his face.

As the mirth subsided, I remembered something that had been troubling me ever since my friends rescued Jermaine and me from the hyenas.

'Gloria!' I blurted.

The unconscious part of my brain had known there was something missing from our group. Had Sam's gran been captured like the rest of us? Had she already been eaten, or was she somehow still in the house, unnoticed and unharmed.

Sam already had his phone out, worry creasing his brow as he fiddled with the screen to pull up her number.

Coming to stand by his shoulder, I leaned in to touch the speaker button when the call connected.

Gloria answered after just a few rings. 'Sam? Where are you? You are missing all the fun.' In the background behind her voice, I could hear the auctioneer calling. People were bidding on a giraffe family.

I couldn't believe my ears. 'Gloria, this is Patricia. Are you at the auction?'

'Yes!' she cackled. 'I haven't had this much fun in years. Where are you all? You should join me. Everyone is dressed really nice and there is champagne. Lots of it. I bought two marmosets, a howler monkey, and three alligators so far. Good thing this isn't real, eh? I haven't got two hundred grand to spend.' She cackled at the idea, the champagne doing its trick.

My heart was thumping with worry. If she was at the auction, surely Jeeves knew who she was.

Barbie, Alistair, and everyone else were crowded around me, listening in.

'Gloria,' Alistair tried to get her attention. 'Does Jeeves the butler know you are attending the auction?'

'Oh, yes,' she giggled drunkenly. 'He came and found me in my room and even brought me a dress. I think he is a little sweet for me. Never too old for romance, eh. I should have worn my good knickers.' Gloria guffawed this time, though whether she was making a joke or was deadly serious, I wasn't able to tell.

We were all silent at my end. Lady Mary's plan was going to be dangerous for the people in the marquee. How much could we tell Gloria? She sounded three sheets to the wind. Again. If we told her what we planned, would she blurt it to everyone else?

We couldn't risk it. And we couldn't risk leaving her in the marquee.

Sam came to the rescue. 'Gran?' he called to get her attention.

'Yes, love?'

'Mrs Fisher and I will be there really soon. Can you help me get into my suit? I want to look right for the party.'

'Of course, love.' We heard her take a loud slurp of her champagne. 'I'll just finish this drink, then I'll meet you in your room.'

I breathed a sigh of relief as Alistair clapped Sam on the shoulder. A simple ruse, but an effective one. The task of getting Gloria to somewhere safe now complete, it was time to set Lady Mary's idea into motion. With two sets of zookeepers' keys in our possession, we were letting animals out of their cages. Some were already missing, taken away by the keepers earlier to be sold at the auction, and there were many, many species which Lady Mary said were not safe to be allowed to roam.

Others though, she deemed as perfect for raiding the auction.

I thought I was going to have to slog back up the hill to her house, but I was wrong. Lady Mary had a plan for that too – we were going to ride there.

On the back of her herd of elephants!

There were rhinos beside, around, and ahead of us, gazelles, wild pigs, gorillas ... Lady Mary knew them all by name and she was at the front, leading her menagerie toward the lights of her house. Esme the tiger waddled along at her side and most unbelievable of all, my dachshunds were either side of Esme.

It was the strangest procession I had ever heard of, let alone witnessed. Yet here I was taking part in it. Sitting astride the lead bull elephant, high up above the road, I glanced across to my left.

Barbie caught my movement and waved back with her free hand – the one not holding a tranquiliser gun. Alistair was to my right, with Sam holding on behind him. Jermaine was just behind me, and Hewitt was to his left. There were another ten elephants without riders all following. According to Lady Mary, she has the largest herd in the Northern Hemisphere.

Due to our raised position, we saw the auction before the people there saw us. They were in a large white marquee in front of the house and sitting on rows of fold out chairs. The hum from a generator explained the lighting inside and now they were in sight, I was better able to make out what was being said.

The man from last night, the one I mentally labelled as Drago, stood on a dais at the front. His voice was amplified as he auctioned off a pair of Bald Eagles. Unlike a farm auction where the lots must be moved fast and the auctioneer gabbles incoherently, Drago was talking at a speed we could all understand.

'This magnificent pair are prime for breeding, ladies and gentlemen. Endangered and protected in the wild, I know we have a lot of interest from buyers across the pond. Who will become the lucky owners of this breeding pair? I have sixteen bids from the internet already. Let's start in the room at one hundred thousand pounds.'

Barbie said, 'Wow.'

Lady Mary said something different. In her posh, upper-crust accent, she held a hand aloft and screeched, 'Un-Gowwa!'

I had no idea what that meant, or even what language it might be from, but the elephant I was riding on did. Lumbering along one second, it was running the next and it was all I could do to hold on and not be shaken loose.

Barbie whooped with delight, no doubt pinching her ridiculously strong thighs together to secure herself in place as her elephant picked up speed. I caught sight of her as I hugged the top of my elephant with all four limbs and prayed I was going to live through the next two minutes.

There were faster creatures than the elephants – namely all of them. I got to watch as they streaked ahead. The rhinos made grunting noises as they ran, the wildebeest too, and the gazelles, antelope, and bongos bounced and pranced as if their legs were made of rubber.

They flowed around Lady Mary who continued to shout unintelligible instructions. Somewhere in the mess of animals, a dachshund barked. It was the same bark Anna reserved for threatening death to the postman.

It took a few seconds for the people inside the marquee to spot the herd of animals bearing down on them, but when the first persons glanced, performed an epic double-take, and then screamed, the others swiftly followed suit.

As the men and women inside the marquee panicked and ran for the exits, the fastest of the animals met the clear plastic side and went straight through it.

Bedlam ensued.

Drago the auctioneer was calling for calm one second, then squealing like a frightened child the next. A pair of zookeepers, ones we had not yet encountered, came running around the side of the marquee to see what on earth was happening.

At an enraged shout from Lady Mary, they quickly performed a U turn and ran back the way they had come.

The side of the marquee facing us was reduced to tatters in seconds, and several of the uprights holding the roof in place were bent, twisted, or otherwise smashed into oblivion when the rhinos arrived.

Across the marquee, the humans were running for their lives. I saw black dinner jackets and glittering cocktail dresses jostling each other in their haste to evade the pack of angry animals.

I saw Heath Martin frozen to the spot at the front of the marquee. He was safe, or as safe as anyone could be, since the animals running through the marque were bunched in the middle.

To his side, the withered form of Jeeves the butler, without his rifle loaded with tranquilisers darts this time, looked set to keel over.

As I watched, he did exactly that and there was no mistaking what I heard when Heath caught him.

'Grandfather!'

An itch at the back of my head filled in another piece of the puzzle.

Alistair drew my attention with a shout.

'The cars!' He shouted to be heard above the trumpeting, crashing noise of our elephants and all the mayhem around us.

I saw what he meant, but how did I steer the three-ton beast I rode? Alistair seemed to have the knack for it, his own giant grey steed veering around the marquee followed closely by Jermaine, Hewitt, and the rest of the pachyderms.

Barbie, on my other side, was going straight through the marquee with me whether we liked it or not.

With a trumpet I could feel vibrating through his entire body, the bull elephant lowered his skull and ran right through the side of the marquee. The aluminium rafters bounced up and over me and suddenly I was bathed in light.

Briefly, I noted how nice it looked. The team had done a marvellous job of erecting and decorating the place in the short time since they knocked us out and took us captive.

The sound of rending metal rang through the night, accompanied by car alarms. I hadn't understood what Alistair meant when he shouted to me earlier, but now I did – he was cutting off the chance of escape and making it more likely we would catch everyone involved.

My elephant trumpeted again and ground to a halt. Now he was inside, he didn't seem to know what to do and was stamping his feet nervously on the artificial floor.

I took it as a sign that it was probably time to get off. Easier said than done. For the last two hundred yards, I had been flat to its back and holding on for dear life. It was ten feet to the floor and once there I would need to avoid the nervous elephant.

As if by magic, the giant beast calmed.

'That's enough now, Gary,' cooed Lady Mary, stroking the elephant's trunk. 'Go and join your friends.' Esme was by her side, placidly observing the mayhem around her with a twitch of her tail. Turning her attention to the big cat, Lady Mary told her to rest and crouched to pat the floor. The tiger obediently slid its front paws out and lowered her ripe belly.

Someone tapped my left foot, and I was able to convince myself to move my head enough to look. Barbie was grinning up at me.

'That was fun,' she chuckled. 'A bit like riding a horse, but with a lot more between my legs.'

With her help, I pulled my right leg over and slid down the side of the elephant until Barbie grabbed my waist and pulled me to the floor.

My legs were a little wobbly, but as Gary the elephant trotted away – I was going to have to ask her who named them later – I spotted Lady Mary heading for the dais and had to hurry after her.

In the disarray of the ruined marquee, people were clambering out from under tables and from behind plants. The animals had rampaged, but most had continued straight through. Lady Mary had been adamant they would wander around the grounds of her house, eating her azaleas but doing little damage otherwise. Those keepers she still had in her employ the following morning would be able to round them up.

I guess Lady Mary spotted someone amongst all the debris because she made a beeline for them. Drago emerged from behind the dais, and she snatched the tranquiliser gun Barbie was holding, lined it up and shot him. The dart with its fluffy red tail embedded in his breastbone.

Drago gasped once, staring down at the dart just as I had when Jeeves shot me, then keeled over backward.

Seeing his partner hit, Shiny popped out from behind a table and ran for it.

Lady Mary Bostihill-Swank, one of the richest women in the country, and the sort of person who got invited to parties at Buckingham Palace, shrieked her outrage and swore like a dockworker because she had no second dart to reload her gun.

Instead, she threw it at him. The long metal weapon scythed through the air, tumbling over and over like a tomahawk. It missed its target by a mile, bouncing harmlessly off the side of the marquee whereupon it clattered to the floor.

Shiny didn't escape the marquee though. He was about to run through a fluttering gap in the shredded material but stopped a yard short. Inexplicably, he then put his hands up and began walking backward.

A second later, as Lady Mary, Barbie, and I watched in confused disbelief, the muzzle of an ugly black machine gun came through the gap. It was followed by Gloria, who was holding it steady as a rock and pointed firmly at Shiny's centre of mass.

It was one from George's collection in his study.

'You gotta ask yourself one question, Baldy,' Gloria paraphrased terribly. 'Will the old lady shoot me if I go for the gun? Or will she shoot me anyway? Well? Will I, Baldy?'

Shiny said, 'I don't want to come over as pedantic, but that was definitely more than one question.'

'Shaddup,' Sam's gran snarled.

Hewitt dashed into the marquee, skidding to a halt as Gloria swung the gun in his direction.

Shiny saw his chance and knew it might be the only one he got. He was going for the gun, and we all gasped in horror because there was nothing we could do to stop him. That didn't stop us from running across the marquee in a bid to tackle him before he could use it.

He swung an arm, ripping it from Gloria's grip in one move.

Barbie, moving at three times my speed, was almost there when he dropped to one knee and twisted his torso to bring the weapon to bear.

He was going to shoot Barbie!

She threw herself down to the floor, but inertia carried her another yard so she was almost at his feet when he pulled the trigger.

Click.

Shiny looked just as surprised as the rest of us.

Click.

Hewitt picked up a handy fold-out chair and whacked Shiny in the face with it. Then, fuelled by bravado, and desperate to impress the drop-dead gorgeous blonde, he delivered his cool line.

'Take a seat!'

In a movie, people might have laughed. It was all I could do to not wet myself with terror.

Hewitt leaned down, offering Barbie his hand to help her up.

'Thank you, sweetie,' she gave him a peck on the cheek as she bounced back to upright. 'That was very helpful.'

Shiny was on the floor but not unconscious. He had blood coming through his fingers where the chair had mashed his nose.

Gloria picked up the gun again, fiddling with it before declaring. 'It's a dud.'

I turned my attention toward the dais once more, expecting to find Jeeves and Heath Martin there. However, Heath was nowhere in sight and Jeeves was alone. Lying on the floor of the marquee and clearly in a state of distress, Heath had chosen to abandon him.

I heard the shotgun being fired outside. The sound echoed off into the night followed by Alistair's commanding voice. He was rounding people up and challenging them to disobey his orders. Through the tattered remains of the marquee, I spotted him.

Sam was still clinging to his back as my man rode an elephant. I felt a little breathless for a few seconds as I watched him.

'You're dribbling, Patty,' whispered Barbie as she passed me.

I wiped my face and hurried to catch Lady Mary. Barbie was already there, and Hewitt was being dashing again, offering Gloria his arm to escort her.

Lady Mary was on her knees and attempting to check whether Jeeves was dying or not.

'Get off me!' the withered old man roared, flapping at her with his twig-like arms.

Lady Mary rocked back onto her heels, still kneeling over him as she folded her arms and scowled.

'I think it fair to say that you are fired, Jeeves. Do you wish to tell me why you thought it necessary to rob me and attempt to have me eaten?'

'Because you don't even know my name!' the aged butler spat.

Lady Mary looked genuinely confused.

'It's not Jeeves?' she questioned.

'No!' Jeeves shouted, spittle flying from his lips even though he was prostrate on the floor. 'That's your grandfather's doing. He couldn't even be bothered to learn our names, so he just picked one and expected us to be content with it.'

Lady Mary pulled a face. 'I see how that might cause some upset, but it hardly justifies your actions, Jeev ... Sorry, what is your name?'

'Dudley,' the old man groaned, lying his head back down. 'Dudley Martin.'

'Oh,' Lady Mary frowned. 'Well, that would never do as a butler's name. No wonder grandpapa changed it. People might think he was addressing you informally by your first name. That would be so embarrassing.'

I nudged my friend's shoulder and whispered. 'You're off the point, Mary.' Taking over, I asked him a question of my own. 'Heath Martin is your grandson, isn't he, Dudley?'

The old man nodded wearily. 'Yes. My son tried to follow me into service,' he raised his head to glare daggers at his employer, 'but your father said he wasn't suitable for the role. I've been planning this ever since.'

'Ever since,' Lady Mary and I echoed together. 'How long ago did you dream this up?'

'Forty years,' Jeeves/Martin spat. 'You were going to come home and find your zoo in ruin. Your creatures would be gone, and I would be on a beach with Heath. It was all set up. But you had to come home and ruin it.'

'What happened to William Gill?' I asked. There were two questions I needed answers to. This, arguably, wasn't the most important one but Lady Mary posed that one herself.

'What is my husband's role in all this?'

The sound of sirens wailed in the distance, heralding the arrival of Chief Inspector Quinn no doubt and hopefully an entire truckload of police officers. Alistair had some of the guests rounded up outside, but there would be more who had run into the grounds to get away. Or they might be in the house somewhere hoping they could stay hidden. I didn't care much for them or whether they got caught. They were clients, but it was yet to be determined whether they were aware the auctioneer was selling stolen goods.

246

What was important to me was that Drago and Shiny were not going to get away. Nor would Jeeves. Heath was at large but I doubted he was going to escape justice.

Jeeves lifted his head slightly, looking first at me and then at his boss. He lowered it again, resigned defeat on his face.

'William was a necessary part of the plan – we could never have found out which of the keepers were susceptible to being bought without his involvement, but he was never getting a cut. I needed the money for my retirement. Heath was coming with me. William kept the keepers in line and allowed Heath the freedom he needed to plan all of this from within the zoo. William even dealt with one of the keepers who demanded more money yesterday. I believe they came to blows.'

That explained the fight Alistair and I heard.

'What about George,' Lady Mary begged.

'Again, I have William to thank for that. I almost felt sorry when Heath told me the head keeper had performed his final task – the meeting with the auctioneer – and had been disposed of. William intercepted your husband leaving the house yesterday. I called to let Heath know you had returned unexpectedly, and we were scrambling to hide things at the house. The auction was all prepared, you see. The marquee was supposed to go up yesterday. Guests were booked in to stay here and had to be quickly contacted to send them elsewhere.'

'Yes, yes,' snapped Lady Mary her impatience overflowing. 'But where is George? Was he involved?'

'Involved?' The butler lifted his head to see if she were being serious. 'Of course not.'

'So where is he?'

The sound of the police arriving drowned out what the old man said next. Sirens and shouted instructions filled the air. For the last twenty-four hours, I had been hoping George was a spy. It wasn't a romantic notion, merely the acceptance that if he wasn't, it meant he was most likely an innocent and that meant he had been captured by Heath and William Gill or whoever else was involved and thus had to be dead.

I didn't hear what Jeeves said, and couldn't read his lips from the angle from which I was looking. I did, however, see Lady Mary jump to her feet and start running.

Where is George?

I watched her run across the marquee in bewilderment, my head swinging back to look at the old man on the floor and then to her and then back to the old man. Gumption finally found its way to my muscles. Not that I leapt to my feet. The only thing I was capable of leaping to right now was a conclusion.

'Where is she going? asked Barbie. She hadn't heard what the butler said either.

On one side of the marquee the police sounded like they were trying to juggle cats. There were large wild animals wandering all over the grounds and frightened people dressed for a cocktail party. I could hear Alistair attempting to explain that the zookeepers were the criminals and not the ones the police needed to recruit to help at this time.

He probably needed my help, but I was too worried about Lady Mary and chose to race after her.

Barbie came too. 'What is it?' she begged to know as she caught up to me. 'Is it George?'

I nodded, showing Barbie a grim expression. 'I think Jeeves just told Mary what they did with him. She's either on her way to find his remains, or she is on her way to get a shotgun. Either way we need to stop her.'

Coming out of the marquee on the opposite side to the police, we both spotted Lady Mary running for her house. Vanishing through the front door, I assumed it was the latter of my two guesses and she was about to get violent with whatever weaponry she kept in the house.

I had no idea where she kept her shotguns, or if she even had any. However, when I called out to get her to stop, I was surprised when she saw reason and waited for me.

There were no tears on her face. If anything, she looked angry, an expression that failed to fit the circumstances.

'What is it?' I needed to know. 'What did Jeeves say about George?'

Barbie pressed close to me, both of us waiting to hear Lady Mary's response. Instead of answering, she crooked a finger and started walking again, this time at a more normal pace.

I exchanged a glance with my blonde friend who just shrugged.

Lady Mary didn't take us far. Around the next corner was a door. It didn't look like much but when she opened it, we saw that it led to a flight of stone steps going down into the dark. She flicked a switch when she started down them, still not saying a word.

At the bottom, we found a short passage and then another door. This one was locked, a key for it hanging on a hook to the right. It was a large mortice key, that turned easily in the lock.

'Oh, honestly,' growled Lady Mary with a sigh.

I could contain myself no longer. 'What is it, Mary? Is George down here? Is he all right?'

'George!' yelled my titled friend. 'George!'

There was a moment of silence before a voice answered.

'Is that you, my little flower?'

Lady Mary was standing no more than two feet away so when she clenched her fists, Barbie and I got to hear her knuckles cracking. We also heard her teeth grind and got to see her eyes flare when she turned her head to look at us.

Barbie was scared enough to take a pace back.

Lady Mary stomped into the cellar, looking for her husband. A little more cautiously, but buoyed along by our curiosity, Barbie and I followed.

The cellar was dimly lit and carried the familiar musty, damp stone smell one always finds. Ahead of us, Lady Mary rounded a corner and stopped. Her hands went to her hips – fists balled. We caught up a moment later and saw the same thing she did.

George was sitting behind a desk, a huge pile of paper to his left and a typewriter to his front.

'I've nearly finished a whole book!' he gushed, a huge grin pulling his face apart. 'I've never been so productive.' His boasts rolled out of his mouth before his wife's posture and expression triggered a warning buzzer in his head. 'Um, I think there might be a problem with Mr Gill,' he revealed weakly. 'He, um. He sort of led me down here and then locked me in. Did Jeeves not tell you?'

'No, dear,' replied Lady Mary with a voice so sweet I could taste the sugar in the air.

'Um, oh. Are you sure?' he countered. 'Jeeves has been bringing me meals and he brought me paper. He said it wasn't safe for me to leave ...' His voice trailed off, as his attention came back to the typewriter. 'You know I haven't written on a typewriter in ... oh, I couldn't guess how many years.' George momentarily forgot how angry his wife looked as the excitement of his work took over again.

251

'Mr Gill is dead,' Lady Mary revealed much to George's astonishment. 'Jeeves tried to kill us all by feeding us to the animals.'

George reacted as if poked with a stick, reaching for a pencil he had tucked behind his ear.

'Ooh, that's a good one. I've never had a murder by ingestion before.' He started to make a note on a handy piece of paper.

I nudged Barbie with an elbow and jerked my head back toward the door. Lady Mary's head was bright scarlet and much like a volcano, she was about to blow.

Once out of her sight, Barbie and I broke into a run, but the full force of our host's incandescent rage reached us as we ran up the stairs.

'George Brown, I have been worried sick! What the heck is all that stuff in your desk? Why do you have guns and fake passports?' She was screaming blue murder at him and, honestly, I wanted to hear his answers, but getting clear of the domestic violence about to occur felt like the more prudent option.

At the top of the stairs, we ran straight into uniformed cops. They were all holding Heckler and Koch assault rifles which were now aimed at the two people suddenly appearing from the darkness.

I think they were about to start shouting for us to get on the floor when Chief Inspector Quinn's voice rang out.

'Not those two. You can let them pass.'

Aftermath

The chief inspector did not look pleased. In fact, I'd go as far as to report that he appeared to be decidedly miffed.

I could have rubbed his nose in it, pointing out that the crimes he refused to investigate yesterday were far more heinous than any of us ever imagined. He could have been the one to catch the bad men, but then we both knew he was going to claim the arrests anyway.

It wasn't something I cared about.

As the armed officers swept past us to check the rest of the house for any auction guests who might be hiding inside, Chief Inspector Quinn beckoned for us to join him.

'I have the rest of your friends outside, Mrs Fisher,' he was good enough to let me know. 'Your butler was most insistent that I had to find you. Had I not agreed, I suspect he would have started a fight to do so himself.'

I could imagine Jermaine doing exactly that.

I did my best to explain Jermaine's actions. 'Today has been rather trying. He needs medical attention.'

Barbie added, 'I had to put one of his arms back into its socket.'

The chief inspector pursed his lips. 'Paramedics are on their way. There are a number of injured persons including a few broken bones and a man who received a rhino horn to his posterior.' While Barbie grimaced, Quinn glanced around clearly looking for something he could not see. 'Where is Lady Mary?'

'I'm here,' she announced, stepping out from the same dark door from which Barbie and I had emerged. The mortice key on its ring twirled idly around her right index finger.

'Mary did you lock George down there?' I enquired with a chuckle.

She said, 'I think it for the best. I will talk to him when I have calmed down. Now, on that subject ...' she looked around, her eyes roving until she picked a direction. 'I've been dry for quite long enough, and it is a long way past gin o'clock.'

Chief Inspector Quinn held out a hand to stop us going anywhere and I worried he was going to be stupid enough to tell Lady Mary to stay off the drink.

'Do I need to do anything about the tiger, Lady Mary?' he asked. 'I am not content to have my officers moving around with such a deadly creature on the loose.'

Pushing past him, she replied. 'You needn't worry, Chief Inspector. I shall keep her with me from now on.'

Ten minutes later, the first two G&Ts were in me, and I had to concur with Lady Mary's desire for a drink, because I felt a whole lot better already.

We were back in the marquee at a pair of tables pushed close together. Esme the tiger was lying at Lady Mary's feet and looked to have gone to sleep. Around us the police were corralling people and trying to prevent further injury – their opinion was that the wild animals roaming the grounds made the area unsafe.

I could understand their point of view.

In the time that we were away finding George, Jeeves had suffered a heart attack. Paramedics were on scene dealing with the many wounds Lady Mary's animals inflicted but dropped all that to come to his aid. It had been to no avail, the old man lost consciousness and never regained it. There was a sheet over his body now.

Once she had some gin in her Lady Mary regaled us with her husband's confession. His desk was a fantasy piece he'd commissioned from a firm who made movie props. The guns were real but none had firing pins so they were also just props. So too the passports which came via another movie prop firm. The money was real, but then he had enough of it in his bank to think nothing of having a few thousand stuffed in a desk.

Basically, there was a part of George who wanted to be a secret agent. Perhaps that was why he wrote such good books on the subject. Whatever the case, he was a thriller writer and nothing more. He hadn't walked to the tiger cage and his foot really was hurt. William Gill picked him up right outside the house – serendipity on William's part – and convinced George to show him the wine cellar.

George said William had a car coming to take them both down to see Esme and seeing the wines would fill in a few minutes while they waited for it to arrive.

He'd been down there ever since. What irked Lady Mary most about her husband's situation was that there was a key on the inside too. They'd put it there decades ago when an ancestor got locked in.

As she talked, the police were working outside. A mobile command centre arrived, and a mobile generator to power it and the lights they erected outside.

The zookeepers, who were by their absence from the auction almost certainly innocent of any involvement, were arriving to begin rounding up the various creatures. In his unexpected role as temporary head keeper, Hewitt had identified to the police those keepers who were involved, and those who could probably be called upon.

Now he was leading the mammoth operation to get all the wild animals back into their enclosures.

Heath had been found. He didn't get far at all because in his flight from the marquee he came face to face with a rhinoceros. Convinced it was going to charge him, Heath ran, and in so doing tripped and twisted his ankle. Barely able to walk, the ringleader was caught by the police trying to make his way to the road.

We needed to give statements – they were going to be long ones, but for now we were quite content to rest and drink gin in the marquee. Chief Inspector Quinn did not approve of the alcohol but was bright enough to do nothing about it.

I had called fruitlessly for my dogs for several minutes while sipping my first gin. They were out there somewhere in the dark again. I was worried about them, but the only carnivore around was Esme and she was asleep at Lady Mary's feet.

My glass was halfway to my mouth when I heard the peacock again. Stretch squawked in the distance, his threat call answered by the terrified yelping of my dogs once more.

How it was that they could run with rhinos and yet be scared of the colourful bird still beggared belief, but before I could react, Esme leapt to her feet.

The dogs' yelping and the peacock's squawking was coming straight for us from outside the marquee. Esme ran in a direct line for them.

Cries of terror – a natural reaction to a tiger showing up anywhere – filled the air but Esme paid the terrified humans no mind.

We were all watching through the tattered remains of the marquee, getting to our feet, although far too slowly to stop what happened next.

Anna and Georgie had formed a bond with the giant Caspian tiger, which the tiger believed included a need to protect them. We didn't get to see Stretch meet his end because Esme's bulk obscured the view.

The dachshunds whizzed around the tiger's legs, running full pelt to get to me, and the peacock, hard on their heels, had no time to avert his course. All we saw from our vantage point, was the tiger pounce and an explosion of feathers.

Esme stopped, lying on the lawn for a moment to enjoy her snack. When she turned around, there were a few feathers left to show where the annoying bird had been.

I was on my knees to scoop the dogs, both girls running right up my legs and into my arms. They showered me with kisses and this time I was going to make sure they stayed with me.

Lady Mary called Esme back, and as the tiger sauntered through the marquee and the disbelieving faces of cops and criminals, she raised her glass.

'I believe a toast is in order.'

We all followed suit, seven friends around a table with our glasses held high. I was expecting my upper-class friend to say something profound or philosophical and the people around us were all watching and waiting to hear what she might have to offer.

'To gin,' she cheered. 'May we never run out.'

Epilogue

I awoke the next morning snuggled up next to Alistair. He was lying on his front with one arm draped across my middle and there were two warm lumps under the duvet by my thighs where the dachshunds had chosen to make themselves comfortable in the night.

Sunlight shone brightly behind the curtains, welcoming me to the day. I yawned and closed my eyes again, revelling in the knowledge that I did not yet need to get up even though I had no idea what time it was.

It had been late when we got to bed last night, and the police were still on the grounds. Keepers were rounding up the animals – no easy task, and the police were sifting through the ruins of the temporary auction house.

With his grandfather dead, and a pile of evidence against him, Heath Martin had confessed to plotting the whole thing. Murdering Lady Mary and the rest of us had not been part of the plan and he lamented that he should have let Drago shoot us as he had apparently suggested. It had been Jeeves' idea to feed us all to the predators and based on his desire to create an ironic ending for the family who had given him employment his entire life.

We learned Drago's name was really Carl Bucket. His partner, Shiny, was Lionel Smith. They both worked for Rivingtons in London but not as auctioneers. They were delivery men; the ones who took the lots to the winning bidder's location. That's how they came to have a car registered to the firm.

According to the chief inspector, Heath Martin had no idea he hadn't hired one of the London auction house's top men and was incensed that they might have lied to him. They pulled the wool over his eyes but had done a decent enough job of selling the animals.

Had he managed to contact a top auctioneer, I felt certain his plan would have completely unravelled last night. Drago/Bucket had texted Heath to say Sam was spying on them and Heath sent the zookeepers – Dave and Jeff and two more – to help deal with my assistant. I doubted a real high-end auctioneer would have done that.

One thing that stood out, was the lack of jewellery listed. There were brochures in the marquee - we'd looked through one while knocking back gin – and found the auction was almost exclusively animals. There were a few paintings – Lady Mary had paintings by Monet in her collection among other valuable pieces. However, the missing jewellery was not listed which brought us back to the concept that one of Lady Mary's staff was just a little light fingered.

It was the element I had failed to solve thus far but finding the energy to do so now was more effort than I could consider mustering.

Forty minutes later, and dressed for the day in jeans and calf-length tan boots with a low heel and a cashmere sweater, I announced my intention to go in search of coffee. Alistair was in the bathroom shaving.

'I'll be right down,' he called back, his face contorted in the mirror as he tried to get the bit under his nose.

Anna and Georgie trotted along in front of me, wagging their tails with excitement. It was breakfast time for them and that would prompt the desire to get outside for a walk.

There was time for coffee though.

I found Sam, Barbie, Gloria, and Jermaine in the kitchen. Lady Mary's cook was preparing breakfast, bustling about and singing to herself as she whipped up platefuls of bacon and eggs with toast and more besides.

'Coffee, madam?' asked Jermaine.

'You sit still,' insisted Barbie with a warning growl as she left her seat to get the coffee pot. Jermaine had both his arms in slings but had attempted to get up to serve me, nevertheless.

'Thank you, Barbie. Good morning everyone,' I called and waved as I went to the box on the side where I had placed the girls' food.

I got a chorus of replies and a fresh mug of steaming hot coffee placed at an empty seat. While I filled two small bowls with kibble, I enquired as to everyone's health and most especially Jermaine and his injuries.

'The doctors assured me I will recover fully in just a few weeks. I should suffer no lasting ill effects, madam.'

It was refreshing news I was pleased to hear yet my heart continued to feel heavy, for the number of days I had left to spend with Jermaine at my side grew fewer with each rising sun. We were all set to return to the ship, and it was only I who had any desire to put it off.

Barbie's boyfriend, Hideki, was on the Aurelia waiting for her to return. Jermaine needed a little time to convalesce but his role in the royal suite was what drove him to get up each day. And as for Alistair, well the Aurelia was his home and his first love. The crew were his family. He hadn't said anything, but I could tell he was itching to take back his role as the captain.

Feeling the sadness inside tugging at the corners of my mouth, I chose to take my coffee outside. A walk would let me clear my head. In a few hours, we would all be returning to my house in East Malling and starting to think about packing up to leave.

I had no idea how long I might be away this time.

'Patty, hold up,' called Barbie as I let the dogs pull me down the steps at the rear of the house.

I swiped at a lone tear as I turned around to look her way. Jermaine was with her too, walking awkwardly with both arms immobilised.

They both saw my sadness and knew me well enough to guess what was causing it.

Barbie pulled me into a hug.

The dogs were tugging at their leads, wanting to be released to explore. With no peacock to chase them, I saw no reason to resist.

They scampered off together the second I undid the clips on their collars and as I stood up again, I blew out a hard breath and fought to regain my composure.

'Sorry ...' I began.

Jermaine stepped in close, freeing his right arm from its sling so he could slip it around my shoulders.

'Madam, we will see each other quite regularly, I'm sure.'

We had talked about this before; the opportunity to remain in each other's company when he would have a new principle to care for and protect. We would do our best, but it was never going to be anything close to what we had now.

Barbie didn't get in on the hug, which was unusual for her. When I looked her way, she had a worried look on her face. I twitched my eyebrows, using them to enquire what might be behind her concerned expression.

'Um, guys, I have a confession,' she started to say. It got our attention.

'What sort of confession?' Jermaine wanted to know, shifting position so we both faced her.

I twisted my head to check on the dachshunds. We were in the private garden at the back of the house, so it surprised me to find my dogs inspecting a pile of poop. The antelope, rhinos and other animals hadn't found their way into this part of the property last night because it is walled off.

'Girls!' I hissed at them. 'Come away.' Hoping they would comply, I turned my head back to hear what big secret Barbie was about to reveal.

Barbie was rubbing her nose with an index finger and skewing her lips to one side as she tried to work out how to frame what she wanted to tell us.

Then it hit me.

'Oh, my goodness! Are you pregnant?'

Jermaine jerked in surprise, his face breaking into a smile until we saw Barbie's face.

'What? No. Sorry guys, that's not it.'

'So, what is it?' I begged to know, holding out my hand so she would join us and feel the comfort of our friendship. 'You can tell us, sweetie. Whatever it is, we won't mind.'

'That's right,' agreed Jermaine.

'Well, it's about the royal suite,' Barbie raised the subject carefully.

'What about it?' I pushed her gently to get on with spilling the beans.

She took another second, tapping her teeth with a delicate fingernail.

'Well, I know you didn't want to leave it. Not really. And, I will confess that I rather liked staying in it too. I know how stupidly expensive it is, of course; you and I could never afford to actually live there with Jermaine. But that got me to thinking about who could afford it.'

A weird weightless feeling started in my stomach.

'Barbie, what did you do?' I gasped, one hand holding my core to settle it.

'I wrote to the Maharaja.' She shot me an apologetic smile. 'I figured since he gave you the house and all the cars and stuff, and he wants to be your benefactor and supporter, he might want to do something else.'

The weightless feeling spread outward through my chest and down into my legs.

'So he bought the Windsor Suite from Purple Star.'

I could hear Barbie talking still, but I was struggling to breathe and could feel my heart banging in my chest.

'It's yours to use,' she continued to say, 'For as long as you want.'

The weightlessness reached my head and the worst case of the whirlies overtook me. My knees went on strike, and I folded into a heap. Mercifully, Jermaine didn't try to catch me; he might have hurt his arms again if he had.

Barbie got to me on the ground though, stopping me from slumping backward to the grass.

'Oooh,' I gasped, getting my head low so the blood would run back to it.

'Are you all right, Patty?' she chuckled at my behaviour. 'Sorry. I didn't mean to shock you. It just … well, it seemed like a perfect solution to all your worries.'

Jermaine crouched so our heads were all more or less the same height.

'Will you change your plans, madam? Will you stay in the Windsor Suite even though you are set to move in with the captain?'

Oh, wow. I hadn't even thought about what this would mean for Alistair. I'd always felt like we were moving too fast even though he disagreed. He wanted me to live in his quarters. Now I was going to have to find a way to gently let him down.

Nothing else would change; we were not going to break up. Alistair was the man for me, but I only signed my divorce paperwork yesterday – I was still working out who I was.

Now that the giddy feeling was dissipating, I pushed myself off the lawn once more and let Barbie help me to get back to my feet.

'Is this okay?' she asked me. 'Have I messed with stuff when I should have left well enough alone?'

Bless her, she is such a sweetheart. She'd found a way to give me everything I wanted, and she was asking if she had messed up.

We were going back to the ship, but in contrast to how I felt just a few minutes ago, now I couldn't wait to get there.

'Have I missed something?' asked Alistair, stepping out of the house to join us on the lawn.

I was going to have to tell him about the change in plans, but I'd forgotten he is the captain of the ship.

'Is this about the Maharaja buying the Windsor Suite for Patricia to use?' he asked casually, like it was just another topic of conversation.

'How …' Barbie started to say, but I spoke over her.

'The captain knows everything. Did Purple Star contact you?' I guessed.

From a back pocket, he produced a glittering envelope. We all recognised it because we'd had letters from the Maharaja before.

'The Maharaja sent me this a few days ago. I was wondering when you might bring it up. I see from your face though that you didn't know.'

I searched his eyes with mine. 'Are you upset?'

The handsome captain, my lover and friend, poked out his bottom lip, mulling over my question before answering.

'No. Upset would not be the right word.' He closed the distance between us, Barbie and Jermaine backing off a pace to give us room. I could hear them whispering to each other behind me when Alistair put his arms around me.

We kissed, lightly because we were in public, but in that moment, I knew for certain we were going to be all right.

Barbie tapped on my shoulder. 'Um, Patty, I think the girls have found something.'

Alistair removed his arms, taking my right hand in his left as I looked to see what Barbie meant.

My dachshunds had chosen to ignore my instruction to leave the pile of poop alone, opting instead to dig at it with their paws. They would need a bath for sure, but Barbie was right that their exploration resulted in a discovery.

There on the lawn, among the pieces of dried poop, was a diamond earring.

I stared at it. 'That's mine.'

'The other one is over here, madam,' Jermaine tapped his foot to move Georgie a little to her left.

Barbie scrunched up her face. 'What are your earrings doing in poop?'

The answer walked out from behind a clipped hedge the very next moment.

Octavia the Ostrich fluffed out her feathers and glared at us with both beady eyes.

I choked out a laugh. The missing jewels hadn't been stolen at all; the big stupid bird had eaten them. Looking around, the lawn was dotted with little piles of poop. How many of them were filled with gems?

The final part of the mystery was solved. George had never really been missing and he certainly wasn't a secret agent working for another government. The jewels had not been stolen, and Esme the tiger had not produced a cub through immaculate conception. It was just a few disgruntled staff, plotting to sell off the zoo animals to the highest bidder.

Like Dorothy and her friends on the yellow brick road, we all walked back to the house to tell Lady Mary what the dachshunds had found.

We were all going back to the ship, and like the sun coming out from behind a dark cloud, everything in my life was warm and bathed in golden joy.

The End

Author's Notes

Hello, dear reader,

Thank you for reading my twenty-first outing for Patricia and her gang. It seems incredible to me that I can have written so many. I remember so clearly the moment she came to life in my head. She had no name at the time, and I do not recall at what point I came up with it. Regardless, Patricia Fisher is responsible for changing my life. Without her, I might never have realised my dream to write full time.

The idea for the jewel stealing Ostrich first came to me when I was starting to craft the first book in Patricia's second series. I had always intended to write ten books and end her adventure by bringing her home. However, by the time I had done that, and the series was drawn to its glorious end, I knew there was still so much story to write.

Patricia had already become my bestseller, and a character I was in love with. Book two or three in that second series was supposed to be about Lady Mary but I couldn't quite work out what to do with the idea of the missing jewels – there wasn't enough meat to turn it into a full novel. Not only that, but it had also become obvious to me that the readers wanted her back on the ship and back with Alistair.

That was not what I intended, though I left the door open for there to be a reunion. However, listening to the fans of the series and allowing their desires to steer me felt like a wise strategy. And ... well, look at where we are now.

Lady Mary and her zoo is based on a real family and a real zoo not far from me in the southeast corner of England. I have visited the zoo in the recent past with my son and wife. Now that we are coming out of lockdown from Covid, I will visit with Hermione too. The house and grounds described in this book, particularly the undulating nature of the topography, are based on what I found there.

Un-Gowwa is a phrase I might have made up or might have misremembered from old Johnny Weismuller films. I watched them in black and white as a child and for some reason, the made-up word 'Un-Gowwa' stuck with me as what he would say as a command to get the elephants moving. I spent a while trying to sift the internet for any reference to it, but striking out, I chose to employ it anyway.

Omelette Arnold Bennett is a real thing. I expect most of you know that, but if you have never heard of it, or never eaten one, you will find recipes with a simple internet search.

Bringing the Blue Moon Investigation boys into the story was something I have wanted to do for a while. Just like everything else I have done, writing several different series that overlap and intertwine was not a strategy I planned or knew that I should employ, it was just something I did.

Their line about the free floating, full torso, vaporous apparition is lifted directly from *Ghostbusters*, a favourite movie from my youth.

If the idea of a dachshund making friends with a big cat sounds a little too farfetched, I took it from a real-life event. This link will take you to a story on the internet. https://www.teddyfeed.com/nature/lion-dachshund-friendship-ya/#:~:text=The%20lion%20and%20dachshund%20have%20a%20bond%20that,while%20Abby%20also%20helps%20to%20clean%20Bonedigger%E2%80%99s%20teeth. It is yet another thing that stuck with me ever since I came across it.

This story concludes this series of books. In retrospect, I probably should have ended it with the previous book, it had such a neat conclusion. Too late to undo it now though. The new series is shown on the next page, and I hope you will stay with me as Patricia and her friends embark on the Aurelia for new adventures.

Take care.

Steve Higgs

Back on board and back in trouble, Patricia Fisher joins old friends and new for adventures on the high seas in her third series of mysteries.

You'll get mysterious uninhabited islands, invading animals, and deadly old rivals, plus ghosts, volcanos, treasure, and a brand-new nemesis who will make all who came before seem insignificant. Patricia Fisher and her friends are set to test their wits and ability to survive whether they want to or not.

Get plenty of sleep because this new series is going to steal it.

A FREE Amber and Buster Story

There is no catch. There is no cost. You won't even be asked for an email address. I have a FREE Amber and Buster short story for you to read simply because I think it is fun and you deserve a cherry on top. If you have not yet already indulged, please click the picture below and read the fun short story about a dog who wants to be a superhero, and the cat who knows the dog is an idiot.

Baking. It can get a guy killed.

When a retired detective superintendent chooses to take a culinary tour of the British Isles, he hopes to find tasty treats and delicious bakes …

… what he finds is a clue to a crime in the ingredients for his pork pie.

His dog, Rex Harrison, an ex-police dog fired for having a bad attitude, cannot understand why the humans are struggling to solve the mystery. He can already smell the answer – it's right before their noses.

He'll pitch in to help his human and the shop owner's teenage daughter as the trio set out to save the shop from closure. Is the rival pork pie shop across the street to blame? Or is there something far more sinister going on?

One thing is for sure, what started out as a bit of fun, is getting deadlier by the hour, and they'd better work out what the dog knows soon, or it could be curtains for them all.

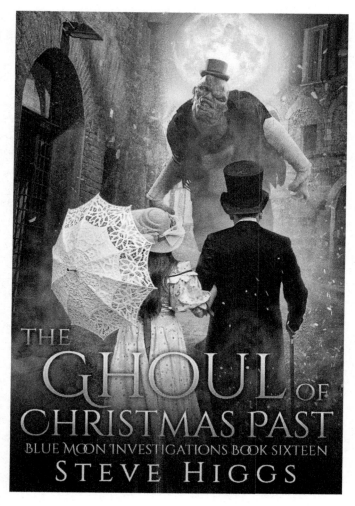

THE GHOUL OF CHRISTMAS PAST

BLUE MOON INVESTIGATIONS BOOK SIXTEEN

STEVE HIGGS

Twas the day before Christmas and Michael Michaels is about to upset his wife.

Recent adventures with his son have piqued his need for a little more action in his life …

… but when he finds himself facing off against a giant ghoul a few hours later, he begins to think he should have listened to Mary and stayed at home.

In trouble with the police, in trouble with his wife, and generally just in trouble, Michael Michaels knows he has uncovered a mystery, but just what the heck is going on? A theft from a museum, a missing man, and a scary figure lurking in the shadows ... what do they add up to?

Michael has no idea, but he's going to find out.

With a little help from a certain bookshop owner and his assistants, Tempest's dad has only a few hours to solve this case. But when the chips are down, does he have what it takes to come up with a cool line at the right time? Or is he just another pensioner trying to do more than his old bones will allow?

The paranormal? It's all nonsense, but proving it might just get them all killed

More Books by Steve Higgs

Blue Moon Investigations

Paranormal Nonsense

The Phantom of Barker Mill

Amanda Harper Paranormal Detective

The Klowns of Kent

Dead Pirates of Cawsand

In the Doodoo With Voodoo

The Witches of East Malling

Crop Circles, Cows and Crazy Aliens

Whispers in the Rigging

Bloodlust Blonde – a short story

Paws of the Yeti

Under a Blue Moon – A Paranormal Detective Origin Story

Night Work

Lord Hale's Monster

The Herne Bay Howlers

Undead Incorporated

The Ghoul of Christmas Past

The Sandman

Jailhouse Golem

Shadow in the Mine

Patricia Fisher Cruise Mysteries

The Missing Sapphire of Zangrabar

The Kidnapped Bride

The Director's Cut

The Couple in Cabin 2124

Doctor Death

Murder on the Dancefloor

Mission for the Maharaja

Get sneak peaks, exclusive giveaways, behind the scenes content, and more. Plus, you'll be notified of Fan Pricing events when they occur and get exclusive offers from other authors because all UF writers are automatically friends.

Not only that, but you'll receive an exclusive FREE story staring Otto and Zachary and two free stories from the author's Blue Moon Investigations series.

Yes, please! Sign me up for lots of FREE stuff and bargains!

Want to follow me and keep up with what I am doing?

Facebook

Printed in Great Britain
by Amazon